Finding Dwain

Finding
Dwain

A Novel

Beryl Cahoon

VMI PUBLISHERS • SISTERS, OREGON

© 2009 Beryl Cahoon

Published by
VMI Publishers
Sisters, Oregon
www.vmipubishers.com

ISBN: 978-1-933204-88-8
ISBN: 1-933204-88-5

Library of Congress: 2009924121

Printed in the USA

Cover design by Joe Bailen

Acknowledgements

I believe the writing of this was in God's own timing. I've written for years but never thought of sharing my stories with others. When I asked Him if I could write something for Him, He truly opened all the right doors. From the family and friends who encouraged me, on to editing and publishing, He has guided this through. I could give no one else as great thanks, as Him.

My friend, Dianne Gentry, whose personal story inspired the writing of Finding Dwain. Her heartache, struggles, and prayers of faith come to life in the pages of this story; a mother who gave up her newborn but could never stop loving him. She trusted God, to watch over him, and someday bring them back together again.

My brother, an avid reader, put many other books to the side, to read and read again, offering ideas and finding spelling errors. Nothing can be harder than to read the same thing over and over again. Thank you, Hugh Cahoon.

Susan Lohrer, truly an inspirational editor, offering a special blend of patience, encouragement, and personal insight, helped so very much in the final presentation of Finding Dwain.

1

Brent Anderson knew he was the last person Zelda Cloud cared to see walking into her office. If she had someone less friendly at the front desk, he would have been told that she was too busy to give him a moment of her time. But here he was, sitting before her desk, as always—praying she would finally do what she always vowed she absolutely was not going to do.

The fifty-five-year-old farmer patiently pretended he hadn't heard a word she said. For the fourth time, emphasizing her determination by slamming a file folder down on her desk, she said, "I *cannot* give you information on a child that has been adopted. You told me to place that baby seventeen years ago. Every time you come in here, I tell you it is illegal for me to give you any information. What makes you think it is legal today, when it wasn't yesterday or a month ago or sixteen years ago, when you suddenly decided you made a mistake by giving him away?"

Brent leaned forward, rubbing the light afternoon stubble on his chin. "What is the legal age? How old does Dwain have to be for us to contact him?"

She gasped. "I…I just don't understand why you *keep* asking me. You cannot contact an adopted child. Period. End of subject. Now, I want you to leave. I have important work to do."

Five-year-old Tammy Rae rushed into the office on abnormally short legs, holding up little arms for Grandpa to lift her. As he set her onto his lap, she excitedly showed him a book the receptionist had given her to read. "It's about puppies. I can read it to you." Moving her stunted little fingers under the words, she read excitedly, "Four puppies in a box."

He shifted her on his lap to keep eye contact with the woman he privately referred to as "Zelda, the witch." He said calmly, to not frighten the little girl, "Zelda, people make mistakes. I made a mistake. I didn't understand about dwarfism. It was an honest mistake. But you knew the baby wasn't mine to give away. Jeff had to consent before you could take his baby."

He looked down and said softly to Tammy Rae, "Yes, honey, I see the puppies. What color are the ribbons they're wearing?"

Looking up he said, "You have to accept your share of the blame in this, Zelda. I was taking Dwain home when you showed up at the hospital and told me, in your experience, you were certain that I wouldn't be able to cope with the baby's handicap. I didn't know you then,"—he let his eyes tell her what he thought of her—"so I had no reason not to believe you when you said the state could care for him better than we could."

Referring to the little one he held, he said, "This one and her sister Teresa could read before they were four years old. Teresa is in the fifth grade."

The woman stiffened. "I have seen Teresa. I am fully aware of how well she is doing in school, and I am also aware of the fact that neither of your granddaughters have had the physical problems that boy was born with." She looked sharply at the young receptionist leaning to lift the little girl into her arms. "In the future, Miss Jennings, you will not come into my office when I am talking with a client."

"I'm sorry." The young lady smiled painfully as she carried Tammy Rae out of the office. To Brent she whispered, "I'll read to her."

"Now, as I was saying." Zelda motioned to the file cabinet. "You gave that baby up because you did not want to bother with future medical problems, and you did not want to pay for operations."

He sighed. "My daughter was sixteen years old and had just given birth to twins. My wife passed away when Sara was fourteen. You told us that the most we could handle was one of those babies."

She glared at him. "No, you knew the normal boy would be able to help you on your farm, but that little one would be nothing but trouble. So if you don't mind, I have work to do. If, I hear of a new law that allows me to tell you the location of an adopted child, I will be in contact with you."

Brent shook his head, stood, and trudged from the office, his shoulders slumped. He noticed a twinkle in Miss Jennings's eyes as he scooped his little one out of her arms. He knew this young woman was alive within, unlike the darkened soul in the inner office.

He carried Tammy Rae out to the car, speaking softly as he secured the straps of her safety seat on the backseat of the car. He told himself giving up Dwain had been an honest mistake. He knew now that seventeen years ago, baby Dwain would have been fine in a little seat like this sitting next to his larger twin.

He looked back at the little girl, winked, and waited for her to smile. He smiled back. "We need to get Mommy's car back to her. You know how she doesn't like driving Grandpa's pickup." As the little girl yawned he smiled, knowing Sara hoped Tammy Rae would sleep in her car seat and not miss her afternoon nap.

After fastening his seat belt he closed his eyes. *Dear Lord, I know you have taken care of him for all these years. Please keep watching over Dwain and keep him safe and bring him home. Lord, we are not a whole family without him.*

❧ ❧ ❧

After Brent left, Rhonda stayed well out of Zelda's way. Her boss picked up and put down one case file after another, making piles and rearranging them. Finally, having accomplished nothing, she stormed from her office, locked the door, and snubbed her nose at Rhonda.

"I have an appointment, and I will not be back today. If you *ever* see that man coming within ten feet of this office, close my door and *you* tell him I'm busy. Do you understand?"

Rhonda nodded. She watched Zelda leave the building, kept watching through the window until she was sure her boss was gone. She remembered Zelda locking her office door when she left yesterday, the same way she had today. But when Rhonda came in an hour before her this morning, the door was unlocked. She always tried the door before Zelda came to work. The bitter woman had fired the last receptionist when she found her office door unlocked one morning. Rhonda couldn't bear the thought of being fired from her very first job.

She moved her stapler and tape dispenser to the other side of her desk. Whoever was coming into the office at night moved things around on her desk. She suspected it was Zelda, who was the only person with a key to her own office.

Knowing, after only working here for a few months, Zelda often made mistakes she would not admit to, Rhonda bowed her head in prayer. "Would you please help Mr. Anderson, Father? There has to be a loophole in the law that pertains to his case."

✿ ✿ ✿

As she drove, Zelda squeezed the steering wheel until her fingers ached. *Why does he bring that awful child into my office? It's bad enough he comes, but why does he bring those horrible little girls?* A sudden chill came over her whole body as she thought of their short arms, and she shivered.

It wasn't just her work upsetting her. In the past six months, strange things were happening that she could only attribute to her own memory lapses. She was also upset over her parents taking her grown sister, Becky, to Disneyland. Her entire childhood, she had begged to go to Disneyland, but there was never enough money. As she turned into her driveway, she held onto her anger; it was because of Becky there was never enough money.

Zelda expected to see a silver sports car in the garage. Because it was gone, she assumed her adorable doctor had been called back to the hospital. Thinking of him, she smiled. Dr. Marcus Bradley Alexander Fitzgerald was everything wonderful in her life. Just thinking of those four words that created his full name thrilled her, as did everything else about him. He was working incredibly long hours so he could be away from the hospital three full weeks while they cruised the Caribbean next month.

As the garage door lowered, she stepped into the kitchen and scooped up her fluffy white cat. She carried her upstairs and set her on the bed.

Stepping into the large tiled shower enclosure, Zelda smiled. She loved everything about her new apartment, but this bathroom was what she loved most.

Thinking of Marcus as she used the shampoo and cream rinse he selected for her "lovely hair," she found herself comparing his accomplishments to men twenty years older, like Brent Anderson, who had accomplished half as much.

Why can't that farmer remember the situation seventeen years ago? Jeff Campbell was a sixteen-year-old spoiled, crippled child, who in her opinion would never be fit to be a father. Sara Anderson was a beautiful sixteen-year-old with her whole life ahead of her. She told Brent at the time, if he were any kind of a father, he would insist Sara give up both of those infants. *Allowing his pretty daughter to marry that horrible little man, and for them to bring two more deformed children into the world, is inexcusable.* Irresponsible parents like him infuriated her. She shuddered, thinking about that awful child, Tammy Rae, with tiny little fingers and impossibly short arms and legs.

ᴄᴫ϶ ᴄᴫ϶ ᴄᴫ϶

Brent had a few more errands before heading back to the farm. Pushing Sara's grocery list into his shirt pocket, he lifted his sleeping granddaughter from her safety seat. He carried her as he shopped, not even noticing the weight on his arm, kissing her a few times on the head as he reached for an item here and there. Still thinking about talking with Zelda, he thanked God for Jeff forgiving him for making the mistake of giving up Dwain. He hated having done something so stupid. Zelda had insisted he was doing the right thing for the baby, but it felt wrong at the time and was tearing him apart now. As he reached for cans of vegetables he thought, *poor little guy. Doesn't even know we love him. Lived his whole life thinking we don't want him because he was born with dwarfism.* He kissed Tammy Rae. *That couldn't be further from the truth.*

Later, in the center of the barnyard, Brent lowered Tammy Rae to the ground and smiled as she ran shouting for her mother to come and see the book Grandpa bought her. He watched her until she was safely inside the house, and then turned toward the barn where he heard teenage voices. He stopped short of the barn door when he saw Teresa closing the door of the chicken house. In her short little arms she carried a basket half filled with eggs. He smiled, waiting for her little legs to bring her across the barnyard to him. His thoughts went back to Sara at this age. Both of the girls, with their thick golden hair and bright blue eyes, looked so very much like their mother.

"Grandpa, I got five brown ones, two green ones, and a white one."

He looked into the basket. "I think we need to get some more hens."

"I could have gotten more, but the red hen pecks me when I try to reach under her."

"Oh, don't be taking her brood, honey. She's sitting on a nest full of young ones."

"Chicks?" She gasped and set off at a run toward the house, shouting, "We're going to have baby chicks, Mom."

Leaning against the barn door, he stood quietly as he watched and listened to three high school seniors working on his old motorcycle. He'd given that thing to Dane when he was eight years old, hoping he would never be able to get it started. As long as it was just him and the neighbor girl, Amanda, working on the cycle, Brent wasn't worried. But with those two farm boys helping, it wouldn't be long before they brought that monster back to life.

The neighbor boys, Kevin and Joe, seriously considered every detail as Dane pointed out what he thought was wrong. "I think this is the trouble. It isn't getting fuel. Feel the spark plug. It's dry."

Joe rubbed his finger on the plug. "Put it back in and kick it over again, and then take it out and see if it's still dry."

When had Dane grown so much? It seemed last week he was six inches shorter.

The boy looked up at him and grinned. "Grandpa, we just about got it started."

It was then Brent realized his tractor was gone. "Where's your dad?"

Kevin handed Dane the spark plug. "Dry as a bone." Kevin looked over his shoulder. "Mr. Anderson, he's over at the school. Principal Campbell wanted him to smooth out the baseball field."

Brent glared at the teens. "Why aren't you boys helping?"

Dane rolled his eyes. "We were. But, Dad didn't just stop with the baseball field. He said that was all we had to stay and help him with, and then he talked Grandpa Campbell into letting him smooth out the whole school parking lot."

As Brent crossed the barn yard to the small house that had been the original farmhouse, he had to chuckle, thinking about Jeff up on that tractor, pulling the field rake along behind. For a man only forty-five inches tall, there didn't seem to be anything his son-in-law wouldn't take on. Stepping into the kitchen, he hung up his hat and washed his hands. Feeling too weary to make a pot of coffee, he sank into an overstuffed chair. No one riled him more than Zelda Cloud. Having to talk to her about the one thing that hurt him the most, drained his strength.

Through the window, he could see his daughter, Sara, standing at the stove in the kitchen of the bigger farmhouse across the barnyard. He saw her raise her head as if hearing something, and then she looked out the window. Then he heard the approaching tractor. Leaning forward, he peered between the faded curtains.

The legs of the little man on the tractor seat could reach only a quarter of the way without the extensions attached to the tractor pedals. His small hands moved easily over the large steering wheel, but the distance he had to pull the extended gear shift lever forced him to shift his whole body uncomfortably. Brent felt guilty sitting in the comfort of his living room, and pulled himself up, snatched his hat off the hook, and hurried out to open the heavy back doors on the barn.

Jeff's mouth moved, and though the rumble of the tractor engine covered the sound of his voice, Brent knew he was asking about Zelda. As the engine silenced, Brent pulled the doors shut from inside the barn.

"She didn't tell me a thing. Zelda is the witch she has always been. I know the answer is in her file cabinet. If I could just get into it, we would know exactly where Dwain is."

Jeff moved stiffly on his short, curved legs. He never complained, but anyone could see that they ached from a long day of work. "Don't do anything that will get us in trouble. When we figure out a legal way to get the information, it won't go well for us if we've broken any laws."

As they walked toward the house, Brent slowed the little man by placing a hand on his shoulder. "But tomorrow is September first. It's going to be another depressing September for Dane if we can't give him some hope of us bringing Dwain home before their birthday."

On the porch, Jeff stopped and peered in through the window. "Good, the boys aren't around. I want to talk to you about something." He shifted his weight from one leg to the other. "I was thinking, you and I could fix that motorcycle for Dane. I ordered a seat and new handle grips."

"That's something we need to discuss, Jeff. It's not a toy. That motorcycle just about got me killed. It's the kind of thing that you get on, and the next thing you know you're going a hundred miles an hour."

Jeff's blunt fingers gripped the door handle. He looked at his hand, then down at the porch. "There are a lot of things we're afraid of. If we approach every challenge with caution, we can do what we need to do." He looked up at Brent. "The first time I got behind the wheel of a car, do you think my dad wasn't scared?"

Brent nodded, respecting Jeff's opinion. *Lord, please help him make the right decision and give me the strength to accept it.* He smiled as the smell of roast beef, mashed potatoes, corn on the cob, and fresh-baked bread engulfed them in the doorway.

"Wash up. Dinner's ready." Sara leaned down and pressed her lips to her husband's. "I fixed all of your favorite things, hon."

Upstairs, Dane could smell the aroma from the kitchen. Kevin sat on the guest bed in Dane's room, rolling a basketball on his fingers.

"Why doesn't your grandpa Anderson help us get the motorcycle going?"

"When I was eight, he told me I could have it if I fixed it. His only condition was that he wasn't going to help me."

"He doesn't want you to have it?"

"Oh, he wants me to have it. He just doesn't want me to ride it." Dane laughed. "He's afraid I'll get hurt."

Kevin spun the ball on the tip of his finger. "So who else do you think will play first string this year?"

Dane shook his head and tossed a motorcycle magazine aside onto his bed. "Anyone who wants to, I guess. In the whole school we only have twenty guys that can dribble, and only about five of them can hit a hoop."

"If you grow as tall as Gramps, you would be awesome," Kevin said.

Dane stood, reached up, and touched the slope of the ceiling. "I grew three inches since last fall. I can touch the rim when I go up for a layup, but I'm never going to be as tall as Gramps."

"How do you know?"

"Because Gramps is my dad's grandfather, and my dad is adopted. I'm like my mom's dad, so I don't think I'll be much taller than I am now."

At the mention of adoption, Kevin stopped spinning the ball. He let it roll onto the bed. "So, what you said before, that tomorrow you won't be depressed and you'll stay that way for the whole month of September." He gave Dane an expectant look.

Something welled up inside Dane. This was a big step for him. "You curious or something?" He grinned.

"I guess. What's different about this September than all the other Septembers?"

"I'm using Faith. Pastor Davis said God wants us to have faith. I have always prayed, and begged God to bring Dwain home for our birthday on September 30. If I'm begging, then I'm not trusting. So, this year, I'm going to do everything I can to show God I believe He'll bring Dwain home."

Kevin picked up the ball again and bounced it on his fingers. "If God wanted him here, don't you think he would've been here a long time ago?"

Dane couldn't let himself think that anymore. Not if he was going to have real faith. "Jesus said a little faith will move a mountain, and Job trusted God and everything was twice as good as it was before."

"Stop....Just stop with the Bible stuff." Kevin looked away.

If Kevin didn't want to hear it, Dane didn't want to force it on him. But he hoped someday his friend would have a change of heart. "I've been thinking, and I figure I need to start with that bed." He pointed to the bed Kevin was on. "I'll take the frame out from under it and cut off the legs."

Dane walked around the room, motioning with his hands as he explained. "I'll trade sides of the room so Dwain has the lower ceiling, and I'm going to get him a short desk. Grandpa Campbell said I can have one of the old desks in the storage room at the school. It'll be in pretty bad shape, but I can paint it and fix it like new. When Dwain comes home, he'll sit at his desk, I'll sit at mine, and we'll do our homework together."

Kevin lay back on the bed, putting his arm above his head. "Not a good idea. Just because he's short doesn't mean he'll like that side of the room. If you like that side, you should stay there or turn both beds so the heads are toward the high ceiling over here, and put the desks on the low ceiling side."

Dane smiled, taking Kevin's advice as his offer to help. "So we start tomorrow. We have to hurry. He could come home anytime between now and September 30."

"What about the Kawasaki? You said we're going to get it started before your birthday too, and if we set a goal like that, you won't be so depressed this year."

Dane looked around. "Dwain is coming home. I have to get everything ready. I'm going to get rid of this rug, because it could get caught on his crutches."

"Dane, why do you think he has crutches? Your dad doesn't have crutches, and neither do your sisters."

"Because Dwain and I are seniors, and when my dad was a senior he had crutches. He had two operations on his legs that year."

"Boys," Mom called. "Come down for dinner."

Dane opened the closet door. What could he do to make room for Dwain's clothes? He could do like Dad did in his closet, put another bar for hangers down lower.

"Your mom's calling us."

Dane sank onto his bed. "We don't have a single picture of my twin brother. Not one."

"I'm hungry." Kevin opened the bedroom door. "That's not depression I see, is it?"

Dane leaped up, smiling. "Not at all. I'm not depressed. Dwain is coming home. I can't be depressed if I have faith."

Jeff waited until everyone was seated at the dining room table, then he nodded at Kevin who, though he was a frequent guest at their table, was given this reassurance of being welcome. When the girls stopped talking and looked at their dad, he said, "Tomorrow is the first day of school. Is there anything we should talk to our Creator about?"

"I'm going to be in the fifth grade."

Jeff smiled. "That's right, Teresa, and you'll do very well in the fifth grade."

He lowered his head. "Dear Lord, thank You for this wonderful meal and this home filled with love. You are so good to us, it's impossible to count our blessings. We ask You to put a hedge around the children as they start a new school year, and to keep the teachers and our principal safe also."

"Daddy?"

He opened an eye and looked at his five-year-old. "Do you want to say something?"

"What about Grandpa? Daddy, you said principal, but he's Grandpa."

Jeff smiled again. "God knows he is your grandpa, but we probably should remind Him." He closed his eyes again. "And keep Grandpa, the school principal, safe."

As Jeff's eyes rested on Dane, his son scooped a large spoonful of mashed potatoes onto his own plate.

Dane smiled, squared his shoulders, and pushed the spoon back into the large bowl of mashed potatoes. "I'm doing something different this September." Dane pressed his spoon into the center of his potatoes, preparing for gravy. "I've decided to believe Jesus. He said, if a man has faith the size of a mustard seed, he can move a mountain. I asked God in the name of Jesus to bring Dwain home by our birthday, and I believe He will."

Brent cleared his throat. "I had another talk with Zelda Cloud today."

Teresa gasped, "The witch?"

Ignoring his granddaughter's outburst, he looked apologetically at Dane. "She still insists that Dwain was adopted, so we can't get information about him."

"Grandpa, my twin brother is still coming home. I've asked God every year, since I first knew about Dwain, to bring him home for our birthday. Now I understand about the faith Jesus wants me to have. To show everyone that I believe I'll receive what I ask for in Jesus' name, I'm going to act like Dwain's coming home. I'm going to fix our room, so it's better for him. Grandpa Campbell is getting a broken desk out of the school storage room so I can fix it for Dwain." He looked at everyone at the table. "I'm putting it in my room. I mean, in our room." He glanced toward the stairs. "Dad, did you test the electric stair-chair to make sure it'll carry Dwain up and down the stairs?"

His son did pay attention to detail—a chip off the old block. Jeff chuckled. "That electric chair will hold three hundred pounds—how heavy to you think Dwain is?"

"But no one has used it the way he'll have to, if both of his legs are in casts like yours were. We have to put the leg attachments on it."

Teresa looked at her mother. "I want to ride on the chair."

Sara looked puzzled, and Jeff knew why. For the past thirteen years, Dane had filled their home with sadness the whole month of September, as he prepared everyone to be as miserable on his birthday as he was, because his twin was not home. She too must wonder how this September could differ.

After dinner Jeff accepted Brent's offer to drive them over to the men's Bible study at the church. He didn't like it when his father-in-law came around to the passenger side of the pickup, but did appreciate it when he allowed him to climb down without help.

A few minutes later, seated on a chair much too high for his feet to touch the floor, Jeff considered the outline for the Bible study, but his thoughts were at home with Dane. Pastor Davis asked him if something was wrong.

Jeff sighed. "Dane is challenging God. I'm worried that he won't understand if God doesn't give him what he wants."

Pastor Davis nodded. "And I stand guilty of encouraging him to have faith. I can only speak from experience. Dane has never tested the 'Word of God' in reference to Faith. Each of us has trusted God before. We have experienced enough to encourage others to have faith. Even David, who was about Dane's age, had experiences in faith before he faced Goliath. God doesn't tell us not to test Him. He said He will move a mountain if we have the faith, and I believe He will. What Dane finds out might not be what he wants to find out. He may be praying for the impossible, but God knew Dane would make this stand of faith when He allowed them to be separated."

Jeff held tight to his own faith that one day the boys would be reunited—even if not this September as Dane believed. "God let Job go through losing everything, and being sick. Job kept his faith, and in the end everything he lost was doubled."

Pastor Davis smiled and held up his finger. "He doubled the material wealth. When all the hardship was over, Job had double the wealth and was given exactly the same number of children he had lost. But that is a whole sermon in itself."

Brent found the book of Job in his Bible. "I never noticed that before. Why didn't God double the number of children that He allowed to be killed?"

"He did, but not on earth. Job's children were in heaven, so he had not lost them. The material wealth in animals, crops and land, wouldn't go with Job to heaven, so God doubled them while Job was on earth. In heaven Job is with all of his children, both the first group and the second group. He has twice as many children with him for eternity."

Jeff wiped a tear from his face. "Maybe it won't be here that the twins will be together on their birthday after all."

Brent shook his head. "I can't let myself believe he's dead so let's not think that's even possible." He put his hand on Jeff's shoulder, and glanced over at Jeff's father.

Jeff knew Ben Campbell didn't hold a grudge against Brent for not bringing both of their grandsons home from the hospital. But, the fact that Ben and his wife had adopted Jeff, a baby in the same condition as Dwain, and had raised him to be a good husband and father, couldn't have made Brent feel any better.

Jeff asked, "What do Sara and I say to Dane? What if God has another plan for Dwain that's better than what we think is best?"

Pastor Davis laid a hand on his arm. "I believe that Dane has enough faith to accomplish God's will, so if we all just encourage Dane to keep that faith, I don't see how we can be wrong."

As the study session ended, Dr. Larry Atwood, a regular member of the Bible study group, reached for his pocket and pulled out a cell phone. It vibrated, and he flipped it open. Excusing himself, he moved over by the wall to talk. "This is Dr. Atwood." He listened and said, "No, this is Dr. Larry Atwood. You can reach my brother, Terry, at the clinic."

Jeff looked back at him and whispered, "Dr. Atwood, I presume."

Larry frowned and shook his head as he sat next to Jeff. In the fifth grade he had regularly thumped Jeff on the head with his textbook for teasing him that way, but Jeff was safe tonight—Larry would never whack him with the Bible. Larry ignored his teasing and opened to Job to read the passage the pastor was referring to.

Knowing Brent wouldn't mind waiting, Jeff turned to Larry as the others started to leave. "What's your opinion of Zelda Cloud?"

If it were anyone but Jeff asking, Larry wouldn't have replied. He looked around the room, and then lowered his voice to almost a whisper. "She encourages giving up a child when, in my opinion, it's not necessarily best for the mother or child. When she finds out an unmarried young woman is pregnant, she contacts the family, which in my opinion, is not professional. If they need her services, it's their place to contact her."

Jeff clamped down on his frustration at the unfairness of what Zelda had done to his family. "Without saying names, have you noticed whether they go to good homes?"

Larry chuckled. "The only placements I know of are the five boys that George and Thelma adopted, and they're certainly in a good home. But in my honest opinion, Zelda overextends her qualifications, and she is going to get herself into trouble."

Whispering, Jeff asked, "How, exactly, does she overextend?" If they could prove she'd done something unethical or illegal, they would have a better chance of getting Dwain back.

Larry's mouth tensed. "I operate on bones and muscles. If I were to try brain surgery, I would be attempting something I know very little about. Zelda moves through life with blinders on, seeing only what's right in front of her, and only what she wants to see."

Jeff hated it when Larry talked so enigmatically. He wanted specifics, but with doctors, there were so many privacy limitations to what could be divulged. Instead of pressing Larry for details, he presented him with his own situation. "I've been to court three times, trying to approach this from different angles, but as soon as Zelda told the court Dwain was adopted, each of my petitions was denied without allowing me to plead my case."

Larry nodded. "That may be a good strategy before some judges, but not Judge Roy Bain. He's a Christian and honestly pursues his profession. I suggest you ask for a hearing before him, and request that he review the adoption record rather than just settling for Zelda's testimony alone.

2

Dane listened halfheartedly to Mr. Tims, his homeroom teacher. He rubbed his thumb over the top of his desk, wondering how much he would have to sand on Dwain's desk to smooth away the gouges of student destruction.

Mr. Tims said, "As you know, all of us need to know how to do research using the Internet. I want you to choose a subject I approve of, and use only the computer to research. You will document the location of the information, and present your findings to the class."

"Mr. Tims?" Kevin raised his hand. "I was wondering if we could use the Internet to find a missing person." He cocked an eyebrow at Dane.

Bobby Miller yelled, "Like solving a mystery. We could go online and see what criminal the FBI can't find, and we could find him. Like a serial killer. Maybe someone with a big reward."

Kevin glared at Bobby. "You know what I mean."

Dane looked at Kevin and a light went on. "Great idea!" He looked at Mr. Tims. "It's a great idea. We could all search. We can work together. Fourteen minds are better than one and besides, God is with us."

"You've lost me." Mr. Tims raised his hands to quiet the class. Everyone else seemed to know what Dane was saying. "What's this about?"

Kevin looked around the room. "We all know what month this is. We have been in school together for eleven years now, so what is September for Dane?"

Three boys said at the same time, "Depression September."

Annie shook her head. "I'm sorry, but this is my second year in this school. I don't know what you're talking about."

Dane turned to her. "I was born a twin. The state took my twin brother. My grandpa and my parents have been trying to get the state to at least let him know he has a birth family that loves him, but there's a lady at the Social Services office that won't even consider helping us."

Karen, a dark-haired girl who seldom spoke, said shyly, "I know a Web site we can begin with. My cousin found her real mother that way. In fact, her mother was also looking for her on the same site."

Dane's eyes widened. "So I'll tell you all the information I have and we can start with that site."

"Wait a minute. Wait a minute. Wait a minute." Mr. Tims raised his hands again. "Let's redefine this project. We can't just say it's to find Dane's brother, or you will all fail if you don't find him. So this is the assignment. What I want you to do is find, and document, everything you can about searching for a missing person. Each of you is to attempt to find—" He looked at Dane. "What's your brother's name?"

Four boys seated behind the teacher yelled, "Dwain Campbell."

Without waiting for further instructions, the students separated into small groups and pressed together around the six computers lining two of the classroom walls. The voices grew excitedly louder, and then softly quiet. Dane grinned. This could really work.

"All right," Edward yelled, "Let's get a list of sites started and write down what's available at each one."

Even Mr. Tims smiled, and Dane could tell he liked the kids' enthusiasm very much. He sat back on the front of his desk, and his gaze met Dane's. For the first time, Dane realized his September depression affected more than just himself.

Dane nodded to Mr. Tims, and feeling lighter than he ever had in September, went to look over Karen's shoulder at the form on her computer monitor. She said, "This is where we put the name of the person we're looking for. What are his name and birth date?"

"Dwain Jeffrey Campbell. He was born September 30 at three o'clock in the afternoon. He'll be seventeen years old, same as me."

Mr. Tims said, "Let's set that date, September 30, and end this assignment at 3:00 in the afternoon."

Sally Yates smiled brightly. "Let's have a birthday party. We could invite the whole school and have a party in the gymnasium at three o'clock."

Dane looked at her. "Do you believe Dwain will be here?"

The corners of her eyes crinkled. "You do, and if two or more pray in agreement…"

Kevin shook his head. "Now we have two crazy people in our class."

Dane wished Kevin weren't so opposed to the idea of trusting in God to help them find Dwain.

Mr. Tims's cell phone vibrated, and he stepped out of the classroom to answer it. It was his wife, a nurse at the county hospital and adjoining Atwood Clinic. "I'm between patients. How did your idea go over with the kids?"

"Fantastic. You should see them. They changed my idea into something they're excited about, so I'm going to let them go with it. It doesn't matter what they're researching as long as they learn about finding information."

"What are they researching?"

He said, "They're working together to find Dwain Campbell."

"Honey, I don't think that's legal. You might get into trouble."

His shoulders tightened. "I'll check into it."

"What'll you do if they actually find him and decide to contact him?"

Bowing his head, he half hoped it wouldn't come to that. "Then I'll have to end the assignment."

❧ ❧ ❧

As the morning progressed, news of the senior class project seeped into the community. One of the first to hear was Mabel Oxford, the head waitress of the Dine and Drive truck stop restaurant on the edge of town. As she considered the implications of the project, she listened to a conversation between two city investors and George McCain, the wealthiest landowner in the county.

"Mr. McCain, the land we are interested in purchasing isn't farmland. It's not being used for anything, so if we develop that property, it won't put you out in the least bit. Every farmer in the state is hurting right now, so we know you can use the money."

Mabel knew by the way George was turning his coffee cup from one side to the other, he was considering their offer. She snatched up a fresh pot of coffee. Filling George's cup, she ignored the fancy city man who pushed his cup toward her.

"I need to do some thinking." McCain looked at Mabel as though he knew something was bothering her.

"Mr. McCain," one of the other men said, "we have serious investors who need an answer right away. If you won't sell to us, someone else will."

Mabel wiped a counter that needed no cleaning, sending George a clear message in her motion.

One of men reached into his briefcase and pulled out a folder. "We are willing to offer you another hundred thousand dollars. All you need to do is sign this."

McCain said softly, "I'm not in the habit of repeating myself. I don't deal with anyone who can't hear me the first time. I said I need time to think about this before making a decision."

"We are offering you over a thousand dollars an acre for land you have absolutely no use for."

"You want forest property in the middle of my land. You'll have to show me your plans, and let me decide if it's something I want in the middle of my property."

The two men left without McCain's signature, and Mabel stacked their plates to take them back to the kitchen. As George started to leave, she slid into the booth across from him.

"Nobody ever offered anyone around here a dime they weren't making a dollar on. As soon as those two showed up in town, my girl looked up their land development company on her computer. They're for real, but they've been in some lawsuit trouble. What they do is buy forested land and clean it off and put a golf course alongside a whole bunch of condominiums. A man could do that hisself, I'm figuring. Why would you need a developing company if you own the land?

"But what's got me thinking, George, is what Amy found out about those lawsuits. They're selling those condominiums to elderly and retired folks. Why would they want to settle clear out here anyway?"

McCain shrugged. "It's always greener on the other side of the fence."

She rested her elbow on the table, planning to begin a serious conversation. He cut her off, saying, "Now, if you'll excuse me, Mabel, I have a field of alfalfa to cut."

Determined to tell him the news she had, she scooped up his cup. "Do you know about the senior class project? It's getting all around town, so you might want to hear about it."

George smiled. "Did this news just get to you?"

"A few minutes ago, why?"

He chuckled, "It has to get to you before it gets all around town."

Not giving him the satisfaction of letting him know that bothered her in the least, she said, "My girl, Amy, said they're learning to use their computers to find information. What they're doing might interest you."

He jingled his truck keys and edged toward the door. "Come to the point, Mabel, what are they doing?"

"They're searching for Dane Campbell's twin brother. The whole class is searching for every bit of information on finding an adopted child. They're going to contact the boy and let him know where his birth parents are. Dane is telling everyone that God is going to bring Dwain back here by the end of the month."

The man's jaw tightened. "What makes you think that would interest me? I have five legally adopted sons." He pointed at her. "Every one of their parents, both mothers and fathers, signed off on them."

Mabel looked at him, holding back what she was aching to say. "But there is always something you don't know about. Whoever got that boy thinks he is all signed off on too, but Jeff Campbell never signed anything letting anyone take his son away from him. You can figure Zelda Cloud messed up on at least one of your boys."

McCain stalked from the diner.

Looking angrily back at the Dine and Drive, he slammed his pickup door. He had known Mabel since kindergarten, and not once did she use that tone of voice without there being a good reason. He and Thelma had adopted five healthy, strong babies, and all five were growing up exactly as he had planned. He had the biggest farm in the county, and his boys would be the best farmers around. There wasn't a thing that would stop what he had put into motion.

As he drove he thought about his sons, one at a time. Teddy, the oldest, now fifteen, was the image of his birth father, which was what George had hoped for because Teddy's mother wasn't from farming stock.

He remembered when Trenton was born thirteen years ago, they had only a few hours to consider adopting him. Zelda Cloud called, saying she had a newborn that they had better snatch up quickly if they wanted him. The baby was taken in C-section from a young high school girl who had been in a coma for more than a month. George and Thelma had been watching that situation along with the whole community, aware weeks earlier that she might not live long enough to give birth. Both the birth father and the birth mother were from well-established farming families. There was no question, Trenton's blood line was that of a strong healthy farmer. That was how it was with all five of their boys. Before he would adopt them, they had to meet his requirements. Every one of them came from prime farming stock. He insisted that the mother or father be from a farming family, because if he planted poor seed, he would get a weak crop.

Greg, twelve, was perhaps his greatest pride. That boy could outwork a man twice his size. He was smart, fast, and willing to start a job and finish it right. George knew he would be big and strong, most likely the biggest and strongest of all five once they were all fully grown.

Tommy, now eleven, was taller, but more slender than Greg. That wasn't surprising since both his birth mother and birth father were tall. George wanted to name all of the boys after their real fathers but he didn't like the name William or Bill so he named him Thomas.

Zelda assured him, Tommy's parents were both hardworking people but he had never seen the father. The baby's mother and her parents, he had known all of her life. She would have kept her baby, but no one in town knew she had him and that was the way she wanted it. The only thing that bothered George was that Tommy was born in the Atwood Clinic. He didn't believe a child with farming qualities could be one born in a clinic that specialized in the treatment of handicapped children. Zelda assured him that nothing was wrong with the baby. She said the girl had chosen that clinic for additional secrecy when having her baby out of wedlock. That made sense, but he still had his doubts until he saw the big healthy baby. Only then did he agree to go through with the adoption.

Their youngest, Alex, was a special kind of boy. The seven-year-old had a way of touching a soft place in George's heart. George smiled, thinking about little Alex. Since he first started to crawl, he stacked and organized everything around him. If he was in the kitchen more than ten minutes, every can in the cupboard faced the front and sat evenly on the shelf, and all the pots, pans, and lids were organized.

Just yesterday, the little guy climbed on a stool at the workbench to watch George fix a crankshaft.

"What's this stuff?" Alex pointed at a large coffee can filled with odds and ends.

"Just nails and screws, and other things I haven't had time to sort and put away."

"I can do that, Dad?"

George opened a new box of small plastic bags. He took one screw out of the can and put it into a small bag to show Alex how he could sort the items using the little bags. He left him to his task, saying only, "Have at it."

A little while later, he heard Alex say he was finished, and saw the barn door open and close. Looking at his watch, he knew his son would go into the house, take a bath, and go to bed. He smiled, liking the fact that his little future farmer liked working with him in the barn.

He was surprised, though he shouldn't have been, by what he found when he went back to the workbench. Alex had removed about twenty empty pegs from higher up, and placed them evenly in a long row near the bottom of the Peg-Board, just above the workbench. Onto the pegs he had pushed the tops of the small plastic bags. He filled the bags with the items from the can. The screws had been placed with matching size screws, the smallest on the left, and the largest on the right. Beyond the screws were plastic bags of nails, all carefully sorted. On a higher row of pegs, plastic bags contained washers, nuts, tiny odd pieces of wire and clips. On the workbench were the larger items; laid out in a single row were a few large nails and screws, a light switch, and a small bent screwdriver.

George stood looking at the workbench, wondering what kind of farmer organized everything the way Alex did. He went into the house, and up to the boys' bedrooms. Alex was already asleep. His clothes were neatly folded, schoolbooks and papers centered on his desk, and slippers beside his bed, positioned for him to easily step into.

He looked in on the oldest two boys. Teddy and Trenton were arguing over something to do with the wrestling team. In contrast to Alex's room, theirs was a shambles.

"I would like you to pick up this room tomorrow," he said, knowing he wouldn't be back to check on the progress and nothing would get done.

Looking in on Greg and Tommy, he saw a similar mess, but before he could say anything, Greg said, "We'll have the room picked up in no time, Dad." That was his Greg. Oh, he was proud of Greg. If the boy said he'd do it, it would be done.

 props

At the county courthouse, Jeff Campbell stepped up to a counter he could not see over the top of. "Excuse me."

A chair squeaked on the other side of the counter, and he heard a gasp. Tentative footsteps sounded.

Finally the legal secretary peered over the edge of the counter. She blinked down at him. "What may I help you with?"

"I'm Jeffery Campbell. May I set up a hearing on behalf of myself and my family?"

"Let me get a legal pad." She shuffled papers on her desk. "And this pertains to what?"

"We want custody of our son. If it is not possible, we want the court to assure us he has been adopted by a loving family." He pushed a sheet of paper onto the counter above his head. "These are the details."

"Just a second." She looked at something behind the desk, and he heard her tap a computer keyboard. "I have an opening on September 14 with Judge Emerson."

"I would like Judge Roy Bain, please."

She looked sharply at him. "We don't permit picking and choosing. You are scheduled for the fourteenth at two o'clock. Is there a party in opposition that must be present?"

"Miss Zelda Cloud, of Social Services."

The woman looked at him over the top of reading glasses, and then her expression softened. She firmly crossed something out. "You will be standing before Judge Roy Bain, at noon on the fifteen of September."

Jeff smiled. "Thank you." *And thank You, Lord.*

She looked down at him. "You are quite welcome, Mr. Campbell."

An hour later, Jeff was too excited to hide his enthusiasm as he rushed into his father's office at the school. "Dad, good news. In fact, great news!"

The man calmly removed his glasses and put the temple of one side into the corner of his mouth, biting down lightly. "The last time you came in here and said that, your next words were, 'We're having another baby.'"

"Almost." Jeff smiled. "We have a hearing set before Judge Roy Bain on September 15, so between now and then, we need to get what you filed before, and everything Brent has on trying to get custody of Dwain. Larry knows this judge, and he thinks we have a fair chance with him."

"Larry." Jeff's father chewed the temple of his glasses. "Larry? The last time you came in here and told me that Larry thought you had a good chance of doing something, the two of you got me in trouble with George McCain."

Jeff laughed. "Dad, think of it. We could have Dwain home by the end of the month. This could be how God is going to do it. I believe God expects us to do something, not just sit around waiting."

Ben Campbell rolled his chair back and over to a file cabinet. Reaching inside, he withdrew a computer disc. "I scanned everything onto this, and I have another copy in my safety deposit box at the bank. You can take this and print it off."

Holding the disk, Jeff started to leave. Biting his lower lip he said, "Dad, did you give Dane a desk, for Dwain?"

"Not yet."

"Did you keep the one you took away from me?" He grinned. "It had some of my best carvings on it."

After his son left, Ben sat thinking, *Jeff, Jeff, Jeff, what will you get us into next?* He looked out the window. The parking lot was greatly improved. His son had pulled the rake back and forth over the gravel lot until almost dark last night. He could not be more proud of him. Leaning back, he wondered if he could find that desk in the storage room. It was in good shape except for the top, and that had been nice until Gramps gave Jeff a wood-carving set for Christmas.

Sara was stirring soup on the stove when Jeff rushed in. Her father, seated at the table, set his coffee cup down, thinking something was wrong. Jeff handed Sara the disc, "Honey, when you have time will you print everything on this?" He looked at them, and burst with the news. "We're going back to court. We have a hearing set with Judge Roy Bain on September 15 at noon. Larry says it's our best chance to get to the truth. This time, I requested the Judge review Zelda's records."

"You did it?" Brent nodded over and over again. "We're going forward again. Thank God. We're going forward."

❧ ❧ ❧

George McCain watched the movement of clouds over the valley below; he didn't like what he saw. A month from now, that cloud formation would be a welcome sight. If his father or grandfather saw this, they would have said to keep the tractor running to cut and dry as much hay as possible before the heavy rains of fall came. He felt despair that it might already be too late. If school had started a few weeks later or if the boys didn't have after-school activities, there might have been enough time to get all the hay out of the fields.

Not a man for making excuses, he drove into the field and climbed into the tractor cab. It was long after dark when he turned off the bright tractor lights, and climbed down, satisfied he had done all he could physically do for one day.

Stepping into the kitchen after washing his hands at the sink on the back porch, he sat alone at the table, eating while listening to the voices of Thelma and the boys upstairs. After placing his plate, cup, and utensils in the dishwasher, he went up to see what was going on. He wasn't surprised when he checked on the boys, and found Greg and Tommy's room neatly organized. After saying good night to the boys, he walked downstairs to his and Thelma's bedroom.

He unbuttoned his sweaty shirt. "We have good boys. Every one of them is exactly what we need to make this place work."

Thelma shut the dresser drawer as she watched him in the mirror. His routine was always the same. She knew it by heart and could close her eyes and see the movements in her mind. At fifty-six years old, he was still a fine-looking man, and she never tired of watching him as he slipped out of his soiled work clothes and stepped into the shower.

"Last night Alex organized my workbench." He poured shampoo into the palm of his hand.

"He's a lot like you." She smiled, appreciating him for always leaving his boots by the kitchen door, and helping her by using the three sections of the laundry chute. He had tossed his pants into the first section, his shirt into the center and the whites into the farthest. Alex had done the same with his clothes, and tomorrow, if the other boys bring their laundry down from their rooms, she could only hope they would do the same.

As he toweled off he said, "Maybe some of the behavior is learned. I don't organize the way Alex does, but I do try to put things where they belong."

Later, as they lay in bed, he turned to her. "Mabel thinks I shouldn't sell that forest section. Her daughter did some looking into what those developers do with the land they buy."

Thelma wondered if Mabel had mentioned the senior class project. Not wanting to bring it up first, she lay still, thinking. She remembered that adopting had been very fearful for her until everything went so well with Teddy. They had not considered adopting another, when Trenton was offered to them. As soon as George could take the two little boys with him in the cab of the tractor, he was ready for another baby in the bassinet at home. When Greg was up and running, George was so fascinated with how strong he was, he insisted they adopt one more. The fascination with Tommy was over how fast he grew. And now, everything Alex did was a wonder for George.

She moved her hand to her stomach, feeling a flutter like a butterfly. "What if one of our children were to have a physical problem?"

"Not a chance. That's why I was careful when we adopted them. I left nothing to chance. I'm not putting all I have into someone that can't do anything but let me down." He looked up at the ceiling. "We chose healthy, strong sons, so nothing will go wrong."

3

The senior class named their project "Finding Dwain." On the fifth day, Mr. Tims found it necessary to change the rules of the assignment. He no longer allowed interruptions from other students coming in with ideas. They had to make a Web site, and post the URL on the school's bulletin board. Within three days of posting their new Web site, they began compiling bits and pieces of information. The first big breakthrough in the search came from the most unlikely source.

Karen Sanders was often too shy to share her ideas with the senior class. She was more comfortable working on their project with her younger sister, Cathy. At home they searched the Internet using Cathy's laptop, and sent anything that might be helpful to the senior class Web site. Then, remembering how their cousin found her birth mother, Cathy got an idea.

Their adopted cousin, and her brother Michael, had gone to the office where the adoption records were kept. He created a diversion in a restroom, by moving the float in the toilet tank, causing it to overflow. When the office staff rushed to clean up the water, the two of them slipped into the office and looked through the files.

Lying in her bed Sunday night, Cathy told Karen her plan, "All we have to do is go to Zelda Cloud's office. We'll say you need to interview her for an assignment in school. You talk to her, and I'll figure out how to get into the file cabinet."

Karen said, "Maybe next week, when we go shopping for mom."

Rolling her eyes, Cathy shook her head. "Why not tomorrow, when we go shopping for mom? Why put it off? You are just afraid to do it, so you're putting it off."

Just thinking about doing something so bold gave Karen goose bumps. "I don't think I can do it. You know how Miss Cloud is when she comes to the school. She always dresses in black and she gives me the chills. She'd probably phone Mr. Campbell, and ask him why he is letting a student bother her."

Cathy expected this. "Then I'll interview her."

At 10:03 Monday morning, September 12, the girls walked into the county office of Social Services. Karen waited shyly as her younger sister stepped boldly up to receptionist's desk. Cathy quickly read the name plaque and smiled at the friendly-looking woman, saying, "Rhonda, I'm Cathy Sanders and this is my sister, Karen. I have a school assignment to interview someone who impresses me. I can't think of anyone who impresses me more than Miss Cloud. I would like to speak with her, if I may?"

Rhonda frowned toward the clock as she set her purse under her desk. She gave the girls an apologetic look.

"She should be here by eleven. You're welcome to wait." She motioned to empty seats by the window.

The girls sat on seats with the sun to their backs, absorbing the warmth. After only a few minutes, Cathy said, "I'll wait here while you get Mom's sewing material."

Rhonda looked up at the clock again and nervously picked up file folders. "Will you excuse me? I have to make copies and a pot of coffee."

Cathy watched Karen drive away, then sat impatiently for a minute before looking into the hallway to see if Rhonda was coming back. Not seeing her, she tried the handle on the closed door behind receptionist's desk. It was unlocked, so she slipped into the office, quickly locking the door before moving to the file cabinets. Pulling open a drawer labeled, "A–C," she moved her fingers over the folders, while listening for sounds in the outer office.

Cadle, Cacine, Cambell, Cammen, Campbell. Now, Dwain Campbell. Case, case, oh here it is. She lifted the file out. A metallic rattle behind her made her freeze, eyes open wide. Someone was trying the door handle! She knew she was caught.

A woman yelled, "I'm here to see Zelda from hell." Rhonda said something softly. The woman said, "I'm not waiting. Tell her she'll hear from my attorney."

Holding in her hands the key to everything, and not knowing how to hang onto it, Cathy almost cried. Then, she saw a very familiar sight: little blue lights across the front of a closed laptop. She eased the top open. The screen was dark, but touching the shiny pad in the center brought it to life. To her amazement, the social worker had left her computer on. Not only was it on, but it was connected to a scanner, both of which she knew how to use.

The folder was thick, consisting almost entirely of notations about Mr. Anderson coming in over and over again to inquire about his grandson. Scribbled below each entry were words and phrases like "such a pest," "idiot," "can't make up his mind what he wants," and "troublemaker." And some other words that Cathy wouldn't want to repeat. Selecting the few pages with pertinent information, she created a computer file she named "Dwain." As she scanned pages, she sent the copies to the file "Dwain." Hearing voices outside the door, she quickly attached "Dwain" to an e-mail addressed to the students' Web site, www.findingdwain.com.

Zelda Cloud said firmly, "Georgette, I'm not going to discuss this with you."

The door was being unlocked. There was no time to write a quick message in the e-mail. Closing the lid, Cathy grabbed the file folder and leaped into a closet behind the desk, pulling the door shut as quietly as she could.

"You cut off my assistance. I have a legal right to know why."

Zelda said, "You have a legal right to know *only* what I say you have a right to know."

Cathy eased the door open just enough to see a pretty, but very angry, black woman seated facing her. The woman's eyes opened wide when she saw Cathy peering from the closet behind Zelda.

"Let me get your file." Zelda moved to the file cabinet. "From what I see here, you are abusing your privileges."

"In what way am I abusing my privileges? I entered the program that you asked me to enter. You're the one who told me I should get an education. You told me that your department would be given more funding if you enrolled some of your welfare cases in classes. I was doing you a favor by starting classes. You knew I had five kids and a sick husband at home."

"You have a dog. If you can't feed your children, why do you feed a dog?"

"That little dog doesn't eat very much and he gives my husband a whole lot of joy while he's in bed all day."

Cathy eased the door open just enough to point over the back of Zelda's head, toward the closed laptop in front of Georgette. She pinched her fingers to her thumb and then mouthed the word, "Open," as she raised her fingers to represent something opening. Holding up one finger as if pushing on something, Cathy mouthed, "Send."

Zelda snapped at Georgette, "You are using the system to go further than I could ever go. You have no right getting an education to be a lawyer at the expense of taxpayers."

"Miss Cloud, I sat right here in this chair, and you told me that if I expected any more help from you, I had to start doing something for myself. You told me to enroll in classes, and you promised me that if I did, I would have child care."

Zelda shook her head, "Yes, typing classes or secretary classes. I'm shocked that you went into a full academic program. You are in your third year in the university."

Georgette leaned forward, placing her fingers on the desk in front of the closed laptop. "I qualified for a federal grant and a student loan to cover my tuition. You know I qualify for state-funded child care."

Zelda opened the file cabinet, forcefully shoving the file back into the drawer. Turning, she saw the woman touching the laptop. "What are you doing?"

"Dreaming," Georgette smiled, moving her fingers along the side of the open laptop, as if admiring it, as her other hand hovered above the keys. "Just dreaming, of how nice it would be to know how to use one of these."

The bitter social worker seated herself again. "Well, that, I assure you, will always be beyond you. And I will personally see to it that you will *never* use this office to become anything beyond your station in life."

The woman smiled, looking over Zelda's shoulder at the Cathy. "Oh, Miss Cloud, I realize I have limited capabilities, but even I have the right to dream?"

Zelda stood and went back to the file cabinet. "I will approve of your child care assistance, but I expect you to enroll in more practical classes."

At Cathy's prompting, the woman lifted the computer lid, moved the curser to the upper right corner, and clicked on the red *X* to close the program. When Zelda turned to face her, the lid was securely closed and the woman's eyes looked only at her.

"Stop this nonsense about becoming a lawyer and stop sending your friends in here for assistance to go to college. This is not a…"

Cathy almost whispered, "Social Services office." She pressed her ear closer to the door. She could hear muffled coughing and wondered what it was.

"Thank you, Miss Cloud, and I think you better take that poor kitty to a veterinarian as soon as possible. I take my little dog to Jeff Campbell's clinic. He is very good with animals and very reasonable. His clinic is only about forty-five minutes up the highway."

Zelda stepped to the door and handed Rhonda the folder. "Start her child care again." To Georgette she said, "The well-being of my cat is not your concern, and that man couldn't possibly know how to care for an animal of such fine pedigree."

While Cathy waited, hoping the social worker wouldn't open the closet door, Zelda spoke on the phone and tapped on the keyboard of her desktop computer. She then placed her laptop into a carrying case and told her cat she was going out for a little bit.

"Keep an eye on Fluffy," she said to Rhonda.

"Will you be gone long? There were two girls here earlier. Should I tell them when you'll be back?"

Without responding, Zelda rushed out.

Rhonda watched her boss struggle to open the door of her shiny red sports car, while juggling the file folders and computer case. She tossed everything inside and got in and slammed the car door. Without looking back, she accelerated in reverse, causing an approaching car to come to a screeching stop. Rhonda shook her head, relieved that Zelda's awful driving hadn't caused an accident. She waited for the car to go around her, then backed onto the street, again without looking behind her.

Karen was safely parked, but shaken by the close encounter. She reached the office door as Rhonda turned to lock it, saying, "I'm sorry. Miss Cloud was just here, but she ran out for a few minutes, and I have to take this poor kitty to the veterinarian." She held up a cat carrier.

"But..." Karen looked through the glass door into the darkened office. "Where is my sister?"

Rhonda called over her shoulder as she rushed out, "I'm sorry, I haven't seen her."

Karen stood with her back to the locked door, wondering what she should do. So far nothing had gone as they had planned. The click of the lock behind her startled her, and she jumped. Opening the door a crack, Cathy said, "I can't lock the door if I come out this way. Go around and help me out the window."

That was easy. Karen pulled as Cathy wiggled, and in just a few seconds, she was out and they both pushed the window closed. Then Karen had to know. "What did you find out?"

⚘ ⚘ ⚘

As she drove to the vet clinic, Rhonda wondered about Zelda. It seemed as if she was determined to serve only the intelligent, handsome, and strong while being a discouragement to those who really need the services offered by the state. When Zelda had vowed she would never have an animal without the finest breeding, she added that if people would just keep to their own kind and stay in their place, the world would be a better place for everyone. This was completely contrary to providing the helpful service Rhonda believed someone in Zelda's position should. She thought about that poor man, Mr. Anderson. He had come in three times since she started working for Zelda. It seemed a simple thing to her. All that needed to be done was for Zelda to contact the adoptive parents and convey the man's request. If they didn't want him to have contact with their son, they could say so, and Zelda wouldn't have to worry about the man coming back again. What Rhonda suspected was that something horrible had happened to that baby, and in some way, Zelda was at fault. Perhaps she had placed him in the wrong home or hadn't authorized proper medical care for him. And when Zelda formed an opinion about someone, nothing would change her mind. Even when proven wrong, she wouldn't accept it.

Rhonda listened to Fluffy coughing and thought about Zelda bringing her into the office and then remembered that Zelda hadn't been carrying her laptop when she came in. Though she denied it, Rhonda was absolutely certain that Zelda was coming back to the office at night. She had the only key to her office door, and her laptop wasn't in the office when she left yesterday. Then this morning it was. It didn't make sense. Not much about Zelda did.

She parked next to the only car in front of the clinic. The sign on the door said, "Closed except for an emergency." This, she considered an emergency. Fluffy hacked and heaved in her carrier as Rhonda rushed into the darkened veterinary clinic. She heard sounds in a back room. "Excuse me, is anyone here? I need some help, *please*. Is anyone here?"

Jeff Campbell stepped around the side of the counter, wiping his hands on a towel. "Good morning, Rhonda. What do you have there? Did you get another puppy?"

"It's a cat. Her name is Fluffy. She can't breathe."

Taking the carrier, he walked back into the room he had come from. Rhonda followed, relieved to have placed Fluffy in caring hands. She watched the little man gently ease the white cat out of the carrier. He lifted a penlight from the pocket of his white jacket and opened her mouth, shining the light inside. He spoke softly to her, "Well, you do have a problem here, Fluffy." And he reached into a drawer under the table for an instrument that looked like a small pair of needle-nose pliers.

He pulled a small bone fragment from the back of her throat. "There, we got it." Again he put the instrument in her mouth and lifted out another fragment. Then he caught the edge of a ball of hair and worked that out and set it in a pan next to the bone fragments.

"Let me just dab a little antiseptic on her throat, and she'll be fine."

Rhonda pulled out her checkbook. "How much do I owe you?"

"Nothing. I'm just here to check on a few animals. Taking chicken bones out of a cat's throat isn't a major operation. I will suggest some drops that should help her with the hair balls, and if she has a problem again, don't wait so long to bring her in."

Holding the cat in her case, Rhonda was waiting for a small bottle of drops when Zelda rushed into the clinic, shouting, "You have no right. That is not your cat and I didn't authorize any type of treatment." She grabbed the carrier, tearing it from Rhonda's grip."

Rhonda tried to explain. "She had chicken bones in her throat and a very big hair ball."

Zelda glared at Jeff, who looked a little stunned at the scene she was making. "I'm not paying for your services. I would never have approved of bringing this animal or any other animal to you." She whirled around and stalked out the door, poor Fluffy yowling her indignance.

Rhonda, giving him an apologetic look, whispered, "Thank you," and rushed out behind her boss. "The doctor didn't charge anything. He just said not to wait so long to bring her back if she gets sick again."

Zelda stopped short. "That type of person has no right being a veterinarian. He should be a welfare case and nothing more than that."

Rhonda's mouth fell open. She gasped, "Why? Just because he's short?"

Zelda pushed the cat carrier over onto the passenger side of her car and faced Rhonda. Her face was red, and her nostrils flared. "He is not short. I am short. He is handicapped, and he should not force the world to conform to his condition."

Jeff Campbell stood in the doorway, for the first time understanding why Brent was always upset after talking with Zelda. Now, he too was upset. He shut the door and fell to his knees. "Dear God, I had no idea. I just had no idea. She is evil and couldn't have good intentions for Dwain. Please hear me. I need to know how to pray about this. I don't know what to say. I am *pleading* from the bottom my heart." He lowered his head, closing his eyes, and then he knew what to say.

"I'm joining Dane in faith. In the name of Your son, Jesus, I'm praying with faith, knowing that you're bringing Dwain safely home to us."

He started to explain to God what God already knew. "I was adopted by loving parents who encouraged me to excel. They moved here so I'd have every available medical opportunity to be as capable as possible to take on whatever I chose to do in life.

"Sara and I have continually prayed for Dwain to be in an environment that will allow him to have great expectations for himself. You gave me a clear, sharp mind, and our children are so smart. I just know Dwain is doing well in school, but I can't believe that Miss Cloud is capable of looking out for his well-being. But I know You've been watching over him."

◌ ◌ ◌

Seeing Zelda Cloud's red sports car careen around the corner from the county road and fishtail onto the interstate, Brent Anderson slowed his tractor and wondered why she had been at the clinic. He would have to ask Jeff later. Knowing the field wasn't going to plow itself between now and dinner, he shifted into low gear, lowered the plow blades, and lined up to turn another row of sod.

And then he saw her, Katie Larraine Maguire, standing at the far end of his field, looking at her father's horses as if she didn't know he was there. He smiled, feeling warmth inside that he'd thought he would never feel again.

As he stopped the tractor and walked toward her, she turned to face him. She looked older, but his heart beat faster at the sight of her. He wondered how long it had been since he had seen her last. Thirty years? He remembered hearing she came back after Hilda's funeral, but he hadn't seen her. She smiled but she wasn't fooling him. He had always been able to tell when she was upset.

She said, "The years have been kind to you Brent."

He smiled, resting his arms on the rail next to her. "You look nice, too. You back for long?"

"Daddy lost everything again. I was able to bail him out last time, but the last few years haven't been my best. I came home to sort through the paperwork."

Brent looked toward the farmhouse and barn. The buildings could use a few coats of paint, and the wooden corrals around the barn needed some repair. He could feel her hurt. He could hear it in her voice. He always could. "He lose the horses?"

She smiled sadly and motioned toward a small herd grazing in the field. "All but these twelve mares. I have one more day in court to prove they were mine before Daddy lost his money. Bill collectors are trying to prove he transferred them to me to hide assets.

"You know how Daddy always gets the upper hand when he deals with me, or with anyone for that matter. When he called a few years ago, and asked if I'd lend him ninety thousand dollars, I told him I had to have a contract. But you know Daddy. He has to have a way out of everything, so he made me a deal. He thought he was outsmarting me. I was foolish enough to agree to another one of his schemes, but this time it backfired on him. I signed a contract giving me every filly born on the ranch from then on. After that, all he got was fillies."

Brent had heard Barney Maguire swearing more than once over the deal he had made with Katie. He had taken her money and bet it on a horse race. He won enough to pay off all of his debts and stud fees for his best racing mares. In the spring when the mares dropped their foals, he expected to have to register a few to Katie. Brent was in the Dine and Drive when Barney Maguire came in complaining. Every one of his mares had given birth to a filly. When Barney said, "In all the years I've bred horses, I never got all fillies before," Brent had smiled, so Barney asked him what he thought was so funny. Brent told him, "You still don't. They aren't yours. They all belong to Katie."

She blinked a few times as she watched the horses. "The bank is having an auction Saturday, if you're in the market for all the things you can't possibly need on your farm." Pain filled her voice.

He nodded. "If there's anything I can help you with, give me a call."

She looked up at him and swallowed hard. Her eyes shimmered with tears. He pulled her into his arms, comforting her the way he had when they were nine and her cat died, and when they were twelve and Joey Hamilton asked Cindy Meyers to the Fall Festival dance instead of her, and when they were fifteen and her quarter horse, Perfect Image, had to be put down after breaking his leg in a race he might have won.

In a few minutes, she pulled herself together, as she always had, and stepped back. "So what's this 'Finding Dwain' the whole town's talking about?"

✧✧ ✧✧ ✧✧

The senior class was clustered around the computers lining two walls of the classroom.

Mr. Tims walked along behind them, observing without commenting. The first group was searching a missing-persons Web site. The next was researching hospitals that provided special medical care for children with the problems Dwain might be facing.

Ryan told Jesse, "It says here, the most recommended clinic for the treatment of problems related to dwarfism is the Atwood Medical Clinic."

Jesse shrugged. "We know his doctor isn't at the Atwood Clinic, so keep looking."

Across the room, Walter yelled, "Oh, look at this. Dane, come here. Look at this. It's from Social Services."

Emily pointed at the photograph of an infant. "Look, oh, he's so cute."

Dane leaned over Walter's shoulder, staring at the face of a tiny baby. Under the photo were the typed words, "Three Days Old. Dwain Jeffery Campbell." Dane reached down and tapped a key to advance to the next page. "Where is he? Does it say who adopted him?"

"Don't, Dane." Walter pushed him off his shoulder. "I can't read if you're shoving me. Okay, he was sent to a hospital. And here, he was placed in foster care with adoption open, whatever that means. There's an address and a phone number."

Sally wrote the phone number down and jumped from her seat. "I'll see what I can find out."

The pretty girl's long blond braids bounced on her back as she ran from the classroom. Rushing into the office, she stopped in front of Principal Campbell's desk. "May I make a phone call, please?"

He motioned to his phone, "Help yourself, Sally. Do you need privacy?"

"No, it's okay." She turned his phone toward her and tapped the numbers. A woman answered. Sally said softly, "Hello, may I speak to Dwain Campbell, please."

Ben Campbell sat up straight. A lump formed in his throat. Was this what they had waited seventeen years for?

Sally said, "Oh, I see. Would you please send what you have to us? We're trying to locate him. We have a Web site. The address is www.findingdwain.com. Yes. Thank you. Will it take very long?"

She set the receiver down. "She didn't adopt Dwain but she has information she just happened to be looking at earlier this morning. She said it's quite a coincidence I would call today, because she has everything by her computer."

Leaving, she looked back. "Do you believe in coincidences Mr. Campbell? I don't. I do believe in prayers being answered when we have faith."

Alone, Ben smiled. Dane was lucky to have a friend whose faith was as stalwart as Sally's.

Dane, too excited to wait for the new information Sally assured him was coming soon, rushed out of the school, the information in the Social Services files spinning in his head. He ran across a field, leaped over a narrow stream, climbed a hill, and ran down a trail to the back of the barn. Seeing his dad's car, he ran for the house and pulled open the kitchen door, yelling, "Mom, Dad, Grandpa. Anybody here?"

"Whoa." His dad stepped into the kitchen. "Where's the fire?"

"Look what I got. It's Dwain."

Jeff took the sheet of paper, in the center of which was imprinted a photograph of a newborn infant. He stood for a few seconds saying nothing, then as tears fell on the edge of the paper he said, "My baby. This is my baby. Sara, this is our baby."

Sara came in and set a basket of laundry on a chair and leaned down to see what her husband was holding. She gasped. "I never thought I would ever see a picture of him. That's baby Dwain? Zelda wouldn't let me see him when he was born."

Dane said, "He looks like you, Dad."

Jeff laughed, sniffing and wiping his eyes with his hand. "One of you has to look like me. Four kids, and finally one looks like me."

Dane bounced around the kitchen. "It came from the last place we expected to get anything—from Zelda Cloud. Maybe she had a change of heart."

Still looking at the picture, Jeff whispered, "Where is he?"

Dane said, "His first foster care mother is sending some more stuff. She said she quit taking foster kids because when she tried to adopt Dwain, Zelda wouldn't approve the adoption. She's sending us what she has up until he was three years old."

As the foster care information came over the Internet, Mr. Tims couldn't quiet his classroom. He sat on the edge of his desk, wondering why Social Services had sent his students confidential information. Sally and Michael were placing a row of photographs on the bulletin board. Andy had called his dad at the radio station and caused a chain reaction that brought a reporter and cameraman into the school. Tonight's news would tell the outside world what was happening in his classroom. He was sure there would be some people who would strongly disagree with what he was allowing his students to do.

Dane and his parents rushed in as a photograph came off the printer. Eddy pointed to the bulletin board. Dr. Campbell stepped up onto the stool Sally had jumped down from. He placed his face inches from the row of photographs, looking at each through a haze of tears.

A woman pressed a microphone toward him. "I understand this is the first time you have seen pictures of your son."

Jeff looked at her, not seeing the camera over her shoulder. "This is my son, Dwain. I never gave up my legal right to my son, and even if he has a wonderful adoptive family, I have a right to tell Dwain I love him. I have a right to look into his eyes, and tell him we never wanted to give him up."

The woman turned to the camera. "This senior high school class is searching for a boy who should be in this class. Dwain Jeffery Campbell will be seventeen years old September 30. He has blond hair and blue eyes. He is a little person. The family believes he is about forty-five inches tall. If you have any information about him, please use the Web site at the bottom of the screen."

4

Senior staff surgeon Dr. Marcus Fitzgerald leaned on the counter at the nurses' station of the privately owned Earlington Memorial Hospital. He had completed another successful but exhausting heart surgery and was ready to go home. He asked one of the nurses, "Did you call my wife to let her know I'll be late?"

"Yes, and you have another message from Zellie."

He reached for the note, read it, and handed it back to her. "This time she wants me to buy Fluffy cat food on the way home. I hope she figures out soon that she's calling the wrong number."

The nurse smiled. "She asks for Dr. Marcus Fitzgerald. I don't think there's another one in the whole state of Oregon."

He frowned. "Are you sure it wasn't a long-distance call?" He turned to a doctor approaching. "You have a nice shift, Bradley. I'm going home and try to sleep." Looking back at the nurse, he said, "Try to get a phone number the next time she calls."

She made a pained expression. "Are you sure you want to respond to her?"

"I just want to tell her to stop calling me. This is becoming embarrassing."

Bradley smiled, picking up a clipboard. "It's your reputation. All of the young women want you," he teased.

Marcus shook his bald head. "I don't have the energy to know any young women. One wife, three children, and four grandchildren are all any man my age could possibly have enough energy for."

ᴏᏅꜱ ᴏᏅꜱ ᴏᏅꜱ

Six blocks from the hospital in the county office building, Dennis Drake sat at his desk thinking. He had the means to find Dwain Jeffery Campbell, but should he get involved? Was it worth his while? What was in it for him? As the newly appointed head of all three county Social Service offices, he had full access to all the county files. With a growing file of complaints about Zelda Cloud, he decided to find out what he could. He enlisted a coworker to ask Zelda about the complaints and get her to send over her files, then he set about looking into the Campbell boy's case.

In the computer file on Dwain Campbell, Zelda's name was on every order to move the boy for the first seven years, then the child simply vanished from the system. That didn't make sense. A child doesn't just vanish from the state's data bank. He sat back, thinking. The last place the boy had been was in a foster home only a few blocks from his office.

His coworker called from his desk. "Zelda said no one has complained to her. And, though I won't repeat her actual words, she isn't sending us any of her files."

Dennis shook his head. "I'm leaving for a while. I have to check out a children's home. Call my cell if the old bat comes to her senses and decides to cooperate."

A few minutes later, he walked up to the front door of a huge old three-story home. The home was registered by the state as an infant care center, run by the owner, Agnes Drew. A gruff, middle-aged woman answered his knock at the door. She abruptly instructed him to go into parlor and sit down. She told him she didn't appreciate unscheduled visits from his office, so this had better be for a very good reason. As he sat facing her, a baby cried somewhere in the large old home, and then another. She grumbled under her breath as she closed the parlor door.

He said, "I'm not here to inspect your home, Miss Drew. I would like to see your records on a child we placed with you ten years ago." He opened the folder that contained documents pertaining to the Campbell boy. "He was in your home until the last week of September. That would make him seven years old at that time."

She lit a cigarette. "Name? I can't tell you a thing if you jabber and don't come to the point." She stood and opened the door. Looking up at the stairway she yelled, "Shut that brat up or I will."

He winced. "Dwain Campbell. You might remember him. He is classified as a little person, or person with dwarfism. Our records show he has a common type of dwarfism. Small, six years old, almost seven, with short arms and short legs."

"Dead," she snapped, walking to the window and moving smoke-stained lace curtains to the side. "They send me the babies. I hire girls to care for them. Some of the babies don't live. Drugs, mostly. Their mothers are usually off the street. Some with HIV, even AIDS. The state is lucky to have a place like this to put them."

She looked back at him. "I remember the boy. He was a back talker. I don't do well with children that don't do what they're told. When Zelda asked me to take him, I told her I would but not on a long-term basis."

She shook her head. "Zelda knows I take babies. I don't like children. I have never liked children. I take in babies that are not under my feet, and I can't stand a child who talks back."

His mind raced. A dead child wasn't worth a thing to him. He had to convince the people looking for Dwain that he knew his whereabouts. He had intended to wait until they offered a cash reward for information on Dwain's whereabouts, and then come forward and collect the money—maybe as much as twenty grand. Now, he had to move quickly before they found out the kid was dead. He looked down at the page in his folder. "Do you have any information I can add to our files? Did you take any pictures of him?"

She shook her head. "I provide cribs and girls to feed and change babies. Dwain was underfoot constantly. I was about to have Zelda take him out of here when he got sick. I sent him to the hospital. I remember"—she squinted—"he was talking about his birthday being in just a few days."

Dennis pulled out a hundred-dollar bill. "If you have even one photograph of him, I will make it worth your while."

She said she might have something and led the way to the stairway. Going up, she huffed and stopped to get her breath each time she took a few steps. On the first landing she said, "I only come up here when I absolutely have to. If one of the girls gives me a reason to have to once, she thinks twice before she gives me a reason to come up here again."

She looked into a nursery where a young lady sat rocking a baby while three other babies watched her through crib bars. She said, "Keep it quiet."

The young lady said, "It wasn't mine. It was from down the hallway."

At the top of the next flight of stairs, she unlocked and pushed a heavy door inward. "I have the girls keep this file room in order. I don't come up here very often, but I know where most of the old files are."

He told her the date on the page in his folder and helped her lift down a file box labeled with that year. She moved her fingers over the tops of file folders inside the box and withdrew one labeled, "Campbell, Dwain."

When he saw photographs in the bottom of the file folder, his eyes opened wide. Scooping them out of the folder, he turned over the top few to see what he had. His heart was pounding.

"This is great. This is really great." In each photograph, a small boy held a baby that looked disproportionately large. In none of the photographs did the baby appear to be the same baby. Some were black, most brown, and a few had light skin. He fanned the stack in his fingers as if it were a deck of cards until he found what he was looking for.

"I'll take this picture." He stuffed the hundred-dollar bill into her greedy hand and then looked at what was written on the child's chart. The last entry, dated September 29, consisted of only the word "Deceased."

The woman motioned for him to lift the file box back up onto the shelf. "He stayed up on the baby floor if he knew what was good for him. The girls liked him too much. Always letting him hold the babies and taking pictures of him. We take a few pictures. State requires it so there are pictures to give parents that adopt them, or the mother if she gets her kid back."

He put the photograph into his shirt pocket. "Do very many mothers ask for their babies back?"

She raised her hands. "I don't handle any of the details. Your office does that. I just take them in, and when someone comes to get them, I hand them over. They come and go. I don't want to know where they came from or where they go."

He stopped. "How do you know for sure that Dwain died?"

She pointed up at another box. "Pull that down."

Reaching inside the second box, she withdrew a knitted baby blanket. Knitted into the pattern was "Mommy loves Dwain."

She said, "He came with this. If they come with something like this, they leave with it. If he lived, they would have come for it."

"Did he have anything else?"

"Only the baby blanket. It's in Zelda's file. She asked me about it. I told her she could come and get it. I'm only required to keep it, not send it anywhere. If she wanted it, she would've come and got it."

She lifted a sign-out sheet from the box. "If you take it, put your name and the date and notate that you took a photograph. I don't want anyone saying I lost anything."

Because she was watching him closely, and because it made no difference whatsoever, he clearly wrote his name and notated that he had taken a photograph. He then followed her down to the second floor. She walked down the hallway to where a baby was crying. As he left, he heard her shouting at someone.

Standing on the old wooden porch, he looked around the neighborhood. A few children kicked a ball in the street while others played in a yard under a tree, tossing fallen leaves over their heads. He sat in his car. This would be the perfect neighborhood to raise his family. Looking at the old house he had come out of, he thought, if he could afford to buy a house like that, he would someday.

For an instant, his training caused a twinge of guilt. He considered going back to the office and looking in the files to find out if there were any complaints about this care provider. She seemed completely unfit to care for children. And then, he decided he would be making more work for himself if he caused the closure of a badly needed infant care center. He shrugged. A bad home was better than no home at all.

Dennis Drake was tired of the system. For the education he had, he shouldn't have subordinates like Zelda Cloud, thumbing her nose at him, refusing to show him the respect he deserved. He looked at the picture and thought about what he would tell Dwain's family. He stroked the soft blanket with his fingers. It was sad the little boy had died, but with the physical problems, he might be better off not living in this cruel world.

✿ ✿ ✿

Dennis Drake was the least of Zelda's worries. If she ignored him, eventually he would stop bothering her. In response to his constant requests for copies from her files, she'd sent him absolutely nothing. What she made available on the state data files was all she intended to share of her personal records.

Putting him entirely out of her mind, she huffed into to the county court building. The legal secretary looked at her stupidly over the top of her reading glasses.

Zelda banged her purse on the counter. "I want a court date for a Social Services matter." While the woman meandered to the counter and opened the appointment book, Zelda said, "It's the State of Oregon vs. Dane Campbell and his family. My office was broken into, and records from my personal files were given to Dane's class in school. I want to see that brat put behind bars."

The legal secretary blinked. "Is this a case that's already before the court in criminal justice?"

Zelda glared at her. "Just put it on the calendar and notify Jeffery and Sara Campbell to be in court. I'll have my case ready by then. Make sure it's before Judge Emerson or Datemen."

The woman's jaw tightened as she looked at the schedule. "I have one opening this month. It is on the fifteenth of September at twelve o'clock."

"Fine. I will be here at *precisely* twelve o'clock."

Zelda smirked as she walked the two blocks from the court building to her office. She held her head high, carrying her official-looking black brief that matched her black skirt, jacket, and shoes. As she approached her office building, she would've skipped if it weren't undignified. *When I fin-*

---

ish with that Campbell kid, his class will be sorry they ever started that nonsense project, "Finding Dwain."

As she entered her office, Rhonda held up a sheet of paper. "This fax just came for you."

She snatched the paper out of her hand and read the top few lines, "Summons to appear in court...yada, yada, yada...Campbell family... twelve o'clock on the fifteenth." She let it drop from her fingers into the wastebasket. "I'm aware of this. Respond to the court—let them know I received the notification. Cancel my afternoon appointments on Thursday. I will be in court."

After the office door closed behind Zelda, Rhonda lifted the paper and read, "Jeffery and Sara Campbell, requesting a hearing for the custody of Dwain Jeffery Campbell. Court requests adoption records be presented prior to the hearing." She whispered, "Judge Roy Bain." Looking over her shoulder, at the closed office door, she considered where her loyalty should lie. She closed her eyes for a moment, and then she pushed the sheet of paper deep into the wastebasket. After typing a reply, assuring the court Zelda had received the notification and would comply, she placed the sheet of paper on Zelda's desk for her signature.

5

George was working at the workbench as his oldest son, Teddy, milked the cow. "It's just not right," George said as he lifted the full milk bucket from Teddy's hand. The teenager set the three-legged stool against the wall and led the cow out to the pasture. His father set the bucket down and closed the barn door.

"Dad, I don't think it's the same for them as it is for us. You made sure our parents agreed to give us up for adoption. Zelda Cloud wasn't honest with Mr. Anderson. She knew Dwain legally belonged to Sara and Jeff, and they both had to agree to give him up for adoption."

When Zelda first handed him Teddy, he took one look at that big baby boy and was so happy, he slipped her an envelope of cash. He assured her it was just a token of his appreciation. After that, she was eager to find them another suitable son. It was two years almost to the day when he called about Trenton. By then, she knew exactly what he wanted to hear.

He handed Teddy the milk bucket. "Sometimes, people in positions of power let it go to their heads, but Zelda Cloud has always been helpful to us."

"But you're the kind of person she likes. She doesn't like people that are different. Some people think you can't live a normal life if you are a short person or in a wheelchair or can't see well. But it's inside of a person that makes him what he is."

As he watched a long black car leave the highway and turn onto the dirt road coming up to the farm, George said, "But strong people have an easier go of life. Take the milk to the house. I'll be in, in a few minutes." He walked to the front of the house, hoping to convince the driver to leave without a lengthy discussion. He crossed his arms and stood in front of the driver's door, giving him no room to open it. The driver lowered the tinted window.

"Have you given our offer more thought, Mr. McCain?"

"None of my land is for sale. My grandparents would turn over in their graves if I sold a piece right out of the center, so people like you can clear the trees for a golf course and fancy condominiums."

"George, you'll never get a better offer. A million dollars is a lot of money. We won't touch your farm. You have to admit you have too much land as it is. The county told us you're letting more than five hundred acres of farmland sit empty."

"I'm not selling, so turn your car around and leave."

The man behind the wheel gave him a grim smile. "But, what about Hilda?" he asked, as though the name were an ace he pulled from his sleeve.

"What about Hilda?"

"Maybe she would like to sell the land."

A vein on the side of George's neck throbbed. "Get out of here!"

Teddy carried the bucket of milk to the back porch and poured it through a filter, filling first a gallon glass pitcher and then a gallon glass jar. He placed both containers into a refrigerator on the screened porch and withdrew yesterday's cold gallon jar of milk. Leaving the gallon jar on the counter, he went into the kitchen. His mother stepped past him with the scoop she used to remove cream from the top of the chilled milk.

"After I take the cream off of this milk, I want you to put the jar in the car. I'm going to go take Trudy her milk and eggs."

Teddy washed his hands and sat at the breakfast table. His brothers were already pouring syrup over their pancakes. Seven-year-old Alex stabbed his pancakes over and over again with his fork. Greg smiled, shrugging his shoulders. Their father washed his hands and then sat and watched Alex for a few seconds.

"Developers again," he said to Thelma. "I keep telling them I'm not interested and they keep coming back." He winked at his youngest son. "So what's going on with you this morning, Alex?"

"Greg said that I'm darker than he is because my mother was a no-good Mex."

George forked two pancakes off of a plate in the center of the table. "The Mexicans that come here in the summer are hardworking people. I've never known them to leave a child. They depend on them to help with the family. Their lifestyle is family oriented. Their kids are as important to them as you are to us."

The boy looked up and slowly set his fork down beside his plate. "How am I important?"

His mother set a pitcher of orange juice on the table. "Without you, how would I get the eggs gathered from the henhouse, and who would feed the dog? You help all of us by doing your share of the work around here."

His dark eyes looked up into hers. "So you won't let my birth mother come back and take me away to live in Mexico?"

His mother's eyes turned to George. George cleared his throat. "All this stuff about finding a child that was legally given up for adoption is only causing trouble. People need to let be what is and take care of what they have."

Thelma said softly, "Don't you worry about a thing Alex. As soon as they find out baby Dwain was adopted by a nice family, they will be fine with that. What has them worried is that they just don't believe he was adopted. In your cases"—she looked at their five sons—"your birth mothers were very young and still had to finish school. They were careful about making sure you would be going to a mother and father with a farm, so you would have lots to eat and a dog and a cat and things to do."

Greg said, "What about a horse? Did you give it some thought, Dad? I would really like a horse." He picked up his plate, carried it to the sink, rinsed it, and placed it in the dishwasher. He glanced out the window. "Bus is at the Taylors'. I gotta get my book report."

As her four younger boys ran upstairs to their rooms to get their school things before the school bus arrived at the end of their driveway in five minutes, Thelma set a plate on the table for herself and poured two cups of coffee. "I just wish all of this hadn't gotten started. I don't know what to say to them."

George leaned forward, lowering his voice to avoid being heard by the younger boys. "The law is on our side. A person can't wait seventeen years and reach into a family to take a child they adopted. He may not even know he is adopted. Not everyone tells the kids right from the start the way we did."

Teddy, hunched as though trying to make himself small and invisible, said softly, "Sometimes when a person is like Dwain, he wants to know what is going to happen to him, genetically. He may want to know why he's like he is and if he has children, what the possibility of them being dwarfs will be. And some people have other medical issues they want to understand."

Thelma touched George's hand, "That is true, George. With each of our babies, you asked about the medical history of both sides of his family."

The vein in his neck pulsed. He pushed his chair back and stood. "I have a tractor to fix. Be home after school so we can get that last section of hay cut, Teddy."

"Dad, we have wrestling."

George stiffened, staring out the window. He closed his eyes, clutched his fist at his side, and drew a deep breath. "I'll make it a late night, then," he said softly.

Teddy stood, let his younger brothers push past him, then lifted the gallon jar of milk from the counter. He looked back at his mother, thanked her for breakfast, and said to George, "After practice I'll get right on the hay field."

Alone again in the kitchen with Thelma, George sat looking at his cup of coffee. "I wish this kind of stuff wouldn't happen. Before that class started this project, our boys never mentioned being adopted."

He looked at her. "Strong, healthy people don't challenge the system the way that little midget Jeff Campbell does. Every time the town tries to do something that steps the least bit on anyone's toes, he gets involved. Our taxes went up because he wanted sloped sidewalks for wheelchairs and blue painted parking spaces for handicapped people."

⚭ ⚭ ⚭

Teddy sat looking out the school bus window, seeing nothing. He had decided to do something to stop Mr. Tims's class from continuing to search for Dane's twin brother. He had to do something or other adopted kids would be in danger of being found. Once he turned sixteen in just two months, he could legally choose to stay where he was. But his younger brothers could be taken, especially Alex. He looked over at the seven-year-old. None of them looked at all alike, but all the same, they were brothers. And he intended to make sure no one separated any of them from the family.

Thelma was tidying the porch when she saw another car rolled up their driveway. As the vehicle pulled up close to the house, the driver lowered the window. It was obvious George was expecting someone else. Once he looked inside, though, he stepped back from the side of the car and smiled. Larry Atwood got out, and the two men shook hands.

"What brings you all the way out here?"

Thelma waved from inside the porch and held up the coffeepot, and the doctor waved back. The two men climbed the steps together.

"I was wondering if we could talk," Larry said as he looked around the farmyard. "It smells good out here. The birds are louder than they are in town."

George chuckled. "Wait until the rooster crows and wakes you up every time someone turns on the bathroom light in the middle of the night."

Seated at the table, Larry declined the offer of breakfast and thanked Thelma for a cup of coffee. She moved away from the men, studying the younger man as she busied herself with wiping the kitchen counter. He was too handsome to not be married. She remembered Trudy saying she saw him talking with Ellen James at the church picnic. Both were tall and very nice looking; they would make a nice couple.

Larry said, "I'm having trouble with some land developers. They've been pestering me about buying into a project they're planning out here."

George snapped, "We aren't selling."

"Good. Then I can ask you what's really on my mind. You know that handicapped children are my calling in life. I'm the only child my parents had who was born without hereditary dwarfism. I was the last child my parents had but not the last they raised. They raised sixteen physically handicapped children. From that, I attribute my interest in helping children with all types of physical disabilities. To help children, I support some special projects."

George leaned back in his chair and squinted. "I'm listening."

Oh good. Thelma had always wanted to know more about the Atwood family. Like her and George, they had adopted children. But the ones they adopted were the very ones George would have passed over. *Oh dear, I hope this doesn't upset him more.*

"In the forty years since my parents started the clinic specializing in treatment for children born with dwarfism, several families have relocated to be closer to the help we offer."

George nodded. "That was why the Campbell family moved here, for Jeff."

Dr. Atwood smiled. "I grew up with Jeff. Well I guess I should say I grew up and he stayed little, but we both shared the same interest in the medical field. He has a love for animals and I for children. And this brings me back to what I came out here to ask you about."

Thelma sat slowly at the table, holding her breath. She was afraid he had come to talk about why Tommy had been born in the Atwood Clinic. If he told George what Trudy had told her, she didn't know what George would do, so she was relieved when the doctor said, "That lake property wouldn't be available for anyone to consider developing if it was tied up in a thirty-year lease. If you lease it to an organization that only wants to allow handicapped children to enjoy using it for a summer camp, you would keep your land, and give hundreds of children something very special every summer."

Thelma gasped, "And the horses. George, we could keep horses for the camp. Like your dad used to do. The boys could ride them and we could have them ready for the camp."

George set his cup down. "Whoa, Thelma, have you two been talking about this behind my back?"

She gently touched his hand. "No, but you know we've been talking about letting Greg have a horse, and you've always said that it's cruel to have one horse, or one cow or one chicken, for that matter."

George shook his head. "Larry, what are you asking me to consider?"

Larry smiled. "I got the idea from those overzealous developers. The more they talked about a golf course, the more I saw rows of cabins, a center area for a campfire, and docks out into the water. We have the kids. All we need is a wilderness camp."

George said, "You're talking about making changes that aren't too different from what those developers want to do with the land."

Larry winked at him. "You would still own it. It wouldn't cost you a thing, and we would do all the work without clear-cutting the trees."

The vein in George's neck had darkened at the mentioned of handicapped children. Since his sister Hilda died, he had been determined to keep handicapped children out of his life. Now, she watched him keep his anger in check. Finally, he simply said, "I'll think about it." The doctor stood and shook his hand. "I can't ask for more than that."

As Larry drove away, George looked over at a place where weeds almost hid a white picket fence, framing a small plot of land. He walked across the yard to the low enclosure and stood looking down at the weeds. Thelma had seen him do this many times before and knew he needed to be alone. But this time was different. He leaned down and pulled up a stake of the short fence, and continued pulling until he had the old fence in a pile, away from the plot of weeds. He then walked around behind the barn and returned with the tractor.

Thelma watched as he set the plow into the soil. He drove back and forth over the small plot of land until he had turned all of the weeds under. He parked the tractor and returned with a wheelbarrow filled with manure. Thelma wiped the counter and then remembered Trudy's milk.

A few minutes later, in her neighbor's kitchen, Trudy told her about a new litter of kittens, and then asked what George was doing over there in the front of the house with the tractor.

"I don't know what he's doing and I'm not going to ask him. For six years he has not let anyone touch Hilda's flower garden. Tommy tells everyone that someone is buried in that little spot. It does look like a much neglected grave, doesn't it?"

Trudy laughed. "That Tommy and his imagination. I really get a kick out of him. I don't know what he likes more, eating my cookies or telling stories. Yesterday he told me the life story of a snake that lives under my barn."

A new paperback romance novel lay on the table. Thelma picked the book up and turned to the back cover. As she looked at the picture of the author, Trudy said, "That's her latest one. I think it's her best one so far. That's your copy."

Thelma smiled, touching the cover with her fingers lovingly. "It seems strange. I feel such a bond with her. Because she gave Tommy up, he's ours." She pushed the book to the side, knowing Trudy would put it away with the other books she wanted saved for Tommy.

Trudy was looking out the window. She said, "When Hilda came home. She looked like she was close to dying. I never saw her so sick in all the years I knew her."

Thelma broke off a piece of a cookie. "She was too sick to do anything with that flower bed. George thought she would rest for the winter and be well enough to plant flowers in the summer. When he picked her up at the bus stop, he had to help her into the car. When she took off her coat, we both knew she might not make it through the winter."

Trudy set a clean gallon glass jar on the counter near the door. It was their routine for as long as the women had been neighbors. Thelma brought a dozen eggs and a gallon of milk to the Taylors' every Monday, Wednesday, and Friday. For which she received in trade from Trudy, one of her freshly baked pies or a tray of cinnamon rolls, and always at least a dozen of the boys' favorite chocolate chip cookies. Trudy said, "I saw cars over there this morning. Are those men still bothering him about buying the lake property?"

"He isn't bothered by them as much as he is over the 'Finding Dwain' project."

Trudy shook her head. "When we were kids, George watched out for Hilda all the time. He always said he would never let that bad heart gene be carried down through him. He said he would never have kids."

Thelma looked over at the clock. "I have to go. I let the time get away from me. I have an appointment in town. Thank you so much for the cookies. The boys will be thrilled."

Not giving Trudy time to ask about her appointment, she hurried out to her car. She hadn't gotten around to telling George she was going into town, but it wasn't a good time to say anything to him.

❧ ❧ ❧

In the dark classroom, Teddy walked in front of the computers, touching the tables with his fingers as he considered what he could do to stop the class from finding Dwain. As the door opened and the light turned on, he turned to face Dane Campbell, who smiled and waved to him as he walked to his desk. "How's wrestling, Teddy? Are you going to take our school to state this year?"

Teddy flexed the muscle in his arm. "I didn't toss hay bales all summer for nothing."

Dane grinned. "Your dad took this school to state. My dad told me he was the best wrestler the school ever had."

Teddy shook his head. "My dad never wrestled. It's hard for him to let me because he isn't into school sports."

Dane half sat on his desk. "Your folks told you you're adopted, but didn't tell you about your real dad?"

Resentment coiled inside Teddy. Why couldn't Dane leave things alone? "I thought my parents were from somewhere else."

"I'll show you." Dane led the way down the hallway to the glass display. He pointed at a picture of a senior wrestler holding a trophy. "Theodore Brady."

Teddy read the words on the plaque and then the words of a memorial to the young man who'd died in a car accident before his graduation. Part of him didn't want to know any of this. But another part wondered why no one had told him his birth parents had lived right in their own town. "So how did I get adopted by my parents? What about his parents, my grandparents? And what happened to my real mom?"

Dane shrugged his shoulders. "My grandpa said that after their son died, his parents couldn't live here anymore. They left. Your mom was still in high school. I don't know where she is now. You could go to the office and ask my grandpa."

Teddy studied the face of the boy in the photograph above him. "He was strong."

"He had to have been strong to take us to state." Dane pointed to his name on the wrestling trophy.

Teddy shoved his fingers into his pockets and walked away. Dane caught up with him. "What were you doing in my homeroom class?"

"Checking out how you were doing with your class project."

"But nobody was there."

"I was just looking." So he could figure out a way to stop the class from finding Dwain. But now…was he sure he wanted to stop the project?

Teddy stepped into the office. "May I speak to Mr. Campbell, please?" The secretary waved them ahead, and Dane followed him into the principal's office. Teddy came straight to the point. "Did you know my dad when he wrestled here?"

Principal Campbell nodded. "I was the principal when Ted Brady wrestled here."

"Who was my mother?"

"That is not a secret, Teddy. You can look in any yearbook while they were in school and see her. He stepped to a bookcase, selected a green book from a top shelf, and handed it to Teddy.

Slowly opening the cover, Teddy prepared himself. He recognized Ted Brady the instant he saw him leaning against the school building with his arm around a teenage girl.

Mr. Campbell said, "Her name was Anna Reynolds. She was a very bright and talented young woman."

So she gave me up so she could go to college. "Where is she now?"

Principal Campbell looked at Dane, and then back at Teddy. "Anna left school and went to work in California. A few years later we were told that she passed away. I don't know the details."

Teddy could tell Mr. Campbell was deliberately leaving something out. "Why didn't she take me with her?"

"I don't know the sequence of events leading up to your adoption. It might be best if you asked your parents. I knew at the time, your parents had applied to adopt a child, and Anna's ability to care for an infant as an unwed mother, still in high school, was a consideration."

"What about her parents?"

Again, Principal Campbell carefully chose his words. "You would have to ask your parents."

"Thank you." Teddy placed the book back on the shelf and walked out into the hallway, where he said to Dane, "My mother couldn't raise me, and I wasn't adopted without her permission. So that makes my case different than Dwain's, right?"

"A lot of things make Dwain's case different. The main thing is that Dwain was not a normal baby so there is a possibility he wasn't adopted. In some cases it's more profitable to keep a child as a foster child, for state benefits."

Teddy could see that scenario didn't apply to his situation or to his brothers', but he had to cover every angle. And Dane seemed to know a lot about this stuff. Maybe he could even help. "I need to know if there's a threat of losing one of my brothers. How do I find out about their parents?"

Dane whispered, "Microfiche at the county library. Vital statistics. I'll show you after school."

"I got wrestling practice, but I really want to know. I appreciate it when someone tells me the truth, and I know when to keep my mouth shut. I just"—he looked at his sneakers—"I don't want to upset my dad."

Dane raised an eyebrow, then he shrugged and thumped Teddy's shoulder. "The library is open Saturday until pretty late. Call me when you're ready."

After the boys left, Ben Campbell sat at his desk wondering if he had said too much. The last thing he wanted was trouble with one of his student's parents. The last parent he wanted trouble with was George McCain.

He sat back, thinking. George and Thelma had done well with their boys, but having been the principal of the high school when the parents of those boys were enrolled, he could see how their individual personalities could very quickly take them astray. If McCain were more open to listening to any-one else's opinion, he would be willing to point a few things out. Any other farmer would say it was nipping trouble in the bud if an attentive school administrator were to suggest he keep a closer eye on his thirteen year old, but George would most likely consider it to be no one else's business.

He thought about the night he'd helped carry Ted Brady's body up the steep slope off Dead Man's Curve on the Old Henderson Road. His body was soaked from head to toe in whiskey. The car had rolled three times before he'd been thrown clear of it. He would have survived if a broken whiskey bottle hadn't severed an artery. The boys that had been in the front seat and Ted's girlfriend, Anna Reynolds, sat along the roadway, too intox-icated to walk a straight line. He believed at the time, had any one of them been sober, Ted Brady would not have bled to death that night.

Two years later, the driver of that car proved he didn't learn a thing from that accident. Trenton Jones died in a second rollover that left his pregnant girlfriend in a coma she never regained consciousness from. The baby, born by C-section a few weeks after the accident, was also adopted by George and Thelma McCain. But very few people realized this. If the boy hadn't been named Trenton and if he didn't look so much like his mother, even Ben wouldn't have guessed.

When Ted Brady died, all the community could remember was that he took the state championship in wrestling his senior year of high school. And when Trenton died, they memorialized his greatest accomplishment by naming the Fall Festival pumpkin growing contest the Trenton Tour-nament.

∽ ∽ ∽

Thelma lay on her back on the examining table as the nurse rubbed a cold liquid over her abdomen, and watched the movement of the fetus on the monitor. Dr. Miller leaned toward the screen and motioned to an older man in the doorway. "Thelma, this is Dr. Marcus Fitzgerald. This is what he specializes in. I asked him to take a look at your ultrasound."

Thelma watched the older doctor as he leaned forward putting on his reading glasses, to more clearly see the miniaturized version of what he was all too familiar with. "I have a patient with a heart valve exactly like this. I'll be replacing the valve in her heart tomorrow morning."

He looked at Thelma reassuringly. "Your baby has a slight deformation in one of her heart valves. A few years ago, this would have been something she would have to live with. Now we perform an operation that is more often successful than not. At the least, we can correct the valve shape enough to allow a pretty much normal life, and at best, we can correct it completely."

Thelma nodded. "And this is a girl?"

"Yes," Dr. Miller told her again and then explained to Dr. Fitzgerald, "In her husband's family, there is a history of this heart defect. His mother was always slowed down by the strain of having a bad heart valve."

Thelma said, "Also his grandmother and his sister. He thinks it just affects the girls."

Dr. Fitzgerald nodded. "The way color blindness affects males almost exclusively."

Thelma asked, "What do you recommend, Dr. Fitzgerald?"

"Surgery as soon as she's strong enough. If she begins to show signs of having difficulty, I could go in through the groin and repair the valve. But if she remains strong until birth, I would rather wait."

Thelma looked at the motion on the screen. "My husband is going to be so disappointed. I don't know what to do."

Dr. Fitzgerald looked away for a second. "Before you make any decisions, I would like you to meet the patient I'll be operating on tomorrow morning."

He gave her directions to the room, and she told him she would visit the patient as soon as they were through here. She knew what he meant by *decisions*. As the doctors left her to wipe off the ultrasound jelly and straighten her clothes, her heart grew heavier.

Thelma kept thinking about George as she walked down the hospital hallway. She planned to take only a few minutes to meet his patient before hurrying back to the farm. George had been in such an unhappy mood when she left, she wanted to be home to fix him lunch, and Trudy's cookies were in the car. Having a few of her cookies would surely help his disposition.

She entered the third room on the left. A small girl looked up at her and smiled weakly as Thelma moved a chair and sat next to her bed. "Hello, my name is Thelma. I understand you're having an operation tomorrow."

The little girl smiled sweetly. "It's because I'm tired all the time. The other kids play but I can't. I can go outside when the sun is shining but not now."

Thelma smiled back and looked around the room. It seemed odd to think a child this small would be in the hospital without her parents nearby. "After tomorrow you'll feel better. Where is your mommy?"

The little girl closed her eyes. "She is in heaven with Jesus. So is my daddy. Everybody is."

She opened her eyes. "I have my doll. Her name is Stephanie." She pulled her doll up beside her just enough for Thelma to see her face. "She's my best friend."

"How old are you?"

"I'm seven years old."

"I have a son that just had his seventh birthday. His name is Alex."

She smiled. "Can he run?"

"Oh yes. He likes to run."

Dr. Fitzgerald stepped into the room and joined them beside the bed. "I see you've met Shelly. I wanted you to see how difficult it is for her, to not have that valve in her heart working properly."

Shelly said, "My mommy died because of her valve in her heart. She died because I was born." She shook her head sadly. "Her heart had to work too hard."

Thelma drew a sharp breath and looked up at the doctor. "Seven years ago? I knew someone who died from…" She and George had considered adopting the baby, but the little one's heart had—

Oh my. She touched the girl's small hand.

cᶰᵒ cᶰᵒ cᶰᵒ

George wondered why Thelma didn't come back from the Taylor farm. He had hoped to apologize for upsetting her, if he had, and ask if she would come with him into the city. As he stepped into the farm supply store, he was thinking it would be nice to have lunch with her.

Taking out a list he had prepared after looking at the labels in the boys' clothing, he moved down the rows of western clothes. He selected five pair of western jeans allowing for a little growth, and then moved to the shirts.

"May I take those to the counter for you?" A girl, about twelve years old, reached for his armful of jeans. He slid them onto her arms but not before his eyes met hers. She turned away, but he could not. He stood with his mouth open. Never had he seen anyone who looked so much like Alex. He stepped behind a rack of shirts and watched her.

A woman coming down stairs put her hands on her hips and glared at the girl. "Are you going to fold those pants all day or go back to school?"

"Mom, we have a customer. I'm trying to help him."

"You get going before your lunch hour is over. I'll help the customers."

He selected two shirts for each of his sons, and then looking at his list went to the boxes of work boots. The woman yelled for someone to come and "assist a customer" in the shoe department. A man rushed from another room. Without looking at him, George handed him the pile of shirts and pulled three boot boxes off a stack.

"I also need two pair smaller then these. Where are the smaller sizes?"

George saw familiar motions as the man brought the boxes to the checkout counter, carefully spacing them with the labels forward. He studied his features without letting him know he was doing so and then said, "This is all I need. Could you tell me if you know someone? Maybe you're related to her. Her name is Clara Menton."

"Clara?" He was visibly shaken. "She worked here years ago. I didn't, uh, know her too well."

George handed him his credit card. "Maybe your wife remembers her."

The man looked sharply at him. "It would be best if you didn't mention her to my wife. She let her go. It wasn't pleasant."

As George watched him meticulously folding and sliding each item into the bag, he said, "She had a child."

The man looked back over his shoulder. His wife was waiting on a customer but might be close enough to overhear. He leaned closer to George and whispered, "Clara only worked here for a few weeks."

"What's your name?"

The man looked as if he was about to be arrested. "Nelek Gorzynski."

George caught his breath, picked up two large plastic bags, and turned from the counter, too shaken to say more. In the pickup he sat staring ahead until he had settled down enough to put the key in the ignition.

"A Polack! There can't be an ounce of farming blood in his veins. That girl lied. That's why she didn't want to keep Alex. This can't be happening."

He looked at his watch. Thelma would expect him home for lunch. He turned toward the freeway. Approaching the exit a half hour later, he recognized his wife's car ahead and pulled alongside her, motioning toward the truck stop turnoff.

George saw her wipe her face as she parked in front of the Dine and Drive. He stepped around the side of her car and opened the door. "What's the matter?' Waiting as she blew her nose in a tissue, he touched her shoulder with his finger and said softly, "Let's talk about it over lunch."

Mabel yelled to the couple as they came in. "Your table is empty back in the corner, just have a seat and I'll be right over with a menu. Like you need one. Do you just want your usual?"

George nodded but Thelma didn't look up. Alert to the possibility of hearing a tad bit of gossip, Mabel called their order over her shoulder and quickly snatched up the coffeepot and two clean cups.

They sat quietly wondering what the other had to say, until Mabel was far enough away for them to speak softly without being heard. Then, George told Thelma about his shopping experience, concluding with, "Just like he does. The same way of putting everything back and straightening everything up. The same eyes and the same dark complexion. I swear Alex is the spitting image of that guy, but he is a Polack. I have never heard of one being a good farmer. Have you ever heard of one being a farmer?"

She smiled. "His rows will be straight and the fertilizer will be mixed to the exact proportions. He will probably turn your worst acreage into the best section, if I know Alex."

George thought about it and knew she was right. He nodded. "You always have a way of seeing the good in everything."

Mabel, hoping to hear something, leaned between the two of them, reaching across to the window end of the table to refill the sugar holder. Moving to the next table, she heard George ask, "Why were you at the hospital?"

Thelma looked out the window and took another napkin from the holder to wipe her tears. She held the crushed napkin in her fist, unable to look at him. He looked around to make sure no one could hear and leaned forward. "Were you seeing a doctor?"

She whispered, "I went in for an ultrasound."

His heartbeat suddenly felt far too slow and his pulse far too loud. "Ultrasound. You're…we're…?"

Thelma's eyes filled with tears again, and her shoulders curved forward as she nodded. "George, the doctor said the baby has a problem." She gave a shuddering sob. "I'm sorry, George."

Fleeting joy crashed in his chest, leaving him with a hollow certainty. "The same heart problem that runs in my family."

Her mouth tightened. "Then, the doctor asked me to meet a little girl before I decided if I wanted to terminate this pregnancy."

"Terminate?" He leaned forward as Mabel tried to set a plate in front of him. Raising his hands to avoid placing his fingers in the hot gravy, he said, "It's one thing to not have babies but a whole other thing to end a pregnancy. I don't care what the doctor says is wrong, if we're going to have a baby, we're going to see it all the way through."

She folded and refolded her napkin. "And then—" She looked up at Mabel and said, "Please excuse us." When the waitress walked away, she whispered, "Then *what* are we going to do? Are we going to hand her to the doctor and walk away from her the way we did Hilda's baby?" She blew her nose. "George, all that little girl has is a doll named Stephanie. Her mommy and daddy and everybody else that ever loved her are in heaven with Jesus. And the only good thing about it is that she isn't afraid of dying in surgery tomorrow, because she won't be alone anymore."

They stared at each other, silent. George knew Thelma had always wanted a child of their own, and he'd always insisted it was better to adopt because of exactly what was happening to them. He knew with all certainty he would never want the child to be aborted. But should they give it up for adoption? And what about Thelma's feelings? Now that the unthinkable had finally happened, something shifted deep inside him.

Mabel filled their coffee cups, saying, "I heard Dr. Atwood is going to talk to you about using your land for a summer camp for handicapped kids. Did he get out your way to ask you?"

George looked at Thelma. Handicapped kids were now more than just an issue for a few weeks in the summer. He put his hands over his face. "Go away, Mabel. Wait on someone else."

"Fine, but those uppity city fellas just parked out front. You know they're not going to leave you alone, as long as they think they can make a million bucks off you."

6

Luke Hamilton was warming up his logging truck long before the first light of morning. Leaving the diesel engine idling, he walked back into the house. Moving about the kitchen in a routine, he filled this thermos from the coffeepot, tightened the lid, and set it in his lunch container. He placed his sandwiches into plastic bags and pushed them in alongside the thermos, and then he walked around the house turning off lights.

He stepped into a room at the end of the hallway and stood for a few minutes, feeling the emptiness that the neatness of room left inside of him. Three little beds lined the wall, spaced evenly in a row. At the foot of each bed in a plastic bag were the sheets, blankets, and pillowcases beside another bag that held the pillow for the bed. He crossed the room and looked out the window and checked the latch. In a bathroom attached to the bedroom he turned on the light. He had remodeled this bathroom himself, a perfect replica of an adult-sized one, complete with a low-edged jet tub, a shower, spacious but with low water controls, a toilet and sink so low that he had to smile at the impossibility of his using them. He turned out the light and walked back to the kitchen.

He stopped short of the kitchen and shook his head before confronting his thirty-year-old son, who was pulling slices of bread out of a new loaf. "Greg, I thought you were all moved out. If I knew I was still feeding you, I would have bought two loaves yesterday."

Greg said, "Me and the guys were playing poker. When I went home, Lucy told me to come back when I can get home at a decent hour."

Luke picked up his lunch container. "What time was that?"

"Two, maybe three this morning." Greg grabbed a can of soda out of

---

the refrigerator and ran out behind his dad. Climbing into the cab of the semi-truck, he quickly changed the subject. "I seen you washed the blankets for the little beds. Are we going to have company?"

"Jake is bringing Butchie to the Atwood Clinic for that operation they've been putting off."

As the truck rolled onto the highway and they passed by darkened homes and empty streets, Greg said, "That school project "Finding Dwain" is all the guys wanted to talk about last night. It scares me. I thought that when you give a kid away, he never is allowed to find you. I sure don't want my kid finding me. The kid would hate me."

Luke shifted down as the big rig began to climb a winding road. "Why would little Greg hate you? You did what you thought was best for him. You couldn't raise him. After your mom died I did a poor job of raising you, so I wouldn't have been any help. The best thing you could do for that baby was let him be adopted by a family that would raise him right."

Greg popped the top of his soda. "I gave him away. Simple as that. No kid wants to know that someone didn't want him when he was born. And when I signed those papers, Zelda Cloud told me and his mom that we didn't have to worry about running into him. She said he was going to be adopted in another state. But just as soon as she got our baby, she gave him to George and Thelma. They knew he was mine because they named him Greg.

"Dad, why else would they name him Gregory? There are thousands of different names they could have chosen. They named the first one Teddy after his dad, Ted Brady. Trenton might not look much like his dad, but he acts like Trenton Jones did when we were in school together. Greg is bound to figure out that his dad's name is the same as his, and he'll come looking for me."

Luke swallowed, trying to clear a lump from his throat. "Have you seen little Greg?"

"A lot of times. He got my hair. Can't do a thing with it but lucky kid got his mom's looks. But if you ever see him, don't act like you're looking at him if George is around, or he'll put you in your place. He told me not to come within a hundred feet of that kid, and that suits me just fine, as long as he never finds out that I made him in the first place."

Luke looked at his son. "That's not what scares me. There are people who know about our family, and it's just a matter of time before someone says something to George or Thelma."

Greg smiled, thinking, *I'd like to see McCain's face when he sees Uncle Jake and little Butchie.*

Luke said, "That boy is my grandson and I want to see him the same way the Campbells want to see Dwain. Every time I hear about "Finding Dwain," I know that somehow I have to get a chance to see little Greg." He shifted down and rolled to a stop at a stop sign and waited for an approaching car to pass by.

As the car passed, he said, "That's George and Thelma right there in that car. I wonder where they're going. I would think George would be racing the weather to get his hay in."

Greg watched the car until the taillights were out of sight. "If he lost a crop it would probably kill him."

⚬⟆ ⚬⟆ ⚬⟆

George followed Thelma into the intensive care ward of the hospital where he moved two chairs closer to the bed so they could sit quietly beside the sleeping little girl. As an IV dripped and a heart monitor thumped to a steady beat, he motioned to the lines on the screen. "I wonder what it means."

A nurse stepped into the room. "Are you supposed to be here?"

George said softly, "This is my sister's little girl."

She looked at a chart. "Shelly's here from the Trellon Home for Girls. Are you sure you have the right room?"

He looked at her sleeping face. "I'm sure."

Dr. Fitzgerald walked into the room. "Good morning, Thelma. It's nice of you to come by and see my patient." He looked at the concerned nurse and said, "I asked them to visit with Shelly." He then extended his hand to George, but before the man could say his name, Dr. Fitzgerald said, "We met before." He smiled, remembering, "I was your sister's doctor. How is she?"

He took the doctor's hand. "George McCain, and"—he motioned toward the sleeping little girl—"Hilda passed away when she had Shelly. How's she doing?"

The doctor said, "I didn't even suspect this little one was your sister's. I am sorry if I…"

"It's fine," George said. "Can you tell if she's going to be all right?"

He smiled. "Our greatest hope is to reach perfection, but that is out of our hands. We are settling for a steady, strong beat." He nodded toward the heart monitor. "And we hope her heart continues as it is. I had to replace the valve and give her a pacemaker that will keep her heart beating should she have difficulty."

"Great," George said. Why was God punishing him like this?

"But if we repair the valve in your baby's heart, her rapidly growing body should do naturally what I had to do this morning for Shelly."

George asked, "And if you can't fix her heart and if this fails?"

Dr. Fitzgerald pulled a chair closer and sat beside him. "In the beginning, when man was first made, there was no mistake. We caused our own misfortune and now we struggle to fix what has gone wrong."

George sighed. "We cause it by having babies with problems. It just keeps happening generation after generation."

"George, I have seen the smartest, strongest, most advanced medical student doing well one day and then the next, lying in a coma because he took one too many pills off the nurse's cart.

"I have seen a healthy straight-A student suddenly unable to say his name, because the gearshift of his car was imbedded in his skull when he rolled his car after drinking a half a bottle of rum.

"You can have the most successful, brightest child and lose her, while you have a child born with a physical defect grow up and change the world and make it a better place. And when it's all over, every person dies. Our Creator has promised us an everlasting life. We will see each other after we leave here because life has no end. My patients who know this fact and know our Creator are not concerned over living a long time or a short time."

George looked at the sleeping child. "My mother was a Christian. She talked about God and then one day, she just fell over in the kitchen and I couldn't wake her up."

The doctor said, "And you saw it as her being taken away from you, but she accepted it as a gift, of suddenly being able to draw a deep breath for the first time in her life. She could dance and sing and laugh for the first time. Your mother had a new body that didn't have a bad heart. She was not at all worried about you, because she knew, as long as you keep the faith she gave you, she will be with you again."

George nodded. "I never thought about what she might have thought about dying. I suppose it was easier on Hilda, too. She left for a long time and came back with a Bible and"—he blinked away tears as he watched the little girl—"and then she gave up her life to have a very sick baby."

He had been wrong. All this time, he had been so very wrong.

The doctor sat speechless and then looked at Thelma. "I understand now why you are considering aborting your baby. I won't…"

George looked sharply at him. "We're keeping our baby girl and we're taking Shelly home, too."

᭨᭨ ᭨᭨ ᭨᭨

When Zelda Cloud received a call on her cell phone from George McCain, she was almost to the veterinary clinic. She was so shocked by his request, her foot eased up off the accelerator. "Are you sure you want Shelly?" He confirmed she'd heard him right, and she said, "But how did you find out she was having surgery? That isn't something that should have gotten out of my office."

A car veered sharply, just missing her back bumper. As it came up beside her, the driver glared, raising a finger at her. He shook his head, pressed on the horn, and sped on past.

"How rude. Honestly, Fluffy, some drivers don't belong on the road.

"We're almost there, Fluffy." Into her phone she said, "If that is what you want, I will prepare the papers, but you will have to see your attorney. I'll fax what you'll need over to him. I have no problem with your taking custody of her. I'm just surprised you want to."

This didn't make sense. George McCain would no more adopt a feeble, disabled child than she would take her precious Fluffy to the horrid little vet—unless her own exclusive cat specialist in the city weren't on vacation in the Caymans, that is.

She closed the cell phone and rammed her foot down on the gas pedal until the last second before she pulled off the road at the veterinary clinic. From her car she could see the sign on the door. "How can he run a business if he's closed all the time?" She backed around, spitting gravel from the tires, and headed for his home.

She had never been on this road before. She had imagined the Anderson farm was a rundown pile of junk but to the contrary, a charming cottage sat on the right, with a large red barn straight ahead and a well-kept two-story home on the left.

Tapping lightly on what appeared to be the kitchen door of the large home, she waited, hoping not to see those hideous little girls. She was very much relieved when Sara opened the door and asked her to come in and then called her husband to come down from upstairs.

He appeared quickly and smiled warmly as he reached for the bundle of white fur she held in her arms. "Miss Cloud," he said softly, more to Fluffy than to the Zelda, "Is Fluffy sick again?"

"It's the same thing. She was fine until this morning and then she started choking."

He motioned to a room behind the kitchen, allowing her to enter first, and then he stepped past her and set the suffering animal on a low desk. From a drawer he withdrew a pair of needle-nose pliers and from his pocket, a small flashlight. Looking in the back of Fluff's throat, he continued speaking softly to her. "Let's get this out, Fluffy, and give you something that will help you not to have this problem again."

As he cared for her cat, Zelda looked about at the intolerably disgusting office. Never before had she seen an adult's office in such disorder. All of the drawers and shelves were much too low to be functional, and the walls above three feet were a wasted space covered with photographs and children's drawings. *For a child this would be suitable but not for an adult.*

The little man reached over on a low shelf for a pamphlet, and he gave it to her. "This will help you understand her condition. I see this in pure-bred cats like Fluffy, more so than in other cats." He handed her a small bottle of liquid. "Put three drops on her food each time you feed her and let me know if she has any more trouble."

Lifting the bottle from his small fingers, carefully so as to not touch him, she put her nose up. "Why didn't you give this to me when I was at your office? If you had, I wouldn't be here now."

He smiled. "You left rather abruptly, Miss Cloud, and we weren't sure she would have a problem once the bird bones were no longer blocking her throat."

She looked away. "Incompetence." Then she added, "I have never given Fluffy anything with a bone in it. Her diet consists entirely of the finest small cans of cat food." Taking out her checkbook, she snapped, "How much is this?"

"The liquid is $6.59. The home visit is free."

She glared at him. "You can't support a family if you don't charge for your services."

A cell phone rang, and moving toward the kitchen, he opened his phone. To the caller he said, "I know. I'm sorry. Something came up but I'm on my way." Over his shoulder, he tossed a casual wave to Zelda. "I'm sorry. I need to go. It's calls like this that feed my family, not three-minute hair ball removals. Thank you for bringing Fluffy in and feel free to bring her back for any reason."

He rushed out, leaving the kitchen door open for her to leave, but as she stepped into the kitchen, Sara offered her a cup of coffee. Feeling over-whelmed and grateful for the presence of a normal person, Zelda looked about the kitchen while she gathered the shreds of her composure.

Soft calico curtains fluttered by the window, and the motion drew her gaze to a hand-stitched wall hanging that reminded readers, "God is Love."

As Sara set a miniature pitcher of cream and a matching bowl of sugar next to her cup on the table, Zelda sat slowly. Not accepting this as kind-ness without a motive, she said, "I can give you no information about Dwain. You realized that, don't you?"

Sara said, "It's in God's hands. I'm just watching the month go by and expecting Him to do something."

"Your God is not going to suddenly cause something to happen just because you want it to." Zelda sipped her coffee. "All of a sudden, the whole world wants Dwain to be brought to a specific place at a specific time, and it's just not possible."

Setting a small plate of wafers on the table, Sara sat and reached for one. This, she calmly dipped into her coffee. "When God created the world, He knew that His only son would come to earth and die as a sacrifice for the sins of the people that He created. He told us that from the beginning of man, He already saw His son die on a cross, and Jesus told us that He already saw the end of the world. God has seen the end, and I believe He saw this very moment, before you and I were even born."

Zelda glared at Sara. "Why are you and that…" She shook her head. "Why are you people being nice when you know I'm doing everything I can to stop you?"

Sara smiled. "Because I know that greater is He that is in me than he that is in the world. I know that Christ in me, can overcome every obstacle. I just need to follow Dane's example, and believe Dwain is coming home, and also follow Christ's example. When He was crucified, He asked His Father to forgive those who killed him, because they didn't know what they were doing."

Zelda rolled her eyes. "You're saying you forgive me because I don't know what I'm doing?" Her cell phone rang, and she jerked it from her small black bag lying on the table. After listening a few seconds, she snapped, "I know you are his attorney. I told him I will fax you what I have, as soon as I have time. I'm not deliberately delaying anything to do with that child. This is ridiculous. If 'Finding Dwain' hadn't gotten started, George wouldn't have even considered adopting a sick child."

She stood, clutching Fluffy. As she left she said to Sara, "I'm putting an end to 'Finding Dwain' tomorrow. And I will get to the bottom of how records from my office got to that school. Someone is going to be in a great deal of trouble."

Brent heard Zelda before he saw her. He opened the barn door only enough to watch her leaving. He waited for her car to reach the paved road, then crossed the barnyard and stepped into his daughter's kitchen.

"She causing trouble?"

Sara handed him a cup of coffee and reached for bread to make him a sandwich. "No, not at all. Fluffy had another hair ball."

He laughed. "Doesn't it seem strange that Fluffy was perfectly fine until now."

She shook her head. "Dad, she isn't deliberately causing that cat to have hair balls, just so she can snoop around here, if that's what you mean."

"No, but it does seem odd that she would be around here at all. For seventeen years she hated the sight of us. All of a sudden, she's out here twice in one week."

Sara looked out the window at a yellow truck pulling up in front of the old farmhouse. "Now what would Jeb Ranger be doing out here?"

"Nothing, just dropping off something." He set his cup on the counter and wandered outside, even though he wanted to rush.

Brent walked around to the back of the truck to help his friend, as the lanky mechanic pushed on the door, rolling it up out of the way. Stepping onto the hydraulic lift, Brent rode it up to the level of the back of the truck. "Anyone figure out what you were doing?"

Jeb gripped the leg of a heavy dark maple chest of drawers as Brent pushed it onto the lift. "Not as far I could tell. No one but me was even bidding on the stuff. I would think that city folks looking for antiques would be out by the dozens. Someone said the newspaper ad for the sale had next week's date. Instead of just a few things, you got all the furniture."

Brent stood, mouth open, looking at the fully loaded truck of furniture. "This is all mine?"

Jeb chuckled. "That's what happens when you want to help someone and God gets involved. I've seen this before. One time I donated money to buy some mattresses for a shelter. I asked God to make that money go a long ways. Sure enough, a surplus place suddenly had too many mattresses and sold them to the shelter for a dime on the dollar."

Jeb gripped the mirror on the dresser as the lift lowered it down to the ground. "Katie's brother, Rodney, was being a tough egg. He acted like he didn't care one way or the other about any of his parents' stuff. Katie tried not to show it, but I could tell, every time something sold, it about tore her apart."

Brent handed him an oak coat stand. "It's all money to him. The banker is holding the cash box, so Rodney doesn't care. It's Katie that's getting hurt."

They each took an end and lifted a heavy dresser up onto the porch. As they rolled it through the doorway, Brent said, "We can put all the heavy pieces down here. Set the light stuff to the side. I'll take it upstairs later. It looks like we'll just about fill all the space I got."

Jed rolled a dusty rug and stood it on end out of the way. "Is there any possibility of Katie coming to church?" he asked softly.

Thinking before saying something he shouldn't, Brent rode the lift up again. He handed a couple of lamps down to his friend. "When we were in the young adult class, thirty years ago, she challenged God. What He showed her scared her so badly, she won't talk about it even now."

"What kind of challenge?"

"She told Him to talk to her." He lifted an end table, lowering it until Jeb had a good hold. "She thought God only speaks with words, in your head or out loud. I pointed out the obvious ways He speaks to us. Like in the very fact that the earth is round and not a mass of jagged edges, the way we can eat just about everything that grows, the blue of the sky, patterns in clouds, and the way those horses she loves so much, grow to be so beautiful."

After carrying two heavy headboards to the far end of the living room and pushing the maple chest of drawers against them to utilize space, Jeb asked, "What happened that scared her so much?"

"She was in the field when Eddie was run over by the plow. I wouldn't have known she was there if his brother hadn't seen her. He said, when Eddie stood up without a scratch on him, Katie turned her horse and raced off. She's never said a thing to anybody about being there." Jeb stepped back, mouth open. "She saw it, and up and run off? I would have been dancing in the streets if God had let me see a miracle like that. I'd build a house right on the very spot and put up a big sign that reads, "This Is Where it Happened."

For years Brent had been angry with God for causing Katie to leave the way she had. Now, listening to the excitement in his friend's voice, he wondered why seeing something that would have thrilled anyone else, had scared her so much.

പ്ര പ്ര പ്ര

Zelda cancelled her afternoon appointments to allow herself enough time to prepare a convincing case to present in court tomorrow. After calling Rhonda and instructing her as to what forms to fax to George McCain's attorney, she left the freeway and turned onto Crest Top Drive. Unbuttoning the top two buttons of her blouse and lowering the convertible top, she let her hair down to blow in the breeze, and sped up, enjoying the smell of the forest and the feel of the sun on her face. Passing a public park entrance sign on her right, she was reminded of the proximity of the less desirable individuals of the world, and shuddered to think that they were camping practically in her backyard.

As she turned in the wide circle to line up with her driveway, she pressed the control to raise the garage door. She parked beside Marcus' lavish silver convertible. Very quietly she stepped into the kitchen, letting the cat slide from her hand she as she whispered, "I want you to eat and go straight in and get a nice nap, my sweet."

She reached back to close the door very softly, not to make a sound, but before her fingers could grasp the handle, the door shut. She stood perfectly still, listening. The only time the door shut that way was when there was an exterior door or a window open somewhere in the apartment. It wasn't like Marcus to leave open a door or window. Just to make sure, she opened the door, just enough for it to close again by itself. But this time, it didn't move. She pushed it shut and then walked cautiously though the rooms, looking for anything out of the ordinary. Everything looked fine. Despite that, her scalp prickled, and she spun around to look behind her. Nothing.

The air smelled stale, so she lit a candle in the living room. To help shake off the unnerving sensation that something wasn't right, she made a point of admiring the new furniture she and Marcus had purchased only a few weeks ago. Looking out the window toward the forest, she felt a cold gust of air and smelled something unusual. Turning quickly, she expected to see someone standing near the bookcase behind her. Again, there was nothing.

She shivered and reached for a book, looked at the cover, and set it back on the shelf. She admired the evenly spaced rows of books arranged by height, thickness, and color with her leather-bound collector's editions in the center.

Marcus had leased this apartment six months earlier. It consisted of a small kitchen, dining room, and living room on the first level and a large master bedroom on the second. The larger portion of the home, where she assumed the owner lived, she was certain was filled with many spacious rooms. But for her and Marcus, this was absolutely perfect. Thinking of Marcus, she moved quietly up the carpeted stairs and into the bedroom. She stood looking about the room. He wasn't there. The bed was made, just as she had left it. So where was he?

Deciding he may have gone for a walk, she tossed her clothes to the side, selected a lavish silk gown from an assortment in her closet, and stepped into the shower. A half hour later, as she stood before the mirror, Marcus spoke to her from the doorway.

"You are lovely," he said seductively as he stepped into the bathroom. He put his arms around her, standing behind her, rocking from side to side, as he looked at the two of them together in a mist-covered mirror.

She started to turn into his arms, but he stepped back. "I was in the backyard and didn't hear you come in."

He pulled his money clip from his pocket. As he touched the silver circle in the center, the beeper on his belt sounded. He reached for it, and then for his cell phone, and stepped out of the room, glancing back at her over his shoulder. "I'm sorry, sweetheart. It's urgent." Looking remorseful, he shook his head and smiled regretfully. "I have to go."

As he rushed down the stairs, she stepped into the bedroom and listened for the garage door to open. She stood waiting, wondering why he hadn't left. Going downstairs, she paused in the living room, seeing her laptop computer on the table by the sofa. She was certain she hadn't left it there earlier. She looked out the kitchen door, expecting to see Marcus preparing to leave, only her car was in the garage.

An aroma she hadn't noticed when she came in made her turn to see what smelled so good. The oven was on, and she could see a pan inside. Slipping an oven mitt on her hand, she opened the oven and lifted the lid of a roasting pan to find a chicken, fragrant and nicely browned. The chicken looked as though it had cooked enough, so she slipped on another mitt and pulled the pan from the oven. Setting the lid to the side, she looked more closely at what Marcus had prepared for their dinner. On each side of the plump glazed chicken sat a baked potato, cut in half and filled with whipped potato, then baked to a golden brown on top.

Deciding to make a salad to go with it, she opened the refrigerator. There sat a green salad, topped with a ring of evenly spaced large shrimp. Next to the salad bowl sat two clear glass desert cups, filled with chocolate pudding, lightly topped with whipped cream and a single cherry. She slowly closed the fridge door. This was just too strange. *He's remarkable, but something isn't right.*

She retraced the steps she'd taken when she came home. Marcus's car had been in the garage, no cooking aroma in the kitchen. In fact, the house had smelled stale, so she'd lit a candle in the living room. Walking through her earlier motions, she passed by the candle, which was still burning. She walked to the window and looked out, remembered feeling cold air and smelling something. She thought. *It was stale, the way the house smelled when I came in, but stronger.*

She stared at the top of the table. Her computer was gone. It had been there when she came downstairs just a few minutes ago. Sitting slowly on the sofa, she put her face in her hands, fighting the need to cry. Something was happening to her mind. She had not smelled the chicken baking when she came in. She had not heard the garage door open when Marcus left. She had seen the computer on the table.

She jumped up and rushed upstairs. The computer case sat where she had left it, on the floor next to the dresser. She looked to see if the computer was in the case. It was, and this reminded her of why she had come home early.

She set it on the dresser, turned it on, and found a file named "Dwain."

Closing her eyes, she rubbed her temples. Something was seriously wrong with her mind. She could remember every case for the last twenty years—names, dates, and many of the actual case numbers—but she couldn't remember taking her own computer to her office. She couldn't remember sending information to the school Web site. If she was going to present a believable case against "Finding Dwain," she had better have an explanation before court tomorrow.

7

In the county court room, Judge Roy Bain spread the case out before him, moving sheets of paper and considering both sides of the issue. He stacked the papers, considering the case of the angry woman, dressed in a black three piece suit. He appreciated the sincere testimony of the little man with stubby fingers and bowed legs and the calm presence of his wife. He recalled the honesty in the voice of Brent Anderson, testifying he'd had a change of heart and tried to get the baby back within the first few weeks of his birth. The school principal and his wife had written documentation of their effort to gain custody as soon as they were aware of his birth. Judge Bain also considered the patience of the tall, slender teen and his two very small sisters, who sat quietly throughout the whole ordeal.

"Miss Cloud, was the confidential information sent to the students from your personal computer?"

She said, "I would never send confidential information to a public school. My office was broken into by one of those students. My computer was used without my knowledge."

He looked at the date and time the file was sent and compared this with her appointments that morning. Her own records placed her in her office. The information came from her computer. This wasn't the first thing she'd said that wasn't right. "You stated you have no knowledge of timely requests made by the Campbell families or Mr. Anderson for custody of the infant. But on the copies sent from your computer to the senior class Web site, in your own handwriting, are notations to the contrary. Therefore, it is my opinion that Dwain should have been in the custody of his mother and father."

Zelda shot to her feet. "Those two were not fit to be parents. They were too young, and he was…he was…he was just not fit. Besides, this is not a case of custody. It's my case against the senior high class. That is the only issue being discussed today. I was not prepared for a custody hearing."

Judge Bain looked at her signature on a statement, acknowledging her understanding of what today's proceedings concerned. *Can I believe anything she says?*

She pointed at Dane Campbell. "We have only one issue at this time. I'm pressing charges against that young man and his class, for having information they should not have in their possession."

Judge Bain didn't appreciate the tone of her voice in his courtroom. "Bailiff, would you show this statement to Miss Cloud, please?"

The bailiff complied, and as Zelda read it, her face turned as white as the paper. Slowly sitting, she glared at the judge.

He said firmly, "Dr. Jeffery Campbell has proven beyond a doubt, to me and to the entire community, just how fit he is to be the father of his children."

Zelda raised her chin and stared at the bailiff as though all this were his fault.

"You say that you don't know where this child is," Judge Bain said. "If he is not legally adopted, you are to request this court, return him to Jeffery and Sara Campbell. Miss Cloud, I am ordering you to find Dwain."

She jumped to her feet. "Your Honor, the child was taken out of this state after Mr. Anderson"—she jabbed a finger at Brent—"threatened to remove him from a foster home, if he was able to find that home. I have no idea where that boy is now."

He stuffed the papers into a file folder. "I expect you to find him, and since you seem to have difficulty doing your job, Miss Cloud, I'm going to let the senior high class continue to assist you. I will notify the students that 'Finding Dwain' can legally continue searching for Dwain Campbell."

Judge Bain looked at Dane, whose eyes were glistening. "Let's keep praying, young man. We have fifteen days. We just may be able to reunite the two of you for your seventeenth birthday."

"Thank you, sir."

Brent rested his hand on his grandson's shoulder as they left the courtroom. In the hallway, they walked past a group of people arguing. The
only person in the group he recognized was Katie Maguire. His hand must
have pressed on Dane's shoulder, because the boy's attention instantly
shifted to Katie.

As her eyes turned to Dane, the tall teenager nodded, gave her a short
wave, and smiled. Brent whispered, "Do you know her?"

"Never seen her before." He shrugged. "She looked at me like she
knows me."

When Katie stepped outside, Brent was leaning against his pickup,
parked across the street from the front steps of the courthouse. Crossing
the street, she considered what a handsome model he would have made,
and chuckled as she wondered whether his suit had been in style ten years
ago or twenty.

"You okay?" There was a yearning in his expression, but he stood
straight, his arms by his sides.

"They thought that just because horses are in Daddy's pasture he owns
them. Now that I've proven to them I own the horses, they want me to get
them off their property."

"Lawyers own the property?" Brent asked.

"No, they represent the bank that foreclosed. George McCain bought
the property from the bank. He wants to plow the pasture as soon as possible."

"Buy you lunch?"

She took his arm. "I saw the most charming little place just across the
park. Let's walk through the park."

Walking on a narrow, winding walkway they slowed to watch chip-
munks in a tree and squirrels on a picnic table. As always, she talked and
he listened. She'd tucked her hand in his arm, and now she let it fall. Their
hands touched. He looked at her and smiled, and she saw in his gaze a
depth of emotion that startled her.

As they sat at a small table in the corner of a dimly lit café, she asked,
"Has there been someone else since Emily? I mean, a serious someone
else."

He shook his head. "I've been busy. Sara was fourteen when Emily passed away. When Sara married they took my grandson, Dane, and lived near campus for eight years while Jeff went to college. I built a house for them on my place, hoping to bribe them into staying close." He smiled. "I didn't even have to beg, and I figure as long as I don't get into their business, I won't give them a reason to put distance between us."

She looked down. "You never went anywhere, but you went further than I could dream of going. Your grandson looks like you did, you know."

"What do you mean by my going further?"

"I just…wonder sometimes"—she smiled sadly—"what my life would be like, if I hadn't left."

"You and Hilda must have found something pretty special in New York City. You didn't come back."

"We rented a very small attic apartment. We had to sit on the floor in the kitchen to see outside. Our view was the sidewalk below. Hilda would call George and tell him how happy she was, and then we would try to figure out where our next meal was coming from."

The waitress poured her another glass of wine and returned to fill Brent's coffee cup. Katie said, "Hilda met Jimmy at an art show. I thought he was a little…" She waved her hand, depicting a gay man's gesture.

"We weren't gone from here a year when she found out she was HIV positive. And then New York City just swallowed us up. I went my way and she went hers. It seemed no time had passed before Daddy called asking for a loan and said Hilda had died. He told me she died in childbirth, but I know she had AIDS. I really doubt there was a baby."

She sipped her wine and searched his eyes. "Did you see Hilda when she came home?"

"No. She never came out and George wouldn't have visitors. There was talk about her being sick, but no one said what with. I don't think it's something George would want anyone knowing, but I did hear there was a baby girl." He smiled. "To get the scoop on that, you would have to talk to Mabel."

"Mabel." She grinned. "Do you remember when we were in high school? We were at the Fall Festival dance." She laughed, "She grabbed

George McCain by the ear and pulled him out onto the floor."

Brent laughed. "That was his fault. I was standing with him and Sid, when George told Mabel she was too fat to do the dance they were doing. She wasn't going to let him get away without proving she could dance better than him."

"And she could. Hilda and I laughed so hard, I about peed my pants." He shot a prim glance at the other tables. She turned her wine glass. "So what is it? You're different. In a good way, but there is something."

"I went through a lot, Katie." He shook his head. "My life hasn't been a bed of roses." He looked away, and his Adam's apple bobbed. He sipped coffee and set the cup down. "Emily had a few problems. I believed, if I made a go of the farm, she would be happy."

Katie moved her wine glass from her right hand to her left, and back again. "I was surprised when you did what you said you would never do."

His eyes met hers, wondering, and she said, "Be unevenly yoked."

He spread his hands on the table. "I never, until this very moment, thought about that. All the time I was working at the farm, she was working at something else. We were pulling so hard in different directions, we weren't getting anywhere at all."

She asked, "You stayed in church?"

He bowed his head. "I quit for a while after you left. After I married Emily and she wasn't happy, I got desperate for God's help, so I went back to church. I took Sara to Sunday school, but Emily had no interest and we grew further apart.

"One night, she said she was going out with the girls. I got a call from the hospital about three in the morning. She was clear over in the next county. I didn't even know the guy she was with. He drove through a stop sign and they were hit by a truck. She lay on life support for six weeks. It took every dollar I could scrape up for the next two years, to pay the hospital bill and funeral costs. When Sara got pregnant, I was right back to scraping bottom to pay another hospital bill."

Katie asked, "Do you think God cares what little people like you and I are doing?"

Brent closed his eyes for a moment, and when he opened them again, she could almost swear he was a different person, more...present. He said, "God placed His own seed within a virgin. That baby lived to be the last living sacrifice for the sins of people. He was the last Passover Lamb."

She wanted to know what made Brent feel this strongly about his faith, but she had never been able to see it the way he did. She shook her head. "I'm sorry, I remember us talking about a Passover lamb, but that was thirty years ago."

He looked down again, as though silently asking God to help her to understand. "You remember that God sent Moses to bring the Israelites out of Egypt, but the ruler refused to let them go. God told Moses to have the Israelites kill a lamb for each household, and place the blood over the door of the house. He told them to stay inside because death would pass through the land that night, but would not enter the homes with the blood over the door."

"The lamb died so the people under its blood would not. Death passed over them, so the lamb was called a Passover sacrifice. Every year at that time, they celebrated Passover. That's what they were celebrating when Jesus was killed. The death of the lamb symbolized the death of a Savior. The Savior that was coming to die, for us to have salvation, was Jesus. Everyone who is willing to be under the protective covering of the blood of Christ will have eternal life."

She knew he really believed what he was saying, because the power of that belief shone from his face so strongly that it pulled at something deep inside her. He smiled. "Yes, God cares about what we're doing. I try to keep in mind that God sees everything I do and knows all my thoughts. Jesus cared enough about saving me, to die for me."

She clicked her tongue, then moved her empty glass back and forth on the table. He had a way of explaining things that formed a picture in her mind, but the idea of God knowing what she was thinking was a little too much. "Well"—she looked him in the eye and shook her head—"I still don't know why you never became a preacher."

8

Dr. Larry Atwood sat at his desk reviewing cases as he listened to the Friday morning local talk show on the radio.

The host said, "Does anyone want to comment on what the judge's decision was yesterday in the 'Finding Dwain' case?"

A caller said, "I don't know what is going on but for some reason the state took the baby out of the home when he was born. Maybe there was a good reason at the time."

"That is possible," the host said. "But perhaps the process of the foster care program used should be looked into to determine if the child was taken too quickly. Next caller."

"My name is Andy. I'm in Mr. Tims's class. What I'm wondering is, why the Atwood Clinic can't help us. We have the country's best hospital to deal with the problems of dwarfism, and everyone knows Dr. Atwood is an expert in the field. So why can't he contact other hospitals and find Dwain's doctor?"

"That is a good question, Andy. I'm sure medical records are confidential, and a doctor can't tell you what is in those records. But, I certainly don't see why the clinic can't help, now that Judge Bain has ruled in favor of searching for Dwain. Next caller."

Larry leaned back, tapping a pencil on the edge of his desk. "As if we have the time or the manpower to contact every hospital in this nation to find Dwain Campbell's doctor." He sighed heavily, "Dear God, help me. I can't be everything to everybody."

A voice in his mind set him straight in his seat. "I can be."

He drew a sharp breath, looked around as if expecting to see someone, and wondered for an instant if he had imagined the words. But he knew he had heard them, and it wasn't the first time God had spoken clearly to him. He thought back to times during surgery, when he had prayed for help to complete the operation. Once, his fingers moved slightly to the side as he cut, causing him to miss a vital artery. Another time, he was told to look where he did not expect to find the problem, thus shortening the operation by hours, and possibly saving the young child's life by doing so. *And what about the summer camp for the children?*

When the developers asked him to invest in their new development, all he could think about was what a waste that beautiful property would be if it went to only a few people. Hundreds or even thousands of children could benefit from it every summer. And then, George McCain called, agreeing to lease the land for thirty years, for only one dollar a year. George McCain, the last person who would lift a finger to help the handicapped, was doing this. Only God could have brought this about.

He picked up the medical charts and left his office to begin his early morning rounds, but his thoughts were on those three words he had heard so clearly in his mind. *Yes, God, You can be everywhere and take care of everything, so I give You my concern for finding Dwain. If I can help, use me.*

ฝน ฝน ฝน

This morning, Tammy Rae had begged Sara to take her to the bus stop with Teresa and Dane. Sara walked with them to the mailbox, where they waited for the school bus. Squinting into the rising sun, Sara turned and watched the approaching rural mail carrier's car. She moved the girls off the road as Dane stepped around to the driver's side to get the mail. He handed Sara a package addressed to her. As he looked at the envelopes in his hand, he asked, "What did you get, Mom?"

"I don't know." She slit the tape with her thumbnail, opened the cardboard box, and pulled out a knitted baby blanket. "Now what's this?" She handed Dane the empty box and held the little blue and white blanket up. There was something familiar about it. Then she recognized her own handiwork, knitted into the corner: "Mommy loves Dwain." The reality of hav-

___

ing given birth to a second baby that morning in the hospital hit her. She clutched the soft blanket to her chest. Her baby was to be wrapped in it when he came home with her. Now, the blanket had come home, but where was her baby?

Dane gripped her as her legs buckled and her feet scraped across the gravel.

"Mom? Mom? What's wrong? Mom?"

Grasping his arm, she looked toward the house. "Get Grandpa. Now, honey, hurry." She clutched the blanket to her face and sobbed, rocking back and forth as her little girls clung to her, begging Mommy to stop crying.

Dane ran halfway to the farmyard before he yelled, "Grandpa, Grandpa." He looked first in the barn. As he turned toward the smaller house, Brent rushed out onto the porch.

"What's the matter?"

"It's Mom." He pointed to where she sat on the edge of the road and then ran along beside his grandfather, explaining. "She got something in the mail, and she told me to get you."

"Dad," Sara held up the little blanket. "Dad," she cried, "My baby. My baby. My baby." As he reached for the blanket, she pleaded, "Dwain *is supposed to come home*. Not just his blanket. He *is supposed* to come home."

Her father picked up the box and looked inside. "Is there a note? Maybe he's coming home later."

Dane looked startled and pulled his cell phone from his pocket. He moved away a few feet to answer it. "Ya, I'm at the bus stop. What does it say? Oh, shit."

"Dane!" Sara couldn't let his language slide, though he must be as rattled as she was right now.

He pulled his fingers across his lips in a zipping motion, then spoke into the phone. "I mean. I didn't mean to swear. I'll be there, as soon as the school bus gets there." He closed the phone. Concern crinkling his forehead, he turned to his grandfather.

Brent rested a hand on Dane's shoulder. "What's wrong?"

"Some of my class is already checking our Web site. Someone left a message." His Adam's apple jumped, and all the color fled his face. "It says that if we want Dwain, we have to get one hundred thousand dollars, and wait for another message to find out how to make a trade. And...there will be a package in the mail, to prove this person is serious."

Standing with her father's support, Sara touched Dane's arm and motioned to the approaching school bus. "You and Teresa go on to school. We'll be all right." She stroked the soft fibers of the blanket. "You need to be at that Web site."

Sara let her father guide her to the kitchen table, because her legs still didn't seem trustworthy. They sent Tammy Rae upstairs to get toys she wanted to take to her Grandma Campbell's house.

He ran his fingers down a page in the phone book and snatched up the phone.

Her baby. Where was her baby? She tried to swallow and couldn't. "Dad, would you get me a glass of water, please?"

He filled a glass with the phone balanced on his shoulder. Sara wondered who he was calling as he said, "This is Brent Anderson. We got a package today that proves someone has my grandson. The computer at the high school got a ransom note. Whoever has him wants one hundred thousand dollars."

He shook his head and frowned.

"I don't know where he was last seen. The last place I saw him was at the hospital the day he was born. He was wrapped in the blanket we just got in the mail."

He rubbed the back of his neck with his hand.

"It's hard to explain. Yesterday, Judge Roy Bain ordered Zelda Cloud, over at Social Services, to find my grandson. When she took him from us, he was wrapped in a baby blanket. Today we received the baby blanket and a ransom note."

He listened for a few seconds. "His name is Dwain Campbell." He sat slowly, looking at Sara. "Yes, it is the 'Finding Dwain' thing that the high school is doing, but now it has become very serious."

After a few seconds, he nodded. "Thank you."

Sara waited, unable to speak, while her father hung up the phone.

Finally, he braced his hands on the table. "The FBI has two agents in this area working on another case. They're sending them to talk to Zelda and then over to the school. Someone is coming out here to tap your phone line. She said for us not to handle the blanket anymore, until they run some tests on it."

The FBI wouldn't be coming if they didn't take Dwain's case seriously. Relief flooded through her. "It's all right. Everything is going to be all right. Will you take Tammy Rae over to Jeff's mom?"

He took a deep, slow breath. "I will. I'm not taking any chances with Dwain, though. If someone is holding him, his life is in danger. No one does something like this unless he is a crazy person." He stood and stepped toward the door.

"Dad what are you going to do?"

"As soon as I drop Tammy Rae off, I'm going to the bank. I'll get approved on a loan for a hundred thousand so we aren't scrambling to do it at the last minute."

✧ ✧ ✧

In minutes the news of the ransom demand was all over town. It reached Jeff in his clinic, but with steady hands he carefully removed a nonmalignant tumor and sutured the incision. When he came out to the waiting room, a dozen people besides those holding their pets surrounded him, wanting to know what they could do to help.

He held up his hands until the crowd quieted. "Right now, I have some very important patients that I'm not going to neglect. I have a son that has refused to start with the basketball program and two little girls that believe that something awful, instead of something wonderful, is about to happen in their lives. I'm not going to do anything except wait for a phone call from Brent. I'm sure he's on top of this situation. In the meantime, we would appreciate your prayers. It would help if you bombard the radio station with phone calls requesting more airtime to get the message out. We are asking whoever has our son to return him to us."

ᴑᴑ ᴑᴑ ᴑᴑ

Tamara Campbell moved about her kitchen, all the while keeping an eye on her granddaughter playing on the jungle gym in the backyard. Since her elderly parents moved in with her and her husband, the few moments she had to enjoy little Tammy Rae was all the real joy she had in her daily routine.

Her father poured himself a cup of coffee and stepped out onto the back porch. The little girl yelled from the top of the steps as she reached for the bar on the slide. "Watch me, Gramps. I'm going to slide down."

Her mother, wrapped in a warm robe, positioned a kitchen chair and cautiously sat at the table. "I see she's here again this morning."

"It's almost noon, Mom. You and Daddy always sleep in, remember?"

She heard her dad say, "Go back and climb on that contraption some more. That's the best place for a little climbing munchkin like you."

He stepped back into the kitchen as she took a tray of bran muffins out of the oven. It would do her no good to ask him again to not refer to the little girls as munchkins. He had not listened to her when Jeff was a boy, and he was not going to listen to her now. He sat at the table and reached for the butter. Looking up at her, holding the knife, he motioned to the tray of muffins, silently demanding to be served. It would do her no good to question his rude behavior. This was how he had been all her life, first with her mother, and now with her and her sisters. Being careful to not touch the hot muffin with her fingers, which would send him into a tizzy, she carefully slid a fork down the side and lifted it, placing it on his plate.

The frail woman seated across the table waited until her husband was satisfying his palate, and then cautiously asked Tamara, "Is there any new news this morning, dear?"

"Unfortunately, yes."

Her dad spoke as he chewed, "Court put an end to the nonsense, did they?"

"No, Dad, it's much worse than that. Sara had made each of the twins a baby blanket. Dane's is on the wall in his room. It's exactly like the one she made for Dwain. Along one edge she had knitted into the pattern,

'Mommy loves Dwain' on his, and 'Mommy loves Dane' on the other one."

The old man said, "Pretty stupid to do that if you're not keeping the kid. If you love him that much, keep him."

"Dad, she received Dwain's blanket in the mail this morning. The kids in Dane's class received a demand on their Web site for a hundred thousand dollars for the return of Dwain. Sara is—"

The old man slammed his hand on the table, and she jumped back.

He clenched his fists. "That no-good! Who does he think he is? Someone ought to hang him." When Tammy Rae screamed excitedly on her way down the slide, he looked out the window. Both women were staring at him, expecting the worst from his sudden anger. He slowly stood, towering over them by more than a foot and a half. "I'm going over to find out what Brent is doing about this. You keep that little one out there close to the house. Better yet, bring her inside. I'm not going to let that sicko snatch another one out from under us."

Tamara and her mother watched him until he reached the back gate. He barked, "Tammy Rae, you go on in the house. Your grandma needs to talk to you, right now. Get on in there, right now."

"Well," Tamara's mother said as her slender white fingers carefully lifted a piece of buttered muffin. "He must have work to do on the farm this morning. I must've forgotten."

Little Tammy Rae climbed up on a chair next to her great-grandmother. "Can I have a muffin, Grams?"

Tamara said, "May I, dear, not can I. You must always say may I."

The older woman looked up at her. "I can't remember what we were talking about. Were we talking about something, Paula?"

Correcting her over which of her five daughters she was would do no good, so Tamara simply said, "I was about to ask you if you would like to help me in the greenhouse this morning."

⚁ ⚁ ⚁

When Dane left that morning, his mother was in a state of shock. He didn't expect her to be any better when he came home that afternoon. Too agitated to walk slowly enough for Teresa to keep up, he lifted her to his shoulders. He walked in long strides up the driveway, all the while assessing the situation. The three vehicles in the driveway told him that his great-grandpa Mark Henderson was here, his dad was home, and someone else was here, too.

Pushing his head to the left, Teresa steered him toward her egg-gathering basket that had been set outside on the porch. This Dane figured to be Mom's way of sending her to do her chores before going inside. As he lowered her, she snatched up the basket.

"We might have baby chicks." She ran toward the chicken house, yelling over her shoulder, "If we do, I'll tell you."

Dane didn't care if they had baby chicks. He wanted to know what was so important for Mom to set the egg basket outside. He eased the door open, hoping that by being quiet, he could listen to the conversation in the living room.

Two men were sitting on the sofa. As he quietly shut the kitchen door, his mother motioned for him to go upstairs. He took the steps two at a time and went into his bedroom and shut the door. He sat on his bed, staring at the blank wall over Dwain's bed until someone tapped lightly on his door. He didn't want to talk to anyone, but reached for the door handle and looked through the crack.

"Grandma." He quickly opened the door and helped his grandma with the box she was carrying. She motioned for him to set it on Dwain's bed. "What's this?"

She looked around the small room, smiling as she always did. "He will love being up in this room. Your father liked being up as high as he could. He lost interest in that jungle gym in the backyard as soon as he was able to scurry up a tree."

He lifted the top off the storage box. "What's in here?"

"Clothes that might fit Dwain. I had forgotten about this box. I put it away when your father left for college."

Dane lifted out a pair of pants. "Wow, was Dad really this skinny when he went to college?" Wondering where to put the pants, he considered the empty closet space, where he had placed a low bar for Dwain. He decided to put the pants in an empty bottom drawer of the dresser. His grandma handed him a shirt that he put on a hanger.

"This is a great idea, Grandma." He smiled and then his voice cracked and he sat, trying not to cry. "He's going to be surprised."

She handed him three framed photographs. "These were on your father's wall when he was in high school. I think Dwain will like them."

Dane asked, "Why did Dad have a picture of a basketball player on his wall?"

"Because he was proud of his grandpa, and he loved him even though he was grumpy."

Dane smiled. "So this is Gramps when he was playing professional basketball?"

She touched his arm. "You still have time to make it to basketball practice, and I think he is in the way downstairs. Would you make an old man's day and take him to your practice?"

"Grandma, he always tells the coach what to do. Last year he got in the way. Besides, I don't have time for basketball. I have to work on getting everything ready for Dwain."

Taking back the photo of his great-grandfather, she gazed at it thoughtfully. "I think playing basketball, and not sitting in your room, is a way of showing you have faith in what you believe God is doing."

She laid the three pictures on the bed. "And I hear that this year, you have a new coach, and we don't know how long Gramps will be with us. You are his pride and joy. You have to remember he had five daughters. My sisters only had girls, and we didn't adopt a basketball player. So where does that leave you?"

He reached over for his gym bag. "Maybe he'll let me drive." He tapped the side of the box. "If you want to leave this, I'll put it away later." He saw hurt in her eyes and quickly added, "But if you want to put it away, it would be great."

Jeff stepped into the room and handed Dane a small hammer. "I only found four nails."

Grandma lifted the hammer from Dane's hand and swished him out the door with her fingers as she handed the hammer back to Jeff.

In the hallway, Dane heard his dad say, "Hey, this is my old picture of Gramps. Where did you find that?"

❧ ❧ ❧

FBI agent Dan Marshall was determined to not allow the cantankerous woman to keep him from doing his job. He left her with his partner in her den and walked up the stairs to the next level of the old house. The young women sitting with babies in four of the rooms could barely understand what he was asking them. One said she was from Holland another from Finland, one from Denmark, and the last, a young Mexican, kept insisting she had a green card—he wondered about that. None had been in the woman's employment for more than six months, so they could tell him nothing about the period of time when Dwain had been in the home.

His partner stuck his head in the door, motioning to the angry woman behind him. "We got something. She remembers the blanket. She gave it to a guy."

Unlocking the storage room door, she said, "I told him he couldn't have anything without signing for it."

Taking out a small notebook, Agent Jones asked her, "Which hospital was Dwain sent to?"

She glared at the man through hardened, cold eyes. "I never asked. I keep only the records I'm required to keep. If you want to know anything else, talk to his social worker."

Opening his cell phone, Agent Marshall called an agent at the Campbell home.

At the Campbell home, Agent Briggs listened to Marshall saying, "She said the boy died ten years ago. The blanket was in a storage box until a few days ago. A guy from Social Services picked it up. And get this, the idiot actually signed for it, and the photograph he sent to the student's Web site."

Agent Briggs glanced sadly at the couple on the sofa, who were staring apprehensively at him. He closed his phone and cautiously selected his words. "He never had Dwain, only the blanket and a photograph."

Sara pleaded, "But where did he get the baby blanket?"

"At a foster home. It was left behind when Dwain left the home. They kept it in storage."

Seated on a straight-backed kitchen chair, Brent leaned forward, shaking his head. "That isn't what Zelda told me when she took him. She said if we gave him something, it would stay with him."

Briggs began putting away his electronic equipment. "That would be out of her control. A caregiver could discard something without considering what it might mean to the child."

Brent asked, "Are you sure he doesn't have the boy?"

Briggs nodded. "What we are sure of is that Dwain is not in the Oregon state system. We are in the process of checking records in other states, but it could take a while." He stepped away as he opened his cell phone and listened and then he turned to face the parents. "Our man is in custody. He admits to sending you the blanket and putting the ransom demand on the Web site."

Looking into eyes of the parents, he couldn't tell them the boy had died. That information would have to come from another, more substantiated source.

ᴄⱱᴏ ᴄⱱᴏ ᴄⱱᴏ

Marshall went back to the Social Services office to find out what Dwain's social worker had to say. When he asked Zelda Cloud what she knew about the death of Dwain Campbell, she flew into a rage. Slamming a file drawer, she yelled, "That boy is no more dead than I am. I'm not at all surprised that Dennis was involved in this scandal. If there is a problem, it's in his office, not mine.

"This is a state-run office. You have no jurisdiction here." She opened the door, letting him pass by, then stepped out herself, pulling the door shut.

She raised her nose. "Rhonda, I have an important appointment. I will be gone for the rest of the day."

Jones called Marshall's cell phone to check on the case then, and

Marshall filled him in while he followed Zelda outside. She got into a red sports car and lowered the convertible top. His salary had to be more then hers, but he couldn't afford a car like that. He decided to follow her and see where she was going in such a hurry.

She backed out of her parking space without looking back and turned without using her turn signal. He was certain that she never once looked into the rearview mirror. He called in her license plate number, requesting information as he followed her toward the entrance to the state park. The response to his request came back. The car was registered to her. She had a fender bender six months ago while driving an older model Ford. That car was traded in for a new Ford that was involved in a parking-lot accident, and then traded for the new red sports car. The way she was driving, she wouldn't have this one long.

With her blouse loose at the neck and her hair floating in the wind, she rocked in the motion of music. Her car swerved, and then she held a cell phone to her ear. It swerved again when she set the phone down and turned her head toward the seat beside her.

Realizing he was following her into a dead end, he slowed, pulled over, and watched as she passed by the last house and turned into a driveway. He eased forward until he could see her car entering a garage.

He believed her car was beyond her budget, and unless the place had a rental apartment, it wasn't hers. He requested information on the residence and checked in again with Jones, who he assumed was heading his way. The agent told him, he had turned off into the state park. He was driving past camp areas and parking in a picnic parking space near a public restroom.

Jones said, "It's quiet. Only one family is camping here." Marshall nodded, knowing that what Jones was searching for had nothing to do with Zelda Cloud. They were in the area working on a far more serious case. The state park was on their list of places to check out.

Aware that he could not be seen through the tinted window of his car, he took out binoculars and watched the windows of the house. A light turned on at the end of the house when she first went in. He assumed she had entered through the garage, turning on the light. A few moments later, a green car pulled up to the front of the house. A man wearing a long apron and what appeared to be a towel covering his hair and part of his face came out the front door. He hurried to the car, lifted two sacks from the driver's hand, and hurried back inside. The agent had assumed this was a food delivery, but he wondered about the apron and the covered head. If the guy was cooking, why would he be ordering out for food?

ᴄᴧᴐ ᴄᴧᴐ ᴄᴧᴐ

Thirty minutes after she returned home, Zelda came downstairs wearing a sheer silk gown. As Marcus handed her a glass of her favorite wine, she smiled, admiring his handsome face and slender physique. He motioned to the kitchen table, where fine china was set for the special dinner he had prepared for her.

They sat and enjoyed a savory Greek dinner while he amused her with accounts of the daily challenges of his profession. His vast knowledge of medical terms and procedures caused her to wonder what such a renowned surgeon could possibly see in her. As he spoke, she studied his features. He was ten years younger than she, but his adoration assured her she was as desirable to him as he was to her.

The house phone rang. She knew it could be only one person, and she didn't want to talk to her. Marcus frowned, and she decided to answer the call and make it a quick one. She knew Marcus didn't care to listen to one-sided conversations between her and her mother.

"Yes, Mother." She ate, made faces, and rolled her eyes. Then she said, "I'm happy that you and Becky are having a nice time in Disney World. I have to go now, Mother."

She hung up and sat fuming. Marcus stood, leaned down, and pressed his lips to hers. Instantly, she forgot her anger toward her mother. He said, "Why don't we go upstairs." As she stood, his hands moved over her, turning her toward the stairway and embracing her.

With one hand on autopilot, roaming over Zelda, Marcus reached for his money clip with his other hand. His finger pressed the clip, sending a signal that turned on the beeper on his belt. He quickly tipped up the beeper, as if checking to see who had paged him, and reached for his cell phone.

Outside, Agent Marshall had moved closer to the house, crouching behind bushes. Using a small camera, he adjusted the zoom and snapped a picture of the silver sports car as it backed out of the driveway. He couldn't clearly see the driver behind the tinted window as it passed, but to his surprise the car went no farther than the other end of the house, turned sharply, and backed into a garage.

He checked back in with the agency, saying, "Are you sure that the house is a single-family dwelling? It has a two-car garage on each end of the house. Could it be a duplex?"

He was assured that the home was sold to Zelda Cloud for seven hundred thousand dollars only six months ago. Bank records showed that she put a down payment of a hundred fifty thousand and made three payments of four thousand, and then stopped making payments. She was also two months behind on her car payments.

The agents decided to continue their investigation, of both Zelda Cloud's mysterious wealth, and the possible mismanagement of the infant foster care facility. But the Zelda situation would still be here in a month.

The psychopathic serial killer they were close to apprehending wouldn't. If they didn't find him quickly, he could strike again and leave the state to process the evidence he left behind.

✿ ✿ ✿

After Marcus left for the hospital, Zelda placed their dishes in the dishwasher and filled the teakettle with water. When the kettle whistled, she poured water into a gold-trimmed teapot, adding two tea bags to the top before placing the lid on. This she set on a table next to her recliner in the living room and went back to the kitchen for a cup and saucer. Returning to her chair, she set the empty cup on the saucer next to the teapot. She turned the handle of the teapot to allow her to easily fill her cup as she read her book. She read part of the first page and then felt a draft, so she went up to her bedroom for a light blanket. As she started to sit again, she noticed drops next to the teapot and wondered how she could have spilled, when she hadn't touched the teapot since she set it down. She went to the kitchen for a towel but when she returned, the drops had disappeared. She wondered how they could have evaporated so quickly, without even leaving a water ring. Lifting the teapot, she began to pour and realized her tea was too red. She lifted the lid and looked at the teabag that floated on top. She was certain she had selected a soothing evening tea, not this tart red tea.

She sipped, not particularly enjoying the flavor, and opened her book. As she stared at the words, she realized this was not what she'd been read-ing a few minutes ago. She looked at the cover. It was not the book she had set here before going up stairs for the blanket. She closed her eyes tightly, and then accepted the fact that she was not going to clear her memory that way, and went in search of the book she had before. Finding it on the end table by the sofa, she reclined and began to read again. In a few minutes, she set the empty teacup on the saucer and closed her eyes, feeling extremely tired. She let her head lie to the side as she drifted into a deep sleep in which she dreamed of her Marcus. At first she dreamed of the cruise they planned to take next month. And then she dreamed that he was sitting on the sofa, using her computer.

He said, "Don't feed that to the cat." Another man said, "I thought you don't like Fluffy." And Marcus said, "I don't want to hear about another trip to that vet, so don't give her any more bones."

Zelda, having moved to the kitchen without leaving her chair, opened the cabinet where she had a special selection of small cans of cat food. Since Fluffy always ate canned cat food, she couldn't have choked on bones. And then she heard Marcus talking again, but she didn't care to hear what he was saying, and she sank back into the pleasant darkness.

Marcus looked at Zelda, who was drooling from the side of her mouth, and he shook his head. He picked up her laptop and put it into the case. He pushed the bookcase out from the wall, slipped behind, and pulled it back into place.

ᴈᴣ ᴈᴣ ᴈᴣ

Dane knew this would happen. Gramps paced the gym floor, watching as the boys took turns shooting from the free-throw line. Finally, the coach motioned to him to go ahead and do what he could. The stoop-shouldered old man shuffled to the line.

As boys gathered around him, he motioned to one of them. "Now, you come here and stand, right here, and hold this ball. No, not like that. That's the way a girl would hold it."

Dane sat on the bench next to his coach, who was also his pastor. "I hope you don't mind if Gramps is here. Grandma Campbell asked me to bring him."

Mr. Davis said, "I know I'm not a good coach, but no one else is volunteering."

Dane shrugged. "Pastor, why is God taking so long to bring Dwain home?"

"I never question God. When I was your age, all I wanted was to be a farmer like my dad. Sitting on a tractor, it didn't matter that I was dyslexic and couldn't read above third-grade level."

Dane had heard this story a hundred times, but he leaned forward, placing his elbows on his knees, and listened. "One day, God spoke to me in my mind as I drove the tractor in the field. He told me to be a pastor. I refused to even consider that idea. The very next day, I fell off the tractor, and the plow went right over the top of me. It should have sliced me into pieces, but I didn't even have a scratch.

"I thought I was dreaming, but when I looked across the field, my dad and my brother were running toward me, and the tractor had gone through a fence and stopped against a tree.

"They saw the plow go right over the top of me. And where I had fallen, the ground wasn't plowed for the length of my body. When my dad asked how it could happen, I told him God spoke to me when I was plowing the day before." Pastor Davis shook his head. "Now, my dad wasn't a believer up until that moment, but the very next day he enrolled me in seminary."

He winked at Dane. "God's choice is not always the one that we would make. I was going off to Bible school to become a pastor, and I couldn't read, and didn't know one book of the Bible from another. But the first thing I noticed was that I could see words clearly for the first time in my life."

Dane smiled. "You forgot to say that your dad would have been your greatest obstacle, but instead, he paid for you to go to seminary, and that if God could keep you safe from being hurt when a plow went over the top of you, he can keep one little person safe from whatever is out there in the world."

They watched as the team's poorest player made his first basket from the free-throw line. Another guy yelled, "Gramps, can you show me how to do that?"

The old man said, "I can show you, but I can't do it for you. This team has to play with only two tall boys, so you're going to have to work together and develop your fundamentals. The other team is going to press you to keep the taller boys from getting the ball. They'll use full court pressure to keep you from getting past half court."

"So what do we gotta do, Gramps?"

"Practice." He bounced the ball. "You practice dribbling, passing, and shooting." Dane laughed as Gramps sank a shot from the free-throw line. "He's still good, isn't he? It's his favorite thing, you know."

Pastor Davis asked Dane, "Do you think Gramps would consider coaching this season?"

"What about you?"

He chuckled, "Like you said, he's good."

Dane jumped up and ran across the gym. "Gramps, Mr. Davis wants to know if you'll coach for the whole season."

The boys gathered around the old man. "Would you help us, Gramps? With you showing us all your moves, we could do really good."

The tallest boy said to Dane, "If we win some games, I could get spotted by a recruiter and get a college scholarship to play basketball. I need a scholarship or I can't go to college."

The old man looked straight into that boy's eyes and said, "When I was your age, I was up at six every morning. I ran a mile to school and a mile home after two hours of ball practice. I shot three hundred free throws a week and five hundred other shots. I didn't become a professional ball player sitting on my butt."

Another guy said, "What we really want is to not come in last place again. This school has never done anything, except in wrestling."

Gramps glared at him. "You shape up and you'll win. Start by finding some more basketballs. Get moving, we don't have all night."

ᐁᐧ ᐁᐧ ᐁᐧ

Pastor Edward Davis stepped into the parsonage and hung up his coat. He had heard women talking when he was on the porch, so he slipped in as quietly as he possibly could. Some evenings Jessica had women's Bible studies in the kitchen. She hadn't mentioned having anyone over this evening, but it wasn't unusual, and he may have not been listening.

He slipped his shoes off and stepped softly up the carpeted steps, hoping to walk back to their bedroom without disturbing the ladies. As he turned at the top of the stairs, his wife called to him. "Honey, oh good, you're home. Come and see who came to visit with us this evening."

As soon as he entered the kitchen, his jaw fell open. He almost forgot to close his mouth. "Well, Katie, this is a surprise." He caught himself before he said, since Hilda's funeral, and said instead, "You're looking very well."

Katie said, "Jessie said you're coaching basketball."

He slid a chair back. "Tonight I had a reprieve. A retired professional player helped me with the team."

Jessica said softly, "We were having a little Bible study."

"A Bible study?" They had his undivided attention. He sat at the table with them. "Any particular chapter or verse?"

Katie leaned forward. "I was telling Jessica that I saw the plow go over you. I know something protected you. I've heard about Jesus being some kind of rock or a cornerstone for builders, or something like that. I was thinking that something hard like a rock must have been between you and the blades."

He smiled. "I always imagine angels lifting the plow up as it rolled over me. I don't remember falling, and I know that, if not for God's intervention, I would have been sliced into a dozen pieces."

She leaned forward. "Tell me why God would make a farmer into a pastor."

He grinned. "He started with fishermen. He knows what each of us is capable of, before we're born. I believe He has a plan for each of our lives. Why He chooses, who He chooses, we won't understand until we walk with Him in Heaven and ask Him."

She looked from one to the other. "That's why I left here after high school. You said that God spoke to you and you wouldn't listen, like Jonas in the Bible. You said Jonas died in the fish and was brought back to life to finish the work that the Lord told him to do. You said that you died too, but I saw it happen and I know you never died."

He laughed. "No, you misunderstood what I said. I died to myself. I died to my plans of being a farmer and began a new life, living for Christ."

She nodded, and her face relaxed. "So when God spoke to you, did you hear His voice?"

"The first time, He spoke with words; but the second time, He spoke with action."

She squinted. "I was riding my horse and asking God to speak to me, so I would know He was listening. I saw you fall and get up after the plow went over you. If that was God speaking to you, was He also speaking to me? Saying He could hear me?"

"God chooses who sees what He does. If you saw a miracle, God chose you to see it."

She shuddered. "But what did He want from me? That's what scared me. Brent was talking like he was going to be a preacher, and I couldn't…"

Edward said softly, "Be a preacher's wife?"

Jessica laughed. "It has its rewards, but I understand why you would be afraid of getting into the ministry."

Edward took Katie's hand and squeezed it for a moment. "You could begin by being a witness. Others need to hear what you saw, in order to increase their faith in God. If you're not willing to be a witness, someone else will be."

Suddenly, her shoulders drooped and she sighed. "And that's all God wanted me to do?"

"I don't know," he said. "Try being a witness and find out."

∽ ∽ ∽

Before going to bed, Brent looked out his window and saw the barn door was ajar. He went out and pulled it open, wondering if there was a reason it was unlatched. Seated alone on a bale of straw, Jeff looked up at him as the moonlight cast its glow over him. Brent pushed the door open wider and slid onto a bale across from the little man. After a few minutes of sitting in silence, he asked, "Can't sleep?"

"No." Jeff shook his head.

Brent said, "I was praying about Dwain and looked out and noticed the barn door wasn't latched. Are you thinking about him?"

Jeff gave a rueful smile. "About eleven o'clock I woke up believing that I was to pray for Zelda Cloud. I don't know why God would wake me up to pray for her. Did you ever pray for someone and know the instant that person was out of danger?"

"No. I pray all the time for Dwain, but I don't receive any assurance that he's safe."

Jeff looked toward the doorway. "I want to believe that Dwain is safe. I know there are people who are willing to love and care for children like him. My parents are proof of that. When they agreed to adopt me before I was born, they didn't know my parents had a dwarfism gene. When I was born they could have refused to take me. I couldn't have had better parents." He chuckled. "I was happy, but it wasn't easy being the principal's kid. I got into my share of trouble, like other kids."

Brent nodded. "When the twins were born, I should've talked to your parents about taking Dwain, but I was worried that if you had Dwain and Sara had Dane, the two of you would feel obligated to get married to keep the twins together."

Jeff looked sad. "You did what you thought was best at the time."

Brent looked at his watch. "If Zelda is safe, we should hit the hay."

"Let's pray in agreement for her." Jeff lowered his head. "If nothing else, we should pray for her to be safe until she has the Lord's salvation. For some reason she is important enough to God to wake me up thinking about her. Maybe her parents or grandparents have prayed for her. If she's a hopeless case, God wouldn't have put her on my mind."

Brent shook his head. "All right, but I'm not good at praying for the enemy."

It was almost midnight before Jeff was able to go back to bed. Hoping not to wake Sara, he turned the bathroom light out and walked into their bedroom in the dark. His feet found the ramp on his side of the bed. A few feet from the head of the bed, the raised platform leveled, and he could turn and sit on the bed. As he slid under the covers, Sara turned his way and moved over into his arms.

He sighed and closed his eyes. "I've never seen Gramps so happy in my entire life."

"Your mother is pretty happy too. Dane absolutely loves the pictures on the wall above Dwain's bed and that closet full of your old clothes."

"Those are good old clothes. One of those shirts is still one of my favorite shirts."

She laughed, "I can just see you wearing that shirt at the clinic."

He chuckled. "I like my Donald Duck shirt."

She whispered, "I'm sure your son will, too."

9

At 2:00 A.M., twenty-seven-year-old Arnold Walker slipped out the back door. As he climbed the steps on the hillside, he saw no lighted windows on the house. The rooms on the bigger, fancier side of the house, where he lived in with his older brother, Archie, were hiding behind heavy shades. On the other side, Zelda was sleeping and had been for hours. He had stood at the side of her bed watching her sleep until Archie slid the wall open behind the dresser and made him leave. Arnold had promised he wouldn't hurt her, but he had also promised not to hurt the others.

Archie had said to him, "Don't go near her again. We're leaving in a few weeks. We only have one more big sale. After that, we'll have enough to quit and get out of the country. You mess up, you'll end up in prison and never get out." Archie acted like he was some kind of genius, like Arnold was too stupid to understand anything by himself.

He giggled. Archie always said stuff like that, but when Arnold messed up, nothing bad ever happened. He hummed a tune as he reached the top of the wooden stairway. He was on the top of the world, and the best part was that no one knew he was there. As he walked carefully down the stairs to the campground, he stroked the small bags of white powder in his pocket. Tonight, his new friends would come again. Just like last night, they would have a campfire and roast wieners and make hot dogs. But best of all, this time they promised to bring marshmallows, chocolate bars, and graham crackers.

He stepped behind bushes where he could see his friends sitting around a campfire. He listened to their voices as he studied the faces of the women who had come with the men tonight. A car parked. As the lights turned off, a woman stepped out. Arnold rubbed his hands together. She was alone. She would stay with him after the others left, and if she made him mad, no one would come looking for her right away.

See, he wasn't stupid. Archie was wrong. He planned things, just like Archie. He planned, just in case she made him mad. He would tell Archie he planned real careful. Archie would come and take her body in her car. He would take her car somewhere far away.

He looked back up the stairway. He already had a friend waiting for him. Zellie missed him. He turned to go back, but someone called to him from the campfire.

"Arnold are you here, man? We brought the stuff, man."

ⅾⅼ𝖔 ⅾⅼ𝖔 ⅾⅼ𝖔

Waking from a sound sleep, Zelda lay still, looking up at the ceiling. She couldn't remember going to bed. She tried to remember what day it was. Listening to the shower running, she reached across the bed. The sheets beside her were warm, and she knew Marcus had been there. For a moment, the room seemed to be moving as if she were on a ship at sea. *When did I go to bed? When did Marcus come in? I was reading. I was reading and fell asleep. I remember.* She smiled.

The dizziness faded, so she went into the bathroom and stepped into the shower behind Marcus. "How did it go at the hospital?"

He turned to her, and smiling, pretended to examine her pupils. "You asked me that an hour ago. We were having tea in the kitchen, and I told you about the heart surgery I had to perform. Remember, the car accident victim. We discussed it in depth, darling."

He looked at her lovingly, touching her head lightly with his fingers, as if comforting a confused patient. "You were telling me about your sister, Becky. What kind of retardation did you say she has?"

Knowing she'd had a conversation she could not remember was shocking enough without learning she had talked with him about Becky. He stepped around her, reaching for a towel. She shut off the water. "I would rather not talk about Becky."

He wiped mist from the mirror with the corner of his towel. "And why is that?"

She put her arms around him and rested her forehead on his back. "She ruined my life. Everything changed when they brought her home. At Christmas and on my birthdays, my parents didn't have money to give me anything I wanted because of Becky. I had to settle for a state college because they had to use their money for yet another medical procedure for Becky."

He turned to face her. "Will she always live with your parents?"

Frustrated by her inability to make him understand, she closed her eyes. "She has Down's syndrome. You're a doctor. Surely, you know what that is like."

He rubbed his thumb in a circle on her shoulder. "It's not her fault, and you're not the only person who has a sibling that is retarded. Even a person who is mildly retarded needs someone to take care of him."

She stiffened, trying to keep anger from her voice. "That is what our state programs are for."

As if welcoming her irritation, he shrugged. "Life is a mixture of difficulties, Zellie. You can't honestly believe you will end a family's heartache when you take their child away."

She moved her finger over the dark mark on his chest, following it under his arm. "Your birthmark is darker."

He hated the feel of her fingers touching him. He wiped the mirror, looking at the dark line. It was wider and longer. He would take his pills and make an appointment to see a doctor in the morning. He said, "I'm tired," and turned to face her. "I really need some sleep."

She groped at him again, and realizing that she was not going to stop touching him, he reached over and picked up the money clip he had placed on the counter. He pressed the center, turning on the beeper on his belt on the chair in the bedroom. He stepped past her and snatched up the beeper.

"Looks like I have to go again." He dressed as he held the cell phone with his shoulder, giving instructions about a medication his patient needed, and then he rushed downstairs. He used a remote control to open and then close the garage door.

A few minutes later, Marcus pushed the bookcase into the darkened living room. He listened for Zelda on the stairway as he slipped through the opening and picked up her teapot, cup, and saucer. After rinsing them in the kitchen sink, he placed a small bag of soothing tea in a quarter inch of water in the teapot.

Almost tripping on Fluffy, he stopped to feed her, quietly popping a lid off a can and scooping it into her dish. He hoped she would stay in the kitchen and eat while he slipped back into the other side of the house.

⌇⌇ ⌇⌇ ⌇⌇

In a hotel room, FBI Special Agent Jones placed a map of the United States on the bed, then laid out maps of the individual cities. The maps were covered with color marks depicting where victims of serial killer Arnold Darien Walters had been found. He believed that the movement of the serial killer showed a pattern. He just had to find it and get a step ahead of him. But where was the pattern? The colors he had placed in the cities where Arnold had been seen, or had killed someone in the past seven years, seemed completely random. Moving back as far as the bathroom door, he could see the way the color fanned out from several points like narrow wedges cut from a pie.

Jones believed he was missing something that was obvious. He attributed this to having worked too many years by himself on this case. Each time he had been close to apprehending Walters, the agency dispatched another agent to work with him. It was usually then that a new light would shine on the case. Going over what he had with another agent helped him see things he hadn't noticed before. He wanted Marshall to take a look at what he had here.

In the past, the instant an agency reported a match on Arnold's fingerprints or his DNA, the FBI rushed Jones to the scene. Because the victim was usually a prostitute, he would find out that a series of these killings in the area had not been investigated properly. He would ask for help to embark on a massive search. Every time he began investigating, the killings would stop, then begin again a few months later, in another city.

As Agent Marshall stepped into the room and handed him a sandwich and a cup of coffee, Jones asked him, "What do you see here?

Marshall said, "I looked over the case. I see red-light districts. Arnold kills at night when it's dark. Most of the people around him are so drunk or loaded on drugs, they can't even describe the guy that picked up the prostitute."

Jones said, "But Arnold is never far from his brother. Archie wouldn't frequent those areas. He is more refined and prefers the more affluent environment."

"Arnold must be going out on his own at night, then."

Jones shook his head. "Arnold isn't bright enough to go very far alone. He has never had a driver's license that we know of." He pointed at the map of the United States, touching five cities. "He has killed five women in higher-class residential areas. In all five cases, Archie befriended the woman, posing as a wealthy bachelor, while he was renting another home in close proximity, where he was making large quantities of cocaine. Both locations were covered with Archie's fingerprints, so we know he went back and forth using the victim's home as a comfortable base."

Marshall looked at a sheet of paper. "But when he placed his orders for the ingredients for making cocaine, he used computers located in other places in the city, and different delivery locations. He also used an untraceable telephone to call buyers."

He turned the map. "Why would someone buying that much at one time risk everything by dealing with men as unstable as these guys? They move all around the country. The ingredients needed for making cocaine aren't readily available, so the buyers have to know this guy is attracting attention to himself."

Jones shook his head. "But he isn't. Archie is one of the sharpest men the agency has ever gone after. We wouldn't know anything about him if he weren't sheltering a serial killer. And as far as the buyers go, you have to know the history of this family. Their father is the kingpin in the buyers' organization. He's another one we've been one step behind. Every time we get a tip on his operation, he's gone when we raid the place.

"Arnold isn't real bright, and if it weren't for Archie, he would not be in the family business. Archie started out standing beside his father, watching as cocaine was being tested. He figured out that if he manufactured a quality product, he would always have a ready buyer."

Marshall studied two sheets of numbers. "It's right here. This is Arnold's pattern. You told me that Archie promised his father he would never allow Arnold to be there when he sells the cocaine." He moved the sheets of paper to line up the columns.

Jones looked at the dates on both sheets. "That's it. When Archie finishes making a half a million dollars worth of product, he sets up a rendezvous with the buyer. His dad makes the arrangements, but he doesn't want Arnold messing anything up. Archie drops him off on the way to deliver the drug and picks him up on his way back."

Marshall started pacing. "Archie drives that blue box van when he delivers his product. He drops his brother off in the red-light district before he goes to the location of the sell. That is why witnesses have said that the man who picked up the prostitute got out of a moving van."

Jones added, "And witnesses said a blue van drove up and he got into it."

Marshall ran his fingers down two rows of dates. "But there are more days that we know Archie sold big amounts of cocaine than there were reported murders."

Jones nodded. "There are two reasons for that. First, his victims were drug users and prostitutes. When one is killed, she gets listed as a victim of her profession with no further investigation. Most cities don't have the budget to do much more then notify the families. That's why I believe Arnold has killed more than a hundred, but we only know about the twenty-seven women."

Marshall reminded him, "You said two reasons."

"Women who have been with him say he's a fantastic lover. In reference to his character, I've heard words like *kind*, *sweet*, *nice*, and even *adorable*. He may actually love women, but according to his mental profile, he won't accept the word *no*, and when his temper flashes, he kills before he thinks, and now it's a habit."

cAo cAo cAo

In a back room of the library, Teddy felt more and more frustrated as he and Dane watched the computer screen as the records of births and adoptions scrolled down before them. They had found the record of Greg's adoption. The arrangement for his adoption was prior to his birth. The mother was a junior in the high school. They had already found her photograph in the yearbook. But there was no mention of the father in the birth records.

"Maybe they don't know," Dane said.

"They know. Believe me. My parents know everything that they can possibly know about all of us." He turned the pages of the yearbook. "He has to be in here. I wouldn't be surprised if he was a wrestler or a basketball player. He had to be someone strong and healthy."

They both stared at a picture of a pretty blond girl seated next to a boy with short arms and legs. Dane smiled. "My folks loved each other when they were in high school. Mom may have even been pregnant in this picture."

Teddy pointed at another couple. "There. That's Greg's birth mom, and this guy's hair sticks up in front just like Greg's does. He has to be his dad."

"Do you know who that is?" Dane chuckled. "That's Greggie Hamilton. You know, Greggie at the lumber mill. He's the guy that runs that big loader that lifts the logs off the trucks."

Greg's birth father had been here all along. Even though knowing who he was would've meant risking breaking up Teddy's brothers, it somehow didn't seem fair or right. He glared at the computer screen. "She was seventeen, just two years older than me. So she gave Greg up for adoption, and then where did she go?"

Dane turned the pages of another yearbook, "Christy Mitchell. She was only a sophomore, so maybe she had Greg and stayed in school. Maybe she graduated and went to college."

She probably did; his parents wouldn't have adopted the baby of someone who was too lazy to get good grades. "Are you working on your motorcycle tomorrow?"

Dane turned pages. "I have a more important project. Do you want to help me?"

"Depends on what it is."

"We cut wood in shop today to make a wheelchair ramp. Mr. Miller showed us how to cut each board at an angle so we can make a ramp with a round corner. Now, all we have to do is set the boards down in exactly the order we stacked them in my grandpa's pickup. Grandpa Anderson helped me to make the frame for them to sit on. If enough guys help, we could get the boards down and the rails up tomorrow."

Teddy studied the screen. "After I finish my chores. I'll get up early and be at your place by noon."

Amanda McCormick, a girl from Dane's class, slid a chair between the boys. "What are you doing? Are you looking for Dwain in that?"

"No." Teddy glared at her. "We're doing something that's none of your business."

Dane stood up. "It's getting late. Do you want to walk home with me, Amanda?"

"No. I have to look something up."

After he left, she whispered to Teddy. "I can't hang out with him anymore. My mom was all right with it until all this stuff about 'Finding Dwain' started. Now she's afraid of what people are going to say about us being together. She says that I should look at a boy's parents and grandparents before I date him."

He turned back to the screen. "So you better not be seen with me. I'm adopted. You don't know what runs in my genetic line."

She pushed his arm. "You're preapproved. My dad knew your real dad, and my mom liked your mom. Your mom was a country-western singer. My dad said she was the best singer he ever heard."

"Don't you have something else to do, Amanda?"

He looked back at the screen. Before the search for Dwain started, he had no idea who his birth parents had been, and everything between himself and his dad was fine. Now, he believed he was adopted for what his parents were, and he wouldn't have been adopted if he had the slightest physical problem. That bothered him.

Thinking about Alex's dark eyes, he wondered what special features his parents had that made them strong enough to be acceptable birth parents.

A week ago he'd wanted to take a baseball bat to the computers in Mr. Tims's classroom. Now, he wanted to confront his father with equal fury.

Amanda opened a yearbook. "Do you think Dane likes me?"

"I think he likes everyone. It's his nature. He talks to everyone the same."

"But I always helped him and Kevin on that motorcycle, so I've spent more time with him than other girls have. And his parents always let me come along when they took his little sisters to the Atwood clinic. I've been with his family almost every day since we started first grade."

Teddy stared at the screen. "Can you do something else? I only have a half hour before I have to go home." He put in Alex's birth date and watched as the computer flashed portions of old microfilm. He moved forward and backward over the hospital's birth records. The record he found was for a baby named Alexander Menton, born the day his youngest brother was born.

Amanda interrupted his concentration. "What do you think the possibility of Dane having a dwarf baby is?"

"Does that matter to you? You seem to be okay with his dad and his sisters. If you want to know something about dwarfism, go over to the Atwood Clinic and ask them. I don't know anything about the possibility of something genetic occurring in a person. I suppose, in Dane's case, it's probably high, since he has three siblings that are dwarfs." He reached for the yearbook that corresponded with the year that Alex was born.

The birth record said that Alex was born to Clara Menton and Alexander Blake. He looked through the whole yearbook before he found Clara's picture in the freshman section. Looking at the girl, he couldn't see where Alex got his dark hair and dark eyes. And he couldn't believe that his dad would adopt a baby whose mother appeared to be so sweet and shy. He read under her name about her freshman accomplishments. She was an honor student and freshman class president. He realized then that she wasn't as shy as she appeared to be in the photograph. So, she was smart, but that didn't make her son a good candidate for a farmer.

"So, what's Alexander Blake like?" He closed the book and went back to the computer.

Amanda said, "That old couple on the farm by the old windmill had a grandson named Alexander Blake."

Teddy picked up a pile of yearbooks. "What year did he graduate?"

"He didn't. He was killed by lightning trying to get the hay in before it rained. My dad said the hay field wasn't worth him taking the risk, but he did it because his grandparents were losing their farm."

Teddy turned the computer off. "I've come to the conclusion that I really hate farmers."

Amanda picked up half of the yearbooks. "Want me to walk you home?"

Teddy took the books from her. "Guys walk girls home, not the other way around."

"Who are you taking to the Fall Festival dance?" She hurried to catch up with him.

"Gloria Stanley."

"Gloria's in a wheelchair. How can you expect to dance with her? You don't even know her. Do you ever talk to her? When did you ever talk to Gloria?"

He stopped at the top of library steps and looked down into her eyes. "Amanda, I'm just about ready to start talking to her."

"Are you out of your mind? Teddy, you're the best-looking boy in the sophomore class. There'll be pictures taken at the dance for the yearbook. They'll be there forever. Do you want your kids to see that you took a girl in a wheelchair to the dance?"

When he didn't answer, Amanda yelled, "She is crippled, Teddy."

He said, "She was hurt in a swimming accident. So what? She's pretty, she's nice, and she's smart."

"So how's she going to dance with you? And when did you start talking to her?"

He stepped into the service station and set the pile of books on the glass display case. "Can I use your phone, Joe?"

The mechanic looked out from under a car in the garage. "Go ahead, but no long-distance calls, Teddy."

He picked up a thin, grease-smeared phone book and ran his finger down the names and then picked up the phone and tapped the numbers. Amanda stood glaring at him. He said to her, "I don't dance very well, so we can just talk, drink juice, and eat cake." He shrugged his shoulders. "That's all I ever do anyway."

To the woman who answered the phone he said, "Hello, this is Teddy McCain, may I speak to Gloria, please?" When she answered, he said, "Hi, this is Teddy. I was wondering if you have a date for the Fall Festival dance."

"Very funny, Teddy."

"It's not a joke. I'm serious, Gloria. I thought that if you went to the dance with me, we could talk."

"I'm not going to the dance." She sounded sad. "But we could talk at school, or you could call me sometime."

"OK. Maybe I will. I definitely will." He hung up and picked up the yearbooks again.

Amanda followed him as he walked toward the trees beside the building. "Why are you doing this?"

He stopped and looked down at her. "What about you? You want to go to the dance with Dane but because of his genetic history, you're asking me. You don't even like me and I don't like you. You spend your whole life over at the Campbell house and the first time someone tells you they're different, you walk away."

She crossed her arms and looked away. Leaning against a tree, he made himself calm down and said quietly, "Pastor Davis told me, the Bible tells us, life is like a puff of smoke. Some people live only a few days and some for a hundred years. None of us knows if we'll be alive tomorrow. We can spend our whole life planning the perfect life and miss out on everything we could've had."

She threw her hands up. "I don't understand you. All you used to talk about was planning for the future and making the right decisions. Now you say we don't have to do that, because we might not have a future. You're crazy."

ༀ ༀ ༀ

Dane hadn't left the library. As he was passing a small room to the side of the research section, he saw Sally Yates through the window. He tapped once on the door and then slipped in and sat on a chair next to her. The room was too small for more than two people. The narrow table provided just enough space to spread out a special project. She seemed to be working on just such a project.

"What are you doing?"

"I'm putting together some Sunday school material." She continued cutting a figure out of a brightly colored paper.

"What age?"

"I have Tammy Rae's class. I'm fixing their study books so they won't have to cut out all the pictures. There just isn't enough time in class."

He reached for a pair of scissors. "I'll help."

Neither spoke until all of the figures were cut out and glued onto the students' Sunday school papers. Sally placed the papers into individual student folders and put the folders into her backpack. As they left, Dane reached back into the room and turned off the light.

Walking beside her, it occurred to him that they weren't talking. When he was with Amanda, she kept the conversation going constantly. He wondered if he was supposed to say something but at the same time, it was nice to not be talking. As they passed Joe Bob's service station, they heard Amanda yelling and then saw her run across the street in the direction of the path going toward her home. Concerned, Dane said, "I wonder what that was about."

Sally said, "You could catch up with her and ask her."

Dane looked back at the service station. "It's okay. It's just Teddy. They always argue like that."

They walked on toward 3rd Street where he'd planned to leave her and catch up with Amanda, but when Sally turned the corner, he continued walking with her.

She said, "I'm teaching them about David's faith in God, but it seems to me, you're teaching them more about faith than I am."

"How is that?"

"Last Sunday we were talking about the faith you have. I told them that David was probably about your age when he went to take food to his brothers. He looked at battle they were in and told the king that if he had faith in God, he would have his victory. With faith, David took his sling and just a few stones and walked out in the middle of the battlefield to face the giant. Because David had faith in God, the King also believed enough to let David go fight Goliath."

She looked up at him and smiled. He felt heat run through his body and hoped she couldn't see how hot his face was.

"This is it." She put her hand on the gate. "Thank you for helping me. You could help me with the class if you'd like to. I'll be alone and at times, it is pretty tough with ten preschool kids."

He touched her arm, not wanting her to go. Until this moment, he had not once thought of how beautiful she was. He leaned down and touched his lips to hers. She stepped back and stared at him.

"I thought you and Amanda…"

He stepped back one step. "We're just friends. I've never thought of her as a…I never kissed anybody before. I just—" He stepped forward again.

Amanda watched as Sally put her arms over Dane's shoulders. She stomped back to the corner. Angrily, she looked toward the service station and then back at Dane and Sally, who were still kissing.

A car passed, stopped, and then backed up. Mike Taylor rolled down the window. "You want to ride around with us for awhile, Amanda?"

She could see Doug Porter and Julie Whitman in the front seat. Who was in the back, she wasn't sure, but what did it matter? When the back door opened, she saw that there were already three boys and two girls. As she climbed onto the lap of a boy, someone handed her an open bottle of beer.

"So where're we going?" She tipped the bottle up as Trenton McCain pulled her back against him.

"We're going to have a bonfire at the campground." Trenton handed her a joint. She drew a long drag and wondered if George and Thelma knew that one of their boys was going to a party.

She handed him the joint. "Trenton, how did you get out?"

"I parked the combine under my bedroom window." He grinned and helped himself to a surreptitious feel of her backside, and she let him.

ᘓᘓ ᘓᘓ ᘓᘓ

Dane stepped into the kitchen and looked up at the clock. "I'm sorry," he said before his parents asked. "I was at the library and then I walked Sally Yates home. We were talking about Tammy Rae's Sunday school class, and I lost track of time."

Dad looked over at Mom. "She's a nice girl."

Dane felt his face grow hot and turned to the sink for a glass of water and to cool down for a few seconds. Speaking toward the window, he said, "She said she'll go to the dance with me. I wasn't planning on going. I've been so busy getting things ready, I forgot about it. Usually my friends and I just go together. This is the first time I asked a girl to go with me."

Mom nodded to Dad. "I like her."

Dane looked at her. "Better than Amanda?"

Dad said, "Amanda is nice too, but we would have less to worry about knowing you're with Sally."

Dane sat at the table where he could see them in the living room. "Worry about what?"

"Babies, alcohol, pot, and a few other things," Dad said firmly.

Dane winced. "Amanda doesn't drink or smoke weed."

His dad turned in his chair and leaned toward Dane. He spoke softly. "We don't want anything to happen to you. Things happen to young people. They don't think about the consequences of their actions. Your mother and I have been there and we don't want you to make the same mistakes we made."

Head down, Dane pushed himself up slowly with both arms. "Amanda is all right."

As he walked up the steps his dad said, "I hope so. The police are raiding the camping park tonight. There have been a lot of high school kids out there the last couple of weekends."

Dane waited until he got to his room before he tapped Amanda's cell phone number. Her phone was ringing, but then was turned off. He looked at the screen and closed his phone. The only time Amanda turned off her phone when she saw his number, was when she was really angry with him.

He lay in bed for more than an hour and then reached for his cell phone and tapped a different number. Sally's tired voice answered. He said, "Sorry I woke you. I was thinking about you."

"Dane, what time is it?"

"I guess I better let you go back to sleep."

"Just a minute. What's going on? I need to look out my window....There are a lot of cars at the police station. I can hear Mr. McCain yelling. He just put Trenton in his car. I see Amanda's parents' car and Joe Benson's dad's car."

Dane's pulse hammered. "My dad said the police were raiding the camping park."

"Well, it looks like they arrested half the kids in our school."

"I hope not." He closed his eyes tightly, saying a silent prayer. "If Joe is there, half our basketball team could be there.

She snorted. "If they don't learn now, they'll never learn. I'll be disappointed if they're allowed to play ball, if they were out there tonight. That's the kind of thing that ends in someone getting killed."

Dane knew now why they had never been friends. He searched in his mind for a mature subject. "Sally, what are you going to do when you finish school?"

"I'm going to go to college and be a schoolteacher, if the Lord is willing. And you, Dane? What are your plans?"

"I'm not sure. I'm praying about it and I know, when I know, I won't have any doubt. So, where're you going to college?"

"Oregon State."

"So am I."

She yawned. "It's going to be expensive. My parents worry about sending just me. Haa-oww," she yawned again. "I can't imagine what it would be like to send twins to college. Are your parents worried?"

"Nah, my Grandpa Anderson always picks up the slack. And once he gets Dwain back, he'll make sure he's taken care of."

ᴄᴧⱴ ᴄᴧⱴ ᴄᴧⱴ

When Dane came home, Brent watched him run up the steps and into the kitchen. He sat in the dark watching the kitchen through his living room window. After Dane went upstairs, he saw Jeff and Sara holding hands. Jeff stepped up a step on the stairway, and kissed Sara. They held each other for a few minutes before she reached over and turned off the kitchen light.

He leaned back, feeling guilty for watching them and at the same time, feeling very much alone. He stood, thinking he could walk to the stairway without turning on the light, and then remembered hitting his shin on an end table, somewhere between where he stood and the stairway. He reached over and turned on the light and then looked around the room at the chest of drawers, bed frames, headboards, tables, chairs, and boxes of who knows what. He wondered how it was that so many years had passed and he still cared so much about Katie.

As he lay in bed a short time later, he lifted his phone and turned it to the moonlight to select the right numbers.

"Hello," Katie answered softly.

"Did I wake you?"

"I was just reading."

Brent turned on his side as though he were facing her. "We haven't talked since we had lunch. Are you upset with me for preaching too much?"

She didn't say anything for a moment. "There's a lot going on outside. I think some teenagers were picked up and are being taken home by their parents. Is Dane home?"

"Yes. Fortunately he doesn't do the kind of things that we did when we were his age."

She laughed. "You and I? Brent, you cost your parents ten years of their lives when you started riding that motorcycle."

He smiled. "Another reason I don't drink. Motorcycles and alcohol don't go well together."

She whispered, "You were more inclined to preach than to get into trouble." She was quiet for a few seconds and then said, "Brent, does it seem like all of our old friends are dead?"

He thought about the people they'd grown up with. "Most of them made the wrong choices, but a lot of people die in thirty years."

She sighed. "I think about Hilda."

"Because you blame yourself?"

"Yes. I do. I asked her to move out of our apartment. She didn't want to, but I had someone else I wanted to live with, and I didn't like her friends. I know I upset her."

He said sadly, "I made some wrong choices too. One, I can hardly live with, and when I dwell on how stupid I was, I'm not good company. We make mistakes and the ones we can't do anything about, we just have to ask God to stop us from kicking ourselves over."

He listened to her breathing and wondered if she had gone to sleep. Then she said, "Eddie Davis told me that Hilda was at peace when she died. He said she had a good understanding of how short life is on earth and how long eternity is. Think of it—forever and ever. That's why the symbol for eternity is the number 8 lying on its side. It's like being on a road that never ends. It goes around one turn and then another over and over again forever. Eternally, Brent. Not fifty or a hundred, but billions and billions of years."

Brent interrupted, "Are you sick, Katie?" Had she come home, like Hilda had, because she was dying?

"No, I'm just tired, and very disappointed. I closed my business, Brent. I thought I could live on the ranch and sell my designs over the Internet. The lease for the office space was more then ten thousand dollars a month. Adding an agent and staff to that, I wore myself out just to pay the bills."

She paused, and it sounded like she might be crying. "I always knew that home was here and someday I would come back and ride horses again. But it's all gone. Right when I'd decided it was time to come back home, Daddy lost everything."

10

Teddy and Dane were talking after church when Pastor Davis rushed by, saying that he had an emergency. He handed Dane a box and asked him if he would do the service at the hospital. Teddy had never gone with them to the hospital service and he didn't know why he wanted to this time. He looked over at Dane as they parked in front of the small county hospital. After putting the pickup in park, Dane bowed his head. Knowing, he was praying, Teddy stepped out and closed the door as quietly as possible.

Looking back at Dane after a few minutes of waiting on the sidewalk, he saw that he was still praying, so he walked through the side door of the hospital. His tie felt tight but he didn't think it would be proper to loosen it. He let out a long breath, shoved his hands into his slacks pockets, and then decided that wasn't appropriate either and pulled them out. He walked down the wide corridor and nodded to a nurse at the nurses' station.

She said, "Hello Teddy. How may I help you?"

"Hi, Mrs. Tims. I'm here for the church service." He motioned behind him. "Dane's outside."

She pointed toward a hallway. "Third door on your right."

"Thank you."

He walked slowly, aware of the light clip his new black leather shoes made on the shiny floor. At the doorway he glanced inside. Five elderly residents were waiting, two on chairs and three in wheelchairs. He nodded to a little woman with white hair. She stood slowly and walked toward him, as if she were seeing someone she knew. He waited until she was reaching up to touch him and then said, "Hello, my name is Teddy."

She slipped her frail arms over his shoulders, saying, "I know, dear. I asked God to bring you. I have been praying to see you." She pressed his face between her hands. Tears ran down her cheeks. "I am so happy to see you, Teddy. It is so good to see you." She took his hand. "I'm not crazy, dear. Come and sit with me." She patted the chair beside her as she sat. "My name is Grace Anna Reynolds."

He dropped heavily onto the chair. "My mother's name was Anna Reynolds."

"She was my daughter and you need to know"—she smiled—"that she loved you very much."

"Thank you."

He felt better when Dane finally walked in. Dane smiled and waved. "Good afternoon. Pastor had an emergency."

Grace said, "You'll do just fine, sweetheart. Just speak loudly so Emily can hear you."

"What did you say?" another old lady yelled.

Dane said, "I said, good afternoon, Emily."

"Oh, I wouldn't say it's a good one, but it's good to see you, you young whippersnapper." She clicked her false teeth. "What are you preachin' on today?"

"I was going to talk about faith. I have been praying for something, believing I will receive it, so I wanted to share that with you. Have you ever prayed for something, believing you will receive it?"

Grace gripped Teddy's hand. "Every day for fifteen years, and I finally got it."

Dane smiled, but he looked like he didn't know what she was talking about. "Well, I have been praying for about thirteen years for my twin brother to come home."

Emily yelled, "That's old news, young man. We've been listening to the radio and we know all about that 'Finding Dwain.' Is he going to get here so I can see him before I kick the bucket?"

Dane smiled, "September 30 or sooner. Can you stay alive that long, Emily?"

She gave a huge grin that showed all her false teeth. "I'll make a point of it. Now tell us something that we don't know."

Jed Hillman leaned over and tapped Emily on the leg. "Let the boy talk. He doesn't have all day."

Dane said, "In the truck I was praying and something came to me. It's Jeremiah 23. God tells us we can't hide from Him. The verse tells us He is everywhere, in heaven and on earth. What we say, where we go, and what we do, God knows.

He looked at the five elderly faces, and at Teddy. "God sees us right now. He sees everyone and knows what everyone is doing and saying. And while He is seeing us, He is also seeing everything that is happening in heaven. God is everywhere and aware of everything."

Grace was holding a notebook in her lap, and she tapped it with her fingers every time Dane finished a sentence. Teddy peeked at what was written there—a list. The top name on the list was "Zelda." When Dane finished speaking and had led them in prayer, Teddy asked her what the list of names was for.

"It's my prayer list."

"Why do you have the name Zelda at the top?"

"She needs my prayers more than anyone else. She is a very troubled soul."

Dane was waiting for him with Pastor Davis in the hallway, but Teddy couldn't leave without asking her, "Why did my mom give me to Zelda, if she is a troubled soul?"

Grace looked sadly away and then said to him, "Some things are best left as they are. You just need to know that Anna believed she would become a famous singer, and you would be proud of her. Zelda Cloud may have meant well for you, and when Anna got out to California, no amount of money could make her forget about you."

As he left she said, "Will you come back? We don't have to talk about sad things, Teddy. I would just like you to come and see me."

He said, "I will...Grandma. I promise you, I will. Next Sunday, I'll come back."

After he said good-bye to her, he went to meet Dane and the pastor. Pastor Davis greeted him. "Thanks for coming. Andy Jeppson passed away.

His family asked me to be here." He motioned down the hallway and they walked that direction.

Teddy was shaken when he saw the ashen face of Andy Jeppson. He knew he couldn't be more then thirty years old, and it was just a few days ago when he saw him driving past. "What did he die from?" he asked Dane.

Dane whispered, "The doctor said a blood vessel in his brain broke."

Teddy stepped into the hallway as Andy's wife and four small children came to the doorway. Dane reached down and stopped the children from rushing into the room as he said to her, "I'm sorry for your loss."

On the way home Teddy said to Dane, "I can see now why my parents would ask about hereditary things before adopting a baby. That is so sad. He just died all of a sudden. He had no warning."

He stared out the window. "He never went to church. Will he go to hell?"

Dane said, "That is between him and Jesus. We're not to judge. God knows the heart of every one of us. He sees what we do, where we go, and He knows what we are thinking. We don't know what Andy's relationship with God was. When we get to heaven, he may be there. A lot of people we thought wouldn't, will be there."

Teddy rubbed his face with his hands. "I can't do this. How can you do this? Those old people are going to die pretty soon. It's going to be so sad."

Dane smiled. "Those are the people I want most to get to know. When we get to heaven we'll see them in their new bodies. I think some of the best times I'll have in heaven are going to be with those old people. Emily will probably tease me by pretending she still can't hear what I'm saying. It'll be a lot of fun."

Teddy rubbed his fingers together, wanting not to say something he shouldn't. But someone had to say it. "Dwain could have died years ago. If he did, he won't be here by the thirtieth."

Dane looked at him, tilting his head and raising one eyebrow the way Brent did when he handed Dane the keys to the truck and told him to be careful. "I thought about that a long time ago and decided he has to be alive. Miss Cloud hates my grandpa so much, she would've sent us a singing telegram as soon as she knew he died. It would've been the easiest way to stop Grandpa from bothering her."

Slowing for the turn onto the McCains' driveway Dane said, "I did ask God to give me proof of his death, if he died."

"Will you be all right with that? When you know for sure?" Teddy shrugged his shoulders in a hopeless motion. "What will you do?"

Dane grinned. "I'll tell Emily to give him a hug for me when she sees him."

"How'll she know him?"

Dane said, "Easy. I'll tell her to look for a tall, handsome man with a perfectly proportioned body."

Teddy opened the door and looked back. "Are you going to be a pastor?"

"I don't know. Are you going to be a farmer?"

"Not in a million years."

11

FBI agent Fredrick Jones was introduced to Principal Campbell by the police chief. Both lawmen sat on chairs facing Ben Campbell, seated behind the desk, as he said, "In the twenty-seven years I have been principal of this school, we have had three or four of these bonfires a year without concern from a federal agency. Why were you alerted to this one event?"

Jones leaned forward so he could speak in a low tone that wouldn't carry into the outer office. What he had to say was best kept here. "Saturday night, Officer Gray"—he motioned toward the police chief—"and his men approached a blue van in that camping park. They know now that the two men at the van presented false ID.

"We have been looking for a blue-colored box truck and two fugitives. When we alerted this police department this morning, Officer Gray remembered that one of the men set a bottle in a trash can. We ran prints from that bottle and got a positive match."

Ben Campbell asked, "What does this have to do with my students?"

The agent smiled to put him at ease. "I would like to ask the students who were at the campground a few questions."

Reaching for the telephone, Campbell placed a call. "Stella, this is Ben Campbell. I have a question that I think only Roy can answer. Is he available?"

The agent looked at the police chief, who whispered, "County judge, Roy Bain."

"Roy, thank you for your time. I know you're busy. An FBI agent and our chief of police are seated in my office, asking to speak to the students that were arrested Saturday night." He listened a moment and handed the phone to Jones.

Jones explained to the judge, "We have physical proof, both in the form of finger prints on a beer bottle and the eyewitness of two police officers, that a serial killer on our most-wanted list was in that park with these students."

Students were called to the office one at a time, in ten-minute intervals. When Amanda McCormick's turn came, she sat nervously looking first at the police chief, then Jones. He smiled at her. He didn't want to intimidate her unless he had to. "Amanda, I'm a special agent with the FBI. I have a special assignment that I've been working on for seven years. I've been looking for a man that was at the camp park on Saturday night. From the others who were there, I know that you were talking to him."

She shifted on her seat. "We just walked a little ways from the fire, just to talk. Everyone was so loud, we couldn't hear each other. He was nice. Very nice."

Jones leaned forward, holding a photograph of Arnold. "Is this the man?"

She nodded. "His name is Arnold."

He was using his own name, then. "Yes, and did you see his brother, Archie?"

"He was alone, but I think his brother may have been at the other camp area. When someone honked a horn, he said he had to go."

"Did you notice any other vehicles?"

"A truck was on the road. When it drove away, Arnold said that he had to go pretty soon because that truck was leaving."

"Amanda." Now that Jones had established a sense of trust with her, he moved a chair to sit in front of her. "I know you are seventeen and you are a senior. I know you are a good student from a good family. And I know it is very difficult to rat on your friends, and you might consider Arnold to be a friend."

He looked at the principal and then back at the young lady. "I believe you are mature enough to understand what I'm going to tell you, but I have not told any of the other students." He watched her. She liked the idea of being trusted with information that the others hadn't been. He said, "When Arnold was sixteen, his older brother, Archie, was in prison for making and selling cocaine."

She looked toward the window. He suspected she knew Arnold had cocaine and he may have offered her some. He said, "Arnold went to a school dance where everyone considered him to be a nice young man. That night he asked a girl to step away from the others so they could talk, like he did with you on Saturday night. Like you, the girl was willing to walk with him, but when she tried to walk away from him he became enraged and strangled her."

Amanda looked at him. He willed her to understand the danger she was in. "That horn may have saved your life."

She shook her head. "People change."

"He didn't change. Arnold was placed in a state mental facility for three years. When he was released, he rejoined Archie, who had just gotten out of prison. They make and sell cocaine in very large quantities. They move from one place to another, and leave behind a trail of murdered women. I believe Arnold has killed as many as a hundred women."

Maybe this will help. He lifted a photograph from his shirt pocket. "Do you know this woman?"

Amanda shook her head. He turned it toward Ben Campbell. He tightened his lips, frowned, then shook his head.

"Her name was Christine Whatson. Three weeks ago, her body was found in her car a block from her home. Her parents said she had gone out to meet friends. The smoky smell of her clothing suggested a campfire. Grass stains suggested she may have been with her friends at a campfire in a park. A single fingerprint on a medallion hanging from her neck positively matched Arnold. That is why I'm here, Amanda. Arnold killed a woman not much older than you, three weeks ago, less than sixty miles from here."

She shrugged her shoulders. "We just talked and he left. I don't know anything else about him. Just that he's nice."

After she left the office, Agent Jones closed the office door and spoke softly to the two other men. "Once they're seen, they move. They've been in the area for at least six months. Your students may know more than they're telling us. She does, I know that for sure."

Campbell said, "My concern is how much danger they're in."

For the safety of these kids, Jones needed to underline the gravity of the situation. "Extreme." To the police officer he said, "We need to keep them away from that camp park and close to home until we get these animals."

Campbell asked, "How long will that be?"

Jones frowned. Civilians always thought cases were solved in an hour, the way they were on TV. "I've been tracking Archie and Arnold for seven years. There is no one smarter than Archie. He has a very distinct pattern. He preys on the darker side of people—greed, lust, adoration, and desire. He is right out of the pit of hell. I could corner them today or in another seven years."

"You need to know one thing, Agent." Campbell squared his shoulders. "If you want to find the den of darkness, look beyond this town. The prayers of many believers in this community have surely caused a hedge of protection around us. When those brothers came into this area, they came into the light and were exposed."

The agent left without responding. Alone in his office, Campbell closed his eyes and prayed for his students. He had come here with his wife and small son, twenty-five years ago, in hope of leaving this sort of thing behind. In the four years that he'd been an administrator in an inner-city high school, he attended the funerals of twenty-two students. The first seven had broken his heart, but after that, they weren't even faces anymore.

When they brought Jeff here to the Atwood clinic, it was as if they had stepped into a world filled with light. In the small community, there were five churches, all within a two-mile radius. The prayers of so many believers concentrated in such a small area had surely caused a protective hedge to be placed around the community. He hoped the agent had the good sense to see the truth.

Outside, Agent Jones sat in his car, thinking. He had a Bible somewhere. He wondered if he should take a look in it and see if there was something to what Campbell said about areas of darkness. His hands moved on the top of the steering wheel. If it were true, if there were areas of darkness and areas of light, knowing this would help him to understand the movement of fugitives. Maybe they were more comfortable away from the light and if they came into an area where there is light, like this community with so many Christians, they might be more likely to make a mistake and get caught. It may sound unconventional and unscientific, but Jones knew from experience to trust his gut instincts. And they said Campbell's theory felt right.

He noticed movement near the corner of the school. Starting the car and pulling forward, he recognized the young lady standing behind a bush, speaking on a cell phone. *Amanda McCormick.* He stopped his car and slipped out, leaving the door ajar so he wouldn't alert her to his presence. Approaching from behind her, he moved stealthily. She said, "Did you kill her? Just tell me, please, and tell me why."

She hunched her shoulders, and then relaxed. "OK. I told him you're nice, that's all. I mean, because you are." Relief filled her voice. She cocked her head, listening for several seconds, then she shrugged.

"Just that you're a killer and that you and your brother make and sell cocaine. Is that what you gave us to try?" Suddenly, she whipped her head around and stared directly at Jones. She said quickly, "I have to go," and closed her cell phone.

Agent Jones gripped her arm. "Do you want to go to jail for helping him?"

"I'm not helping him."

"You don't think that by telling him about my being here, you didn't help him to flee? I have been on his trail for seven years. What you just told him might be all he needs to pack up and leave again. And if he leaves and he kills the way he has in the past, those deaths that could have been prevented if we had him locked up are going to be your responsibility, Amanda. It makes you an accessory to murder. That's a major prison sentence."

She put her nose in the air as she shrugged his hand off of her arm and walked away. Looking down, where her feet had pressed the long grass, he saw a piece of paper. He waited until he was sure she couldn't see him and then leaned down and picked it up. On it were numbers, written in clear, square handwriting. His years of tracking Arnold left him no doubt as to who had written them.

⚹ ⚹ ⚹

Emily Baxter sat behind the counter at Earlington Memorial Hospital. For the third time she told the woman on the phone that Dr. Marcus Fitzgerald was not available and would return her call if she would leave a number. She hung up and looked up as the gray-haired, exhausted physician leaned on her counter. "I'm sorry, Marcus, I didn't see you. You just missed another call from Zellie." She smiled, shaking her head. "She refused to leave her number—still insists that you know it." She handed him his phone message, saying, "She wants Chinese for dinner tonight and you're to call and let her know if you will be home."

"My goodness." He chuckled. "I only wish she would realize she's calling the wrong number. I'm certain my wife is making roast leg of lamb this evening. I don't care for Chinese food."

⚹ ⚹ ⚹

Hearing his brother coming, Arnold quickly checked his cell phone to make sure it would vibrate and not ring if his new friend Amanda called him again. "Well, what did Dad say?"

"He got the shipment and he's pleased with the quality." Arnold felt Archie watching him as he reached for a measuring cup, scooped and leveled powder, and poured it into the large commercial mixing bowl.

"Is he happy that I'm helping you? Did you tell him I know how to mix everything just right?"

Archie said softly, "Just be careful."

"I snuck in and checked the messages on the phone. Zellie called you twice. She wants Chinese tonight."

Archie said, "I'll be glad when we pack up and get out of here. That woman is driving me crazy."

Arnold giggled. "Maybe she would be happier if you were home at night more often."

"Listen." Archie gripped his arm. "Tonight I'm taking her laptop to her office to make an order for supplies. I can't take a chance of our location being traced back here or I'd stay here and do it."

"I know that. I'm not as stupid as you think, Archie. I know you have to make phone calls from other places and that you have a key to her office." Because Archie might be smart, but he wasn't sneaky-smart like Arnold was, so he needed a key. "Just like before, at the other lady's office."

"What I want you to do is stay away from her. Don't go in her room anymore after she goes to bed."

Arnold shook his head. *Archie leaves her alone. She doesn't want to be alone. She smells good, like flowers. Like lilac flowers. Her long hair is soft, and tickles.* He licked his lips. "In the dark, she doesn't know I'm not you, and when you see her in the morning, isn't she happier? Don't you want to keep her happy?"

Archie rolled his eyes. "Happy but not dead. If she suspects you're not me, she'll shove you away and you'll kill her, just like you did the others."

Arnold caught a glimpse of himself in a mirror on the wall. He was younger than Archie and way more handsome. He smiled. He liked the way he looked. "Okay, okay, I'll just stay here and mix this exactly right and make Dad happy."

Archie reached for the phone. "Chinese. What do you want tonight?"

Arnold wiggled his eyebrows. Archie glared at him as he moved away to use the phone. Arnold tightened the cloth wrapped around his head and looked into the mixer to make sure there was no hair. Picking up a measuring cup, he paused. He was never to put more than a level scoop of that powder in the mixing bowl. He couldn't remember if he already filled the measuring scoop. Looking at the counter around the bag was usually a good indication. Not seeing any spilled powder, he was assured he hadn't added the ingredient. He carefully measured and poured it into the mixer. He smiled, satisfied he was making a quality product.

He stood watching the mixing motion as he thought about the girl. She'd let him hold her hand as they walked away from the campfire, but when they sat on a log she put her hand in her lap, but she didn't try to push him away, so he didn't take offense to her motion.

"Do you believe in God?" she asked.

"I don't know anything about Him."

"My friend Dane talks about God all the time, and I really like listening to him, but I don't know how I feel about what he believes. He asked God to find his missing brother, and now the whole town is just waiting to see if God will do it."

Arnold said, "I don't think God likes me."

"That's one thing I understand about God, and I think you're wrong. He loves you. The Bible says He knew you before you were born. He knew everything you were going to do. He lets you choose to do right or wrong."

His hand moved behind her back and up to her shoulder. "So if I have done wrong, why should it matter if I keep doing wrong? I will go to hell for what I already did, so why should I stop doing wrong stuff?"

She said, "Because you can't be happy if you're doing the wrong thing. You're always looking over your shoulder and worrying about getting caught. Like when I don't clean the barn the way I should. I don't get in trouble, really, but I can tell my dad is disappointed with me when he sees that I didn't do it right." She shrugged. "It bugs me to feel like I've disappointed him."

She let his hand rest on her leg. He wondered what else she would allow him to do, and he inched his fingers up her thigh. She pressed her hand down on his to stop him. "If you've done things that are wrong and you ask God to forgive you, and you really mean to never do those things again, He will forgive you. After that you need to ask Jesus to be your Savior. Just ask for forgiveness and ask Jesus to help you not to do it again. And when you die you'll go to heaven."

He moved his hand off of her leg, and pouted. "So I can play a harp and sit on a cloud."

She smiled. "I think of it as the most beautiful place there could possibly be, with flowers that are so lovely I can't even imagine such colors. And when a person wants to go in, God sends His Son to the gate to see if He knows that person. Any friend of His Son is welcome to come in and live there forever."

She closed her eyes. "Sometimes I close my eyes and think about what the trees and birds would look like if there was no sin in the world."

He moved a little farther from her, suddenly not interested in touching her. "What is sin?"

"Doing things that God says are wrong. If we do wrong, it doesn't just affect us. It can affect our kids and our grandkids. Like when my great-grandfather had only been married to my great-grandmother for a few years and he had an affair. He thought no one would ever find out. Then, one of his daughters married a man from another town, and he turned out to be her father's own son. It caused a real problem for their children. They had some major medical problems. My mother is afraid I'll marry someone that might cause our children to have physical problems, because she remembers her cousins going to the doctor all the time."

Arnold thought, *I'm going to ask Archie if Dad did something bad, so I was born not so smart. If he did, then his bad thing makes me do bad stuff. Then, it's not my fault.*

She said, "Dane has a dwarfism gene. He is the only child in his family that isn't a little person."

Arnold heard a horn honk and told her that he had to go. It was the signal. The buyers had left. Archie told him not to come back until he honked.

He suddenly realized, he wasn't just remembering the horn honking. There was actually a horn honking. The Chinese food delivery man had arrived. He didn't have to run out for the delivery this time because Archie was home. He took a worn notebook out of his back pocket and studied the list of ingredients until he came to where he thought he was in the mixing process. He looked at the mixing bowl, the containers of ingredients, and then back at his notebook. Everything seemed to be all right.

ᴄᴧᴈ ᴄᴧᴈ ᴄᴧᴈ

Agent Jones leaned against his car, looking at the tree-lined shore across the lake. The camping park was so peaceful. The afternoon sun had warmed the side of the car. He put his hand on the hood, moving his fingers in a circular motion as he thought. Amanda's eyes had told him she didn't know Christine Whatson.

He took the small photograph from his pocket. Only nineteen years old and her life snuffed in one angry moment. Where were you, Christine? Where were you when Arnold found you? In a park. At a campfire. Grass stains on your clothing and wood smoke in your hair.

He sighed. "Christine, where were you? Where did Arnold find you?"

He thought again about the profiles. Archie was educated. He took advantage of the prison system by getting a college degree while locked up. He dressed nicely and spoke well. Women who desired a wealthy, successful male companion were what he preyed upon, but he had in the past lured unsuspecting well-established males with the same desire.

Three years ago, Professor Steowegg of the Stanford University invited Archie into his home. At that time, Archie posed as a doctor from a reputable private clinic. Steowegg explained to Agent Jones that he would never have taken a lover who was not perfectly clean and respectfully employed.

"My blood tested positive for HIV," the professor had lamented over the telephone. Jones could understand the man's despair. For forty years he had carefully selected his partners and now, it was he who had been selected, and with that came his first known encounter with HIV.

Jones's mind followed the trail illuminated by the thought of the disease. *Archie has had HIV for more than three years, so he might be seeing a doctor. A doctor…* He picked up the phone book. *He could be doing exactly what he did three years ago.*

Deciding that it would be below Archie to pose as a doctor from the Atwood Clinic or adjoining community hospital, he decided to check out some of the hospitals closer to where Christine's body was found. In an hour he was parked in the visitor's lot of the private Earlington Memorial hospital. At the front desk he held up his identification and asked if he could speak with an administrator. A nurse introduced him to a senior member of the hospital staff, Dr. Marcus Fitzgerald.

When Jones showed him a photograph of Archie, the doctor smiled and shook his head. "If I could say I've seen this man, I wouldn't be able to tell you whether he's a patient, or for what illness he's being treated."

Jones looked him in the eye. "You're probably treating him for AIDS." He showed him another photograph. "This is his brother, Arnold. He's number six on our most-wanted list. He's a serial killer. In the past seven years, Arnold may have killed a hundred women. He has an uncontrollable temper."

"Well." The older man raised his eyebrows. "In that case, you have my attention."

Jones pocketed the photos. "Archie often preys on older women. He has posed as a doctor. He dotes on his victims hand and foot while he uses them as a cover for a cocaine production and distribution operation."

The doctor sighed. "And you suspect he's using my name. Telling some poor unfortunate soul that he is me?"

"No, I—"

The man raised his hand. "For the past six months I've received phone messages from a woman whom I have never met. She always asks that I return her call and tells my nurse what she would like for dinner. It has been quite embarrassing for me. I've been the talk of the hospital."

Jones drew a sharp breath as his own words came back to him. *He dotes on the victims. Of course, Archie's MO. How could I have overlooked this?* He shook his head. "Oh I'm sorry. Do you have a name or a phone number?"

"No, she only uses the name Zellie. But we do keep records of phone calls coming into the hospital."

Jones said, "I'll get the phone records, but in the meantime, I want you to think about something. Five years ago, we were as close to arresting these two as we've ever been. We walked in before they loaded all their loot. The agency decided that the best thing to do with that money is offer a reward for information that leads to Arnold's arrest. If you call us when one of them comes in here and we're able to nail Arnold, even if you don't want that reward money, I'm sure your hospital could benefit from a hundred thousand dollars."

Dr. Fitzgerald propped one elbow on the other hand and rubbed his chin. "I can't discuss the medical records of a patient. But it's possible that both of these men are receiving the same medication for the same condition, and the younger one might have an addiction to the drug they're selling."

Leaving the hospital, Jones drove around behind a row of Dumpsters, where he parked with a view of the front entrance of the hospital. As he recorded information into a file in his computer, he watched people coming and going through the hospital entrance. How many times had he sat like this, watching places Archie frequented? Why couldn't he be sitting here when Archie drove up? *He's smart. Too smart.* Had Archie spotted him before? Sometime in the past seven years, he may have identified him as an FBI agent.

"All right, where is the case I'm looking for? About three years ago. Woman responding to an *America's Most Wanted* program. Ann Crain." He found the file. "Ann Crain," he read aloud, "biologist, professor." He looked at the details of the case. She had identified both of them from the television program. They had stolen her identity and thousands of dollars. She had been fooled into thinking Archie was preparing wonderful meals for her. After he left, she found credit card charges. When Jones investigated, the restaurant owner said Ann had ordered meals from their finest selection to be delivered to her home at a specific time every afternoon.

Jones realized he had made a mistake. There was no need for him and Marshall to remain in the rural area. Archie used the camping park only to meet with a drug buyer. There was nothing that far out in the county for Archie. He had to be close to fine dining and elegant living. Jones searched through a listing of restaurant businesses and began phoning as he watched the hospital entrance.

He left a message on Marshall's cell phone asking him to gather up their things and check them out of the hotel. After giving Principal Campbell's theory on darkness and light some thought, he decided to set up headquarters in the city, preferably in a spiritually darker section.

*   *   *

Amanda sat on her bed, watching the moon rising over the freshly turned earth. One of the McCain boys was driving a tractor slowly across a field just beyond her father's pasture fence. Trenton said he was grounded and wouldn't be permitted to go to the fall festival events if he didn't finish plowing. She thought it might be him. It didn't matter to her what he was doing.

It's all Trenton's fault.

Something had happened in mid-August that left her feeling ashamed every time she thought about it. She and Trenton were sitting on bales behind the McCain barn, drinking beer and smoking marijuana, when Dr. Campbell's car came to a stop next to the barn. He climbed out of the car and pulled out his heavy medical bag, without speaking or even waving to her. He had never done that to Amanda before, so she knew he was ashamed of her.

She looked sadly at a small chair, painted in the colors that were her favorite when she was little. She smiled, thinking, and then as if coming into her happier memories, little Tammy Rae eased the door open and ran in laughing.

"I came to see you, Amanda." She clapped her little hands and turned around and around before climbing up on the little chair, which she knew her daddy had helped Amanda paint. She said, "Your mommy said I could play with you."

Amanda laughed as she lifted her off the chair and spun around, and then bounced her on the bed. "What are you doing here all by yourself, Tammy Rae?"

"Daddy is here." She pointed toward the barn. "He's doctoring a fat cow named Big Bill."

Amanda looked out the window, hoping to see Jeff. "My dad wants to take Big Bill to the fair again this year. He wants to make some money on stud fees, but Big Bill is getting old and stiff."

"What are stud fees?"

Amanda bit her lower lip. "It's one way farmers make money for their kids to go to college. It's no big deal if we get the money or not, because I don't even want to go to college." She looked at Tammy Rae and wondered why it was so easy to confide her innermost secret feelings to this little girl. "I just want to be like your mom and stay home."

Tammy Rae said, "Mommy helps Daddy. She writes on papers in his office. Today she took me to the thrift store." She held out her blouse. "I got this. Do you think it's pretty?"

"I think it's very pretty. What else did you get?"

Tammy Rae smiled and chattered away, and as Amanda listened to her, she wished her parents would treat her like an adult, the way she treated Tammy Rae like a big girl. "We got shirts and pants for Dwain for when he comes home. Mommy is making the pants shorter right now on her sewing machine."

Amanda sat sadly on her bed. "It must be nice to have other kids in the family. You like having a sister, don't you, Tammy Rae?"

Tammy Rae had to think a moment before she said, "We have the same bedroom. I wouldn't want a bedroom all by myself. Dane has a bedroom all alone, but when Dwain comes home, he won't be alone anymore."

She climbed back onto the little chair. "My daddy painted this chair for you, didn't he, Amanda?" She crossed her little arms. "Now, tell me why you don't want to go to college. Dane is going to go to college and so is Dwain my other big brother." She watched Amanda expectantly.

Amanda wasn't sure if she didn't want to go to college because there wasn't enough money or because she really didn't want to go. She was certain she was much happier when her parents weren't arguing about college money. She didn't know what to say, so she said, "It's a long ways away, and I like being home."

Tammy Rae put her hands on her sides and said firmly, "I don't want Dane and Dwain to go far away." She frowned. "Just how far away is far away?"

Amanda smiled. "Let's go see what your daddy is doing."

Taking her hand, Tammy Rae said, "The big boys are making a wheelchair ramp. Want me to tell you a secret? It's about Daddy and Grandpa and the motorcycle. But you can't tell Dane. Do you *promise* not to tell Dane?"

12

Teddy could hear voices in the barn, but not the ones he'd expected to hear. He stepped in and stood back, watching the two men working on the motorcycle. As his shadow fell on the straw at Jeff's feet, the man looked up.

"Hi, Teddy. The boys are behind the house, but do me a favor and don't spoil our surprise. Dane doesn't know we're fixing up the bike for a birthday present."

Teddy smiled. "Sure, Mr. Campbell. I won't say anything, but I think you should close the door. I could hear you talking outside."

He stepped out and closed the squeaky wooden door.

The men continued talking inside, but they were harder to hear now. "What I remember most about it was the power," Brent said. "Hand me that wrench."

There was a thump, followed by Jeff's distinctive gait. "He's going to like these tires."

Teddy walked around behind the house, where he found Kevin and Dane carefully spacing boards on a slanted walkway.

He picked up a board. "You heard anything else about Dwain?"

"No." Dane stopped pounding. "Are you really interested in Gloria or are you just trying to make your dad mad?"

Teddy reached for a nail and shrugged his shoulders. "I like her. She's real funny and her folks are the nicest people I ever met. Do you know her dad majored in biology just like my dad? They're both interested in improving the farmland by replenishing the nutrients that have been lost out of the soil. And her parents think my parents are the best people in the world, because they leased land for only a dollar a year, to a handicap organization that they belong to."

Kevin smiled as he reached for another board. "If we keep going like this, we'll be able to start on the handrails in about half an hour." He laid the board next to the one that Teddy was nailing in place. Placing two slender pieces of wood between the walkway planks, he made a gap between the boards exactly the same as the gaps between all the other boards.

Dane moved up above him and reached for another board. "Handicapped people are no different than anyone else. Before her accident, Gloria was just as popular as the other girls. Now, she's alone a lot."

Teddy looked at him. "You don't like her, do you, Dane? You aren't making a move for her just because I am, are you?"

Dane shook his head. "I asked Sally Yates to the dance, and we've been talking on the phone a lot."

Teddy said, "Same with me and Gloria. We talked on the phone last night for more than an hour. She understands how I feel about what we found out in the library, and she decided to go to the dance. We're going to sit together for pictures for the yearbook."

Dane looked around. "I found out something, but I don't want to get into trouble, so don't go confronting your parents about it and making it so you can't come over here anymore."

"What?"

"I asked Gramps about that place you were wondering about. He said it was your Aunt Hilda's flower bed, and that Hilda died seven years ago of heart trouble. She would still be alive, Gramps said, if she didn't have a baby."

Teddy looked away. "I remember Hilda coming in the winter, and I remember her funeral but nothing about a baby. Where is the baby?"

"Gramps said he didn't know why your parents adopted Alex and not Hilda's baby, but he's pretty sure she didn't die when Hilda died."

Teddy hit the nail extra hard. "You just answered my question. They didn't want her because she's a girl. You have to be a strong farm worker to be adopted into my family." He hurled the hammer down. "I'll be back."

He ran a full two miles, crossing a field, a narrow bridge, and the highway. Near the porch he slowed to a walk and turned toward the freshly plowed flower bed. The old fence was piled for burning. New portions of fence lay along all four sides. He started to lean down and touch the fence to see if the paint was dry, but he could smell wet paint and quickly withdrew his fingers.

He found his mother in the kitchen. "What's Dad doing out there?"

"I didn't ask." She pulled a roast out of the oven and placed slices of potatoes around it.

He crossed his arms, which for some reason made his mom smile. She put the lid on the pan. "Where have you been?"

"Was that Hilda's flower garden? Dad said we were just leaving that spot to grow weeds, because it's not good for anything but flowers, and we don't have a need for growing flowers on this farm."

Something scraped overhead, and she looked up. "Go up and help your father. It sounds like he's moving something heavy."

Teddy took a step toward the stairway and looked back at her. She was smiling. He thought for a few seconds. *Dad's getting the flower garden ready like he did before Hilda came home. Maybe 'Finding Dwain' is making him want to bring her baby home.*

He found his dad in the hallway pushing Greg's dresser and stepped around to the other side to help. "Where is this going?"

"Your room."

"My room? You're moving this into my room? Are you moving Greg into my room too?"

"Yes. Just lift and let's get this in there."

He backed down the hallway and into his room, where he found Greg, looking down at him from a top bunk of one of two new bunk beds that had not been there that morning.

"We got bunk beds." Greg sat up and put his hands on the ceiling. "It's really cool up here."

Teddy backed into the only empty space in the room and then looked down through the window at the plowed patch of dirt. A warm tingle started in his belly. "Do you want me to help you to put that fence together later when the paint dries?"

His dad stood and looked at him. "Why are you so happy over this?"

Teddy grinned. "I'm sure whatever you are doing is the right thing to be doing, that's all."

"What do you think I'm doing?"

Teddy looked down at the plowed ground. "Maybe you're bringing us home a little sister."

Greg's mouth fell open. "Dad?"

Their dad leaned back and crossed his arms. "Now, how did you figure that out?"

As tactfully as possible, Teddy said, "A little white picket fence around a flower garden is something a girl would like."

His father smiled and looked over at Greg. "You'll have to be careful with her. Her name is Shelly, and she just had a heart operation, but there is no reason she won't live to be a hundred years old if she's careful." He turned and bit his lip to hold back tears. Stepping out of the room, he looked back. "I want you boys to take Greg's old bed down to the storage room so we have more space in Shelly's room."

Greg climbed down and ran out behind him. "Dad, how about adding onto the house? When the Thompsons had too many kids, they added onto their house."

"Greg, good idea." Their dad clapped a hand on his son's shoulder. "Let's see what we can do this winter."

Trenton moaned painfully with his head in his hands. "Leave it to Greg to talk Dad into a big winter project. I was looking forward to catching up on movies this winter. Whatever happened to the good old life, where people sat by the fireplace and watched movies in the winter?"

Teddy looked over at him. "Farmers work all the time."

Trenton grunted. "I'm not going to be a farmer after I get out of high school. Four more years, and I'm out of here."

Eleven-year-old Tommy came to the bedroom door. He looked in at the two sets of bunk beds. "My teacher said I'm the best story writer in my class. I'm going to be a story writer. Do you want to hear my new story?"

Teddy moved quickly to the door. "Sorry, I have to help Dane and

Kevin with something." Trenton rushed out behind him. "Ya, sorry Tommy, I have to help, too."

Looking down from the top bunk, Alex said, "I'll listen if it's not scary. I have bad dreams when you tell me scary stories."

Greg came back in. "We're supposed to clean out the barn. Where did Teddy and Trenton go?"

Tommy blurted out, "They went to rescue somebody from a wild horse."

Greg rolled his eyes. "Stop making things up about the horses. Those are tame horses. If you keep telling stories about them being wild, you'll mess up everything so I can't ride them."

When he left, Tommy whispered, "They're wild horses in the winter. They're only tame in the summer. In the winter, they have to be wild to chase off the wolves."

Alex glanced wide-eyed toward the window. "Are there wolves around here?"

"There's one that has fangs as long as my fingers. Don't you hear him howling in the night?"

Alex slid down and ran out the room, yelling, "Daddy, Tommy said there are wolves."

From down the hallway their father said, "Tommy, stop scaring him with your wild stories. Tame them down or don't tell him any more stories. Do you hear me?"

Tommy sighed. "I hear you."

Later that evening, while Trenton helped their dad in the field, Teddy, Greg, and Alex had to muck out the stalls in the barn. Teddy watched Greg and noticed he responded in an interesting way when he said certain things to him.

"Greg, I never saw a boy your age that could shovel the way you do. You are the strongest boy I ever saw."

Greg puffed out his chest. "I shoveled out that back stall in half the time it took you to do your stall. Want to race, Teddy?"

"Sure. You start on that stall, and I'll start on this one when I say go."

"No," Alex shouted, "Let me say go." He scrambled up onto the top rail of the stall. "Okay, on your mark. Get ready. Go!"

Their father stepped into the barn and lifted Alex off the top rail, giving him a bear hug. "Looks like you have everything under control in here."

"I say go and they race."

"Well that's good, because Momma made a chocolate cake. The faster they get done, the sooner we get to go inside and eat." Alex wiggled as their dad tickled him.

Teddy scooped a shovel full of wet, heavy manure and let it fall into the wheelbarrow. He was thinking about strength and suddenly realized that if he were weak, he wouldn't be able to help on the farm.

Greg finished first, yelling to announce his victory. Teddy smiled. It didn't bother him at all to be beat by Greg, as long as his younger brother was doing most of the work. He grabbed the handles of the wheelbarrow and hefted it to the back of the barn and out the door.

His dad followed him out. "Teddy, tomorrow I need you to load this pile of manure onto the flat bed and take it over to the vet's place. Jeff wants to use it in compost for his greenhouses."

Alex hugged their dad's neck, "Can I go with Teddy? They got a whole bunch of worms that they feed our cow shit to. It's cool."

The older brothers faked coughing to hide their hilarity at Alex's language, waiting for their dad to give the little guy a scolding.

He didn't. Instead, he watched a truck turn off the highway and come their way. His face darkened, and the vein in his neck throbbed. Alex wiggled down and moved away.

Greg stood next to Teddy watching as a gray-haired man stepped down from the truck and their dad walked up to him yelling, "Luke Hamilton, you get back in that truck and get out of here, right now."

"I just want to see him. I've never seen him, and I just want to ask if you will let me see him, George. I'm his grandpa. I'm the only grandpa he has, and he's the only grandchild I'll probably ever have."

Greg asked Teddy, "Who is he?"

Wanting to be brave, but terrified that Luke's arrival meant he would lose Greg, Teddy broke out in a sweat. "He is your grandfather. Your birth grandfather."

"Is he going to try and take me away?" Greg's jaw tightened like he was trying not to cry. He stared at Luke Hamilton.

"I don't think so. He just lives a few miles from here. He works at the lumber mill. He probably just doesn't want to be left out of your life." If he wished hard enough, maybe he could make it true. He wondered how Dwain's adoptive parents would feel when they found out the Campbells wanted him back.

The boys crowded to the barn door to get a closer look. Greg asked, "Like Dwain's family, you mean? Even if Dwain has a good home, they still want to talk to him."

Teddy said, "Maybe he was never going to ask about you until the 'Finding Dwain' stuff started making people around here want to poke around in other people's lives."

George said firmly, "Luke, this is my family. I'm telling you to get back in that truck and drive away."

Greg swallowed hard, stepped around the side of their dad's pickup and boldly offered the man his hand to shake. "Hello. I'm Greg. It's nice to meet you."

Luke's face lit up. "You look like a strong young fella."

"I am strong." Greg smiled proudly as the man shook his hand.

"Wanna arm wrestle?" The man laughed.

"Sure do." Greg raised his hand to grip his grandfather's.

"Okay, okay, you two." Dad looked over at Mom standing on the porch, and gave her a funny look that made Teddy's stomach churn. Why wasn't he sending Greg's grandfather away? "Thelma, would you put another plate on the table? We have company for dinner."

The big man put his arm over their dad's shoulders as they walked toward the house. "Thank you. Thank you very much. You don't know what this means to me. I've been asking God for years if there could ever be a way for me to see the boy. Then, this 'Finding Dwain' stuff started, and I got to praying all the time I was working. Suddenly this afternoon, when I was driving past here on my way home, I just turned and came up here to the house. I don't know what caused me to do that. I drove past here a thousand times and not until today did I go ahead and drive on up here."

Greg shrugged his shoulders and smiled at Teddy. "My grandpa is probably stronger than your grandpa?"

Teddy thought about all the work they had to do tomorrow. "I think he probably is. I bet when he was your age, he could do twice the work I do."

Greg said, "Bet I could feed the cows faster than you can load the flatbed tomorrow."

Teddy looked away, smirking to himself. "I don't know about that. You'll have to open the bales and haul them out to the field on the trailer behind the tractor. I don't know if you can do that in the time it would take me to fill the flatbed."

At the table, Luke looked from the five brothers to their dad and their mom. "This is real nice. You made a real nice home for these boys. I couldn't have done so good. I lost my Lorie when my boy was in eighth grade. After that, it was all I could do to get out of bed and dressed in the morning. I just didn't have the heart to take care of him or keep my place up."

Thelma smiled. "You're welcome here anytime."

Teddy noticed Greg looking at their dad to gauge the vein in his neck. But Dad didn't look angry, he simply leaned back in his chair, looking like he always did after dinner—full. Cautiously Greg asked, "Do you have any pictures of my grandma?"

"Pictures? I have a whole bunch of pictures. I have pictures of us when we were in Minnesota when I was just a boy like you. I came out here with my brother and two of his kids, the same time Ben Campbell brought his family here. I met my sweet Lorie here. I told my brother he could go back to Minnesota if he wanted to. I wanted to live right here with Lorie. Of course, my brothers and their families come out from Minnesota about once a year, but it's not like having my own boy to take fishing. Do you like fishing?"

Seven-year-old Alex perked up. "I love to fish. Fishing is my favorite thing."

Greg said, "I rode my bike up to the dam and caught some fish."

Luke's eyes shone. "I'm not working tomorrow. I could take you fishing."

"Me too?" Alex pleaded.

Their dad looked at Mom. He blinked, and his mouth opened and shut like he'd swallowed a fish bone. "If you finish your chores, you can go fishing with your grandfather, Greg."

Alex pleaded, "Me too? I want to go fishing too. Daddy, Mommy, *please.*"

Luke hopefully looked around at the brothers, and then at their dad. "I could take them all up to the pond. We could catch a whole passel of trout and be back in time to cook them up for dinner."

"I have to feed the cows." Greg looked at his older brothers, and Teddy could see he hoped they would offer to do his work.

Luke solved the problem. "I'll be here in the morning to help you, so we can get an early start on fishing."

Thelma smiled as though a virtual stranger came into their house every day and wanted to be a grandpa to one of them. "I'll fix a lunch for all of you."

"I can't go." Teddy said "I promised someone I would help him in the afternoon." His dad's eyebrows shot up. Before he could ask, Teddy said, "I volunteered to help with the church service at the hospital."

Dad looked down at his plate. Teddy expected him to say he couldn't help with the church service. He waited. His dad looked at him, the way he always did when he was remembering an unfinished job. He said, "My brother had a motorcycle with one of those sidecars on it. I thought he sold the whole thing. The other day when I was digging around in the old barn, I saw that sidecar sitting under some straw, back in the corner. When you haul that load of manure over to Jeff in the morning, you could take that sidecar and see if Brent wants to put it on his cycle. It might slow Dane down a bit so he doesn't crash it the way Brent did."

Luke laughed, "I remember that. Those boys went off the overpass. There was Brent Anderson, Skippy Morgan, and your brother, Sid. That sidecar caught on the railing and held tight, so the bike didn't go over, but Sid fell off and rolled all the way down the hill under the bridge. Skippy was still sitting in that sidecar when we got there. Brent was lying on the side of the road but his cycle went all the way to the highway below and then got hit by a semi."

Greg asked softly, "What happened to my mom?"

Luke glanced at Dad, who nodded. Luke leaned forward. His face crumpled a little more, like a sad hound dog's. "She was a great gal, that girl was. She was a sharpshooter. She could shoot a rifle better than any man I ever knew. Her parents were farmers, but before that they were retired military, so when she graduated from high school she enlisted in the army. She went off to war and unfortunately, like Sid, she died out there on the battlefield. We are downright proud of her."

"And my dad?" He looked at his grandfather and then his mouth fell open. "I know. His name is Greggie and he works at the lumber mill. He drives that truck with the huge wheels." He looked at their dad and then the chocolate cake on the counter and said, "I'm staying right here. This place is looking better and better."

Dad laughed. "And I was afraid you would prefer the lumber mill."

Teddy looked at Trenton, then quickly down at his own plate. He hoped his brother hadn't noticed. He ate slowly, concentrating on keeping his eyes on his plate as he considered the situation. He and Trenton may be the most alike. They wouldn't be finding out they had a dad just down the road.

He looked at Tommy, who wasn't excited about going fishing. He usually spent Sunday afternoons at the Taylors' eating cookies and telling Mrs. Taylor stories. He wondered if Tommy had a mom or dad that would come to the house someday. What would their mom and dad do if that happened?

What about Grandma? He looked at his mom. She smiled. Did she know? Did Grandma call and talk to Mom? Should he ask her? Dad might say he can't go to the hospital. Better, just keep quiet.

13

The town council was meeting this morning to make the final plans for the Fall Festival. George and Thelma McClain had never missed a town council meeting or any of the planning for the annual celebration of the harvest. Thelma had her pickles in jars on the porch for the pickle-tasting contest, and George had the boys out selecting the biggest and nicest pumpkin to enter in that contest. But George was not thinking about this Saturday's festivities as they drove along the highway heading toward the county line.

"That was nice of you to give Dane that sidecar," Thelma said.

George smiled. "Brent and Jeff took it into the barn. When Teddy left, they were painting it the same color as the cycle. They want to surprise Dane for his birthday."

Thelma looked out the window. "I just hope he won't be too disappointed tomorrow. Trudy told me that Sara said Jeff painted the name Dwain on the sidecar. Trudy said they're talking as if they really believe God is bringing that boy home, and he will ride in that sidecar in the parade on Saturday."

George drove up the driveway. Part of him wanted to believe the senior class really would find Dwain Campbell. "I don't know what it is, but since this 'Finding Dwain' stuff started, my whole outlook on life has changed." He put his hand over hers as he parked in front of the children's home and sat looking at the closed front door. He bowed his head to hide the moisture in his eyes. "I miss Hilda, so much. I wanted her to stay home and take care of herself."

Thelma turned her hand over inside his and gently squeezed his fingers. "She had to live her own life and find her own happiness. She was an artist and she loved the bright lights and the people in New York City."

He looked at her sadly, "All the time she was growing up, we were careful with Hilda, and then she left and didn't come back for more than twenty years. When she finally came home, she had full blown-AIDS and was eight months pregnant. All she could talk about was that flower garden. She had me plow the weeds under and get it ready for her to plant flowers in the spring. Then when she died, I was so ashamed all I could put in the obituary was 'a heart condition.'"

Thelma patted his hand. "Hilda knew it was too late for her. She asked for a C-section so her baby wouldn't be exposed to HIV. She knew the operation could kill her. She wanted to save her baby's life."

He whispered, "Shelly loves flowers the way Hilda did. I'm afraid she'll be like her mother, and we'll go through this all over again."

Thelma said softly, "Dr. Fitzgerald said that the Bible tells us to live one day at a time. Dane talks about having faith. I think what we need to do is ask God to help us to raise Shelly and then trust the Lord to guide her because we won't always be here for her."

He knew what she was asking him to do; she wanted to go to church. He cleared his throat. "It's time to go in and get Shelly."

As George pulled the key from the ignition and opened his door, the front door of the building opened. A woman and a little girl stepped out. The little one wore a long coat and carried a small suitcase. She looked so much like Hilda, his eyes began watering again, and his vision blurred. He swiped away the tears with the back of his hand. "Oh, my goodness," George whispered as he slid out of the seat. She waved a small hand shyly.

He walked slowly toward her. "What do we have here? Just the prettiest little girl in the whole world." He knelt down on one knee. "Hello, Shelly." He touched the blade of a small hand shovel that protruded from her bag. "What's this?"

"It's for my garden work." She reached into a small pocket and pulled out a box of crayons. "And this is for drawing pictures."

"Well." He scooped her up and hugged her, careful to avoid hurting the incisions from her surgery. "I will make sure you have lots and lots of paper to draw on so you will always be happy to stay with us."

She looked at Thelma. "Are you my mommy now?"

Thelma touched her cheek. "I most certainly am, and we are so happy to finally be able to take you home with us."

Shelly looked back at the big house and waved sadly to the lady in the doorway. "I'm well enough to go home now."

The woman waved and shut the door.

With their first little girl seated in a car seat and securely fastened with a seat belt with her arms around her doll, they headed home. From the backseat came excited chatter George had never heard before.

"Stephanie, we live on a farm. Kids will come to our summer camp and play with us. We have horses. We have cows. We will plant flowers after the snow is gone. We will have a baby sister and we have a dog, two cats, and five brothers."

George reached over and clasped Thelma's hand. "I haven't gone to church since my mom died. I was thinking we should start going again."

࿊ ࿊ ࿊

As the sun rose on this new morning in the state of Idaho, Phil Drake sat at his desk, studying the information on his computer screen. Receiving an absolute confirmation on his success, he leaned back and shut down the computer.

"Yes, yes!" He formed a fist and shook it at the ceiling. "*I did* it. I did it. Our little nest egg is about to hatch."

He hurried up the stairs and into the kitchen to share the good news with his wife, Brenda. "Everything went through, Bren. We can relax. We won't be spending a dime for Tiff's college." He bounced around the kitchen. "We got in first. He had the highest score on the entrance test. It's a miracle I even found that grant program. Who would believe there is that much money for a handicapped kid to go to medical school?"

Brenda shook her head. "It's too early for this." She motioned out the window. "Speak of the devil. And it looks like she has her friends with her.

Here, take this tray up to Dwain"—the phone shrilled—"and answer the phone in the hallway."

He took the breakfast tray from her, looked out at the girls climbing out of his daughter's sports car and then snatched up the ringing phone on his way up the stairs. Zelda Cloud's voice peppered him with disjointed ravings about a baby blanket. When she took a breath, he interrupted her. "Miss Cloud, you never told me about his baby blanket, and you have never said anything about his parents. You know my daughter's college education depends on the adoption being finalized."

He stopped short of the bedroom door. Turning his back to the door to avoid being overheard, he said softly, "And why would they want him now? Could you do something to hurry the adoption? I'm not going to let anyone snatch him away now. There is too much at stake here."

Pressing "end" on the phone, he stepped into the bedroom. "Hey, champ, how are you feeling today?"

"Not good, Dad. I'm sorry but I'm not hungry. My leg hurts and one side feels like it's burning up. I need to have the doctor look at my leg again. I think something's wrong."

Phil set the tray on the bedside table. I'll go down and call your doctor. We need to get you up and back in school so you can graduate with your class and go to college. You have big things to do in this world, Son."

After his foster father left, Dwain closed his eyes, trying to block out a reoccurring nightmare. Tomorrow was the last day of what he had come to accept as the worst month of the year. As the day approached, thoughts of his birthday were smothered under a heavy cloak of despair. The same nightmare always came more and more frequently until September 30 had passed. He closed his eyes as the pain in his leg forced the vivid memory of the wicked witch into his mind. She hurt his arm when she pulled him from a wheelchair and threw him onto the backseat of her car. As she drove in the dark, he tried to rise up and see out the window, but he was too sick. She was yelling. In his dreams, she was always yelling.

Tiffany, his tall, blond, eighteen-year-old foster sister, stepped into his room, closing the door very quietly behind her. She took a piece of bacon from his breakfast plate and stood in front of the mirror on the dresser, watching herself seductively savoring the slice.

"So you think everything is going so awesome, don't you? Don't think that you're really going to be my brother. And don't think my parents really want you either. You better be reading the fine print on everything that you sign."

"I can read." He lowered his voice. "Unlike some people."

She tossed her hair back and strutted across the room. "Look at you, Dwain the pain. They chose you over a dozen other kids just like you because you had no problems. You could walk and no one had to change your diapers. Almost as good as a pet dog." She sneered. "You weren't supposed to need surgery. It about kills them to have to take care of you while you lie in that bed. If you hadn't complained to the social worker about your legs hurting, you wouldn't have ever had that surgery."

She held up her hands showing him long, slender fingers topped with colored and carefully shaped fingernails. "Why do you think my Mom covered your hands when she took your picture?"

Dwain bit back his resentment, but it boiled anyway. He couldn't help the way he was born, and Tiffany never missed a chance to grind him under her heel for it.

"I have beautiful hands." She put both hands behind her neck and lifted her long blond hair as she looked at herself in the mirror. "I am, in fact, beautiful."

"Until you open your mouth." He made a face at her.

She glared at him. "You may become legal"—she made quote marks with her fingers in the air—"but you will never be in their will. Daddy said that he specifically stated in the will that everything is going to me."

She took a slice of Dwain's buttered toast and picked off the crust. "You know the only reason they want to adopt you is because of your college grant money, and they'll keep getting handicap benefits for you even when you are an adult."

Some of his friends at school had cranky sisters, but for some reason, God had seen fit to stick him with Tiffany, whose tongue could rip a grizzly to shreds. Dwain counted to ten in his head and wished she would go away.

"If someone really wanted to adopt you, and I wouldn't know why, don't you think they would have a long time ago? Instead of waiting until you're a senior in high school. Can't you see they're doing it for the money? Daddy found a new investment, and that's all you are to them. He sits down the basement in front of his computer looking for investments. He can't make enough on the stock market to pay for me to be in the sorority with my friends when I start college next year."

Not that it would ever occur to her to stop demanding the most expensive clothes, the most expensive car, the most expensive everything. He rolled over and faced the wall. Maybe she would get the hint.

"Do you think they made that ramp for your wheelchair because they love you? That was paid for by the state, and next year when they put this house up for sale, all the handicap improvements are going to pay off for them."

Phil stuck his head into the room. "The doctor said to pack you up and take you back to the hospital, champ."

Tiffany swung around. "Not now, Daddy. My friends are here. I don't want them to see him."

He said, "Why don't you take your friends to the mall for a few hours?"

She rubbed her fingers together. "Money, Daddy. I can't go to the mall without money."

He took a twenty-dollar bill out of his wallet. She pouted. "I saw a hundred, Daddy."

He handed her the hundred, reaching for the twenty. She pushed both bills into the back pocket of her tight designer jeans and looked back at Dwain. "Any possibility of him dying?"

Phil shook his head. "I hope not." He spoke louder as she descended the stairway. "For your sake, young lady, you had better hope he'll bounce back and go back to school so he can graduate with you this year."

Her footsteps stopped at the bottom of the stairs. Dwain could visualize her realizing that when the teacher called his name in first-period class, they would have the same last name. She gave a loud hiss and stomped all the way to the front door, slamming it as she left.

❁ ❁ ❁

Zelda was so angry she couldn't do a thing but wring her hands and pace the floor as the meddling detective sat watching her. He had worked for her before and had shown a marginal amount of respect, but today he just sat there like a toad and smirked at her.

He said, "Zelda, you hired me to provide you with information to substantiate your case. From what I have observed, you don't have a case against Jeff and Sara Campbell. They have a more than happy family and the place is overrun with neighbors and friends who are all expecting this kid to come home at any minute. The boys even made a ramp for his wheelchair."

"A what?" She spun around. "Who told them he's in a wheelchair? Someone is leaking information to that family, and I will get the bottom of this."

His head tilted to the side as though he knew something he shouldn't and was wrapping his devious mind around a plan to manipulate her. "I heard he's out of your jurisdiction?"

She spoke to the wall rather than give him the pleasure of seeing he'd rattled her. "That's none of your business."

"But Zelda, the court ordered you to locate the boy so he can be legally returned to his parents. You're in contempt of court if you know where he is and don't notify the court."

She pounded the sides of her fists down on her desk. "I run this office. I have run this office for twenty years, and no one is going over my head to reverse my decisions. I'm perfectly aware of what people in this community are doing. They're not fooling me. I can see it."

"What's that?" he asked stupidly. Or sneakily. They were all out to prove her wrong, but she was *not* wrong. She was the one who had been wronged all those years ago when her sister got special care, expensive care, and Zellie got nothing. Well, she wouldn't let it happen again.

"That…that place, that summer camp for those…those *horrible* little… *Ohhh.*" She shuddered. "They should all be in state-run institutions. Larry

Atwood and that stupid Jeff Campbell are ruining this county."

"But the camp has George McCain's support." The detective used a soothing tone of voice that made the hair on her neck stand up. "I thought you and McCain were in agreement."

"'Finding Dwain' is making everyone crazy, even George McCain."

He stood. "Everyone is affected by it in one way or another. Me, I'm a little wiser. You'll have to make a case in another way. I wouldn't help you, even if I could."

"You!" Zelda screamed, "Get out! Rhonda, Rhonda, I'm ready for my next client."

At the door the detective said, "I just want you to know one thing, Zelda Cloud. I've investigated hundreds of state cases over the years, so I know there are a lot of good people working hard to do their jobs right. But you aren't one of them."

Brent Anderson couldn't help overhearing Zelda Cloud ranting as he approached her office, and he heard the detective's assessment of her personality—and agreed wholeheartedly. He stepped past, making eye contact. "The motorcycle is purring like a kitten."

"I knew you could get it going." The man shook Brent's hand. "I'll be there to see it in the parade on Saturday."

Brent sat in the same chair as always and once again faced the angry woman. "I want my grandson, Zelda. You know where he is. I know you do, and so does Judge Roy Bain. I suggest you put on an act and pretend that you just happen to find him, and let me go get him and bring him home, right now."

She rose, flattening her hands on the desktop. "Judge Roy Bain is on a fishing trip and is not going to be back until long after your precious birthday party at 3:00 tomorrow afternoon, so don't threaten me. Besides, why do you need me? God is going to bring him back to you, so what do you want from me?"

Brent said softly, "God can use the most evil, vile, stubborn person to bring about what He wants to do. I just thought it might be good for you to do the right thing for a change."

He waited, praying she would open her heart and help, but she didn't.

ঔ৯ ঔ৯ ঔ৯

Thelma waited until after Shelly was asleep before she asked George if he wouldn't mind listening for the kids while she slipped over to Trudy's for a few minutes. Trudy was in her kitchen mixing another batch of chocolate chip cookies, and her coffeemaker gurgled with a fresh pot of coffee as Thelma walked in the door.

"I swear I can smell those cookies baking all the way over to our place." Thelma handed her a carton of eggs and slid a large round cake onto the kitchen table. "Are you sure you don't mind bringing this one tomorrow? I'll have a car full with the kids and two other cakes as large as this."

Even with George being so supportive about the new baby and bringing Shelly home, Thelma felt overwhelmed by the flurry of fall activity—and her pregnancy. She was exhausted.

"Not at all." Trudy touched her lightly on the arm as she took her place at the table. "Just sit and tell me everything."

Thelma sighed blissfully. "Shelly is a doll and she has George wrapped around her little finger already. I have never seen him so happy."

Trudy poured coffee. "He was always a happy boy. The only complaint anyone had about him was that he worked so much. After his mother died and Sid went into the navy, his dad depended on him more then he should have, I think."

"So what have you heard about Dwain? Is there any news?"

"Well…" Trudy looked toward the stairway behind her and then sat on a kitchen chair, whispering, "You know that Mabel is sweet on Zelda's detective. Today he put Zelda in her place. She slipped and told him she knows where Dwain is, and then he told Zelda that she's in contempt of court and he won't work for her anymore. On the way out, he walked right into Brent Anderson, and he knows Brent heard everything Zelda said in that office. He listened to Brent tell her to give him his grandson."

Thelma leaned forward. "Did Brent go get him?"

She shook her head. "Mabel's detective friend said he doesn't know how Brent stayed as calm as he did. And Zelda may be in trouble. The FBI agent that was at the school is watching her."

Trudy's timer rang. She slid a tray of cookies out of the oven and placed the hot tray on top of the stove. Moving quickly, she scooped up another tray filled with unbaked dough and pushed it into the oven and reset the timer.

"That's twelve dozen. There will probably be three hundred people at the party. With fifteen cakes, ten gallons of ice cream, and twelve dozen cookies, we just might have enough. I heard that the Atwood clinic is going to bring a bus full of kids and parents over for the party. If Dwain does show up, we wouldn't know which one of those little people he is, will we?"

Thelma smiled, glad Trudy was energetic enough tonight to carry both sides of the conversation. "Did you know that the bank and grocery store have signs in the windows? They're closing tomorrow afternoon for the birthday party."

Trudy seemed to read her mind and said, "I wonder if the Dine and Drive will close. I can't imagine Mabel not being in the gymnasium at three o'clock tomorrow."

Thelma sipped her coffee while Trudy chattered on, and then in a lull in the conversation she said, "Greg is excited about his grandpa, and now all the boys are asking us questions about their birth parents and if there are any grandparents." She placed her hand on her abdomen.

"What did the doctor say?" Again, Trudy seemed to know what was uppermost on Thelma's mind.

"She's strong. We're taking this one day at a time."

"And George?"

"He is so happy to have Shelly. I just can't imagine what he will be like with two daughters, but I'm sure he'll constantly worry about them leaving him to run off and be artists in New York City."

Looking across the field, she jumped up. "The kitchen light is on. I have to go. I'll see you in the morning." A few moments later, hurrying into the house, she was relieved to see her husband heating leftover chicken in the microwave. "I was afraid one of the kids was looking for me."

"Just me having a snack. What did Trudy have to say? Any new gossip?"

"Zelda's detective walked out on her, and she's being watched by the FBI agent that was at the school."

He frowned. "I always thought she did all right by us, but now I'm not so sure she actually checked out the background on our boys."

Thelma looked across the field as Trudy's kitchen light went out. "Poor Trudy is tired. She's hoping to have enough cakes and cookies for the birthday party tomorrow, but if the whole town shows up, I don't know what we'll do."

He looked at the clock. It was almost midnight. He set the plate on the counter and picked up the telephone. She picked up a fork and ate a bite of his chicken while listening to him. He said, "Tony, sorry to call so late. Do you think you could cater that party at the high school tomorrow?" He teased, taking Thelma's fork, smiling as he put it behind his back out of her reach. "The girls have been baking but they could use a—" He laughed as Thelma snatched the fork. He frowned as she moved his plate to the table. He said, "About five hundred. See if you have enough balloons, party hats, and favors for all the little kids."

He listened, and his head bowed. "No, I don't think Dwain is anywhere near here, but it's Fall Festival so let's put some effort into this."

14

Jeff Campbell's morning began at 3:00 A.M. as he fumbled for his cell phone on his nightstand. Looking at the number on the lighted screen, he pressed "talk" and then listened to his neighbor's description of the trouble a cow was having and said, "I'll be there as quickly as I can."

Tossing aside his covers, he considered the situation. Gripping the low handrail, he pulled himself up the stairs to Dane's room.

"Son, wake up. I need you to come and help me."

Dane peered at his clock and rubbed his face. "On a school night? Must be important." He reached for his jeans.

As Jeff put the car in reverse a minute later, Dane ran from the house, still pulling on his shirt.

"Grandpa's light is on," he said tiredly.

"Grandpa doesn't do well with delivering calves."

"Whose cow is having a calf?"

"It's that milk cow Amanda had as her 4-H project a couple of years ago."

"Millie? Already?"

"That is how life is, Son. Babies grow up and start having babies of their own before you know it."

❧ ❧ ❧

Brent looked out as the car left and then saw the kitchen light come on. He stepped out onto the porch and walked across the yard. His daughter poured him a cup of herbal tea as he sat at the kitchen table.

"I just keep saying short prayers for Dwain," he said.

"So you're not worried, Dad?"

He chuckled. "You got me there. I keep forgetting to have the faith to stop worrying." He looked at her over the steam. "Do you think Dane will want to work this farm when I'm too old?"

"I don't know what he'll want to do. Right now it's play basketball and ride his motorcycle."

He winked. "I saw him holding hands with Sally Yates today."

She moved her finger on the table the way she always did when she was thinking of a way to say something. "I'm worried about Amanda."

He winced. "She and Dane are just friends. She isn't going to be upset over him and Sally."

"No, but she is upset about something. I'm pretty sure I know what it is, and I don't know what I can do about it."

He knew when to ask and when to just wait, so he sipped the tea and waited until she quit moving her finger in circles on the table and looked up at him again. She said, "Jeff has let her know, not in words but in actions, that he disapproves of what she's doing. She has always loved Jeff, and he has always welcomed her as part of the family, but lately she's been spending too much time with Trenton McCain."

Brent raised his hand. "You don't have to tell me any more than that. But you know Trenton is younger than Amanda, and I never knew a girl in high school who went for a younger boy. We just don't get as smart as the girls until we get out of high school, and then after we get married, the girl gets smarter and stays that way the rest of her life."

She smiled. "And that brings me to something I would like to ask you about." She moved her finger for a few more seconds. "Mabel said that you and Katie had dinner together."

He almost choked as he swallowed. "She wants me to keep her horses out here. We were talking business."

"Mabel said she kissed you."

He shook his head. "It was nothing. I asked her if she would go with me to the Fall Festival dance."

She touched his hand. "That's good. You haven't dated anyone since Mom died."

"No, I dated a couple of times when you were in high school, before the twins were born. After that, I couldn't mix my feelings about needing to know what happened to Dwain with the kind of feelings a real relationship needs."

"Did you love Katie before Mom?"

"It wasn't like that. We were more like Dane and Amanda. Same grade, same age, and best friends."

Sara questioned him with her eyes so he quickly added, "Your mother was a princess. I was so crazy about her I tripped over my feet when I thought about her. My friends vanished after high school. They literally left the valley and scattered in all directions, but I didn't miss them. All I thought about was your mother."

Sara said, "You must care a great deal for Katie to have purchased so much of her parent's furniture."

He looked down, closed his eyes, and whispered, "You noticed."

"I saw you unloading the truck on the day of the auction. I was waiting for you to say something."

He bit his lower lip then smiled and shook his head. "I just hated for her to lose everything. She doesn't know I bought the stuff. I'm just waiting to see if she's going or staying."

◌▵ ◌▵ ◌▵

When Dane and Jeff Campbell rushed into the barn, Dane could see this might not turn out well. Millie was lying on her side looking dejected and dazed, unable to continue birthing her calf.

"I can't lose this one, Jeff," Tom told his dad. "The whole place rests on being able to get a good heifer out of Millie."

Dane knew the family must be close to losing their farm. Every little thing that went wrong was a disaster. As his dad knelt at her back end, Tom said, "It's just too big. I was afraid of this when she kept getting bigger and bigger in the last month. With you looking at Big Bill, I just didn't have money for you to take a look at Millie."

Dane watched his father glove up and lean as close to the animal as possible, pushing his arm inside in search of the problem. He had carried in the heavy medical case but now didn't know what he could do to help.

After several seconds, his dad looked over at him. "I can touch the leg, but that hoof is just too far. Dane, slide your hand in here and go just beyond mine. See if you can reach that hoof and put it in my hand."

As he pulled off his shirt, Dane saw Amanda. It was like her to be in the middle of everything that had to do with the animals. He wondered why she was just sitting on a bale of hay by the barn door. As he pulled on the shoulder-high glove and squeezed his arm into the animal, he saw Amanda close her eyes and lay her head to the side, as if she was sleeping. That just isn't something she would do, he thought, and then Millie clamped down so hard, he thought his arm might break. Gradually, the pressure eased, and his fingers moved over the back of his dad's hand and deeper in search of the hoof. Gripping the slippery form, he pulled it gently toward his dad's hand. As soon as he knew his dad had the hoof, he withdrew his arm and moved away. Despite the glove, his upper arm was covered in slime. Taking a handful of clean straw, he rubbed himself clean and looked again at Amanda. He wondered how she could sleep through Millie having her first calf.

The birth happened so quickly, Dane missed it. With a wet slithering sound, the calf was suddenly out and his dad was telling him to take her. Dane knelt and pulled her over onto the clean straw, knowing from experience exactly what to do. He rubbed straw over her, speaking softly to reassure the newborn that there was nothing to fear.

Tom was almost frantic. He rubbed his hands together saying, "That dang thing is too small. It's just too small."

"Dane." His dad slid a second calf toward him. "Take this one. She's breathing. Rub her down good and get them both on their feet."

Dane knew by the sound of his dad's voice, he was concerned about something. He wondered if Millie had what his dad called excessive bleeding. And then he saw what might be his father's concern. A third calf slid smoothly out and immediately started kicking. His dad said, "That should make Millie feel a whole lot better."

Dane rubbed the calves with straw, speaking softly to them as he thought about how awful it must have been for them to be stuck in there like that.

Tom shook his head. "Jeff, they're too small."

His dad stood and motioned the man to help him with Millie. Together they got her to stand. As Dane moved the three little heifers under the udder, his dad said to the man, "You've been a dairy farmer for thirty years, Tom. You know multiple births mean smaller babies."

The man said, "They're so much smaller than twins." He spoke softly, as though he were afraid a loud voice would harm the tiny calves.

Dane's dad hitched his thumbs in his belt loops. "They don't stay small for very long once they start eating. Right Dane?"

Dane grinned, thinking of Dwain. His brother was probably big, even for a little person.

✃ ✃ ✃

At 3:20 A.M., Dwain's doctor made his decision. Unable to get the foster father's cooperation, he placed a call to Dwain's social worker. She gave her approval, so he was now legally able to proceed. He stepped into the hospital room where the boy's foster father sat on a chair, leaning against the wall, half sleeping as Dwain lay moaning on the bed.

To Dwain he said, "I faxed your medical records to Dr. Edmonds in Lewiston." He turned to the foster parent. "I contacted his social worker. She has given me her approval. I don't understand what's wrong, and I don't want to let it go on any longer. I need you to take Dwain to the hospital in Lewiston. Dr. Edmonds will see him first thing in the morning."

The man stormed to his feet. "I already told you I'm not paying for a trip to some fancy hospital where they can't do anything for him anyway. You do something here. I'm not driving to Lewiston."

A nurse said, "Doctor, my cousin Gordon works in the garage. He's taking one of our ambulances to Lewiston in about half an hour. They're going to put some new electronics in it tomorrow. If you want, I could ask him if he'll take Dwain and his father to Lewiston with him in the ambulance."

The doctor nodded. "That would be fine. I just want Dwain in the hospital in Lewiston first thing in the morning." He looked sharply at Phil to drive in his point.

With no time to spare, the doctor helped the nurse move Dwain onto a gurney that would slide into the ambulance. He then watched as a nursing assistant pushed the narrow bed down the hallway. Saying a silent prayer, he asked God not to let whatever had gone wrong be a mistake he'd made. He walked away, feeling the lifting of a heavy weight off of his shoulders, and he knew he was doing the right thing.

In the parking lot, as Dwain was being secured in the ambulance, Phil looked for an escape. Immersed in a horrible sense of anxiety, he took a few steps in the direction of visitor's parking and then forced his hands deeply into his pants pockets and walked back to wait until the boy was alone. Then he climbed into the back of the ambulance.

Phil didn't understand why he felt the way he did. He had a foreboding feeling and desperately needed to go home. "Champ, I have too much to do at home," he said quietly. "If I lose more time, we'll lose too much money. I have to get back to my stocks. Can you do this on your own? We'll drive down and pick you up when they're ready to release you. Okay, champ?"

"I'll be fine, Dad."

Phil jumped out, closing the door softly, and stepping straight back so the ambulance driver wouldn't see him in the mirror and know he had gotten out.

Gordon started the ambulance. "Everything okay back there?"

"Everything is fine back here." He thought it might be the kid—the voice sounded thin and tired.

Gordon turned the dispatch radio down and began changing channels as he heard less and less of the city emergency calls. Two hours passed before he decided he should pull off at a little rest stop along the highway to relieve himself and stretch his legs.

"You want to get out for a bit?" When no on answered him, he looked into the back and then turned a knob to turn up the lights. The kid was alone. He slipped between the seats and moved to the sleeping boy's side.

"Hey, kid. You all right? Kid?" The boy's skin was pasty, and his breathing was shallow. Not good.

Leaping back into the driver's seat, he snatched up his mic and located the Lewiston dispatch. "I'm coming but my ETA will be more than an hour and I don't think this boy has that long. This is serious. I have a boy here that is not responding. I need a helicopter real quick." He moved back to the boy and sat with him until he saw the light of a helicopter up to the right in the dark night sky.

He lifted the microphone again. "There's a helicopter out here. Can you get it to stop and pick this boy up?"

Dispatch told him to stand by.

"This is *Helo 57932.* We are en route with a kidney that we picked up in Lewiston. We will land and pick up the boy but we can't return to Lewiston. We have a medical team on board. If he is stable, we'll transport him along with the kidney to Redmond, Oregon where a patient is being prepared for a transplant. Lewiston, will you fax the patient's medical records ahead of us to Redmond?"

Gordon had a hard time explaining, in the few seconds, why he was transporting a patient in serious condition without a nurse or paramedic. "I thought someone was with him. When I left the hospital, someone said everything was all right back there. I guess it was the kid."

Two medical technicians worked over the unconscious teenager as the helicopter flew through the darkness toward the rising sun.

Communicating with a doctor in Redmond, a paramedic assured him that they were right on schedule with the kidney, so the receiving patient could be prepped for surgery. About the boy he said, "Respiration is steady, but he's still unresponsive. Peripheral edema of his left leg. Scars on the leg indicate he had recent surgery, possibly to correct curvature; he's a little person. The other leg has a cast. I can't believe a doctor was transporting him in this condition."

The doctor responded, "Is your patient a dwarf?"

"Yes. He looks like he's in his late teens. Height is between forty and forty-five inches."

The doctor said, "There's a hospital just over the Idaho border on the

Oregon side that specializes in the care of dwarfism. This may be a blessing for that boy. I'll get you the landing coordinates. It's almost in your flight pattern. You could touch down, drop him off, and come on to us without losing any time."

Given the directions, the pilot changed frequencies as instructed and radioed the Atwood Clinic. "We are approaching with an ETA of four minutes. Turn on some lights so I can see your helipad?"

Instantly, bright lights surrounded a round circle behind the L-shaped building. Two nurse's aides rushed out with a gurney as the helicopter touched down. With the rotor still spinning, the small patient was pushed off into the hands of hospital personnel and then the aircraft lifted off.

A nurse hurried toward the patient. "What did they say about him?"

"Only that they picked him up along the side of a highway near Lewiston. They have no medical history and no name."

Another nurse rushed out of the hospital, carrying a clipboard. "I started a chart for him. We received a call from a Dr. Cox in Redmond. He said that the helicopter was transporting a kidney from Lewiston to Redmond when they picked up an emergency dwarf patient. He recommended they drop him off here."

The senior nurse took the chart and scanned it as they rushed toward the Emergency Room. "This has no medical history, no name, date of birth, nothing." She wrote September 30, 5:40 a.m. as arrival date and time, then hung the clipboard on the wall outside the ER.

As a nurse inserted an IV, a doctor passing by snatched up the chart and wrote "Tiny Tot" in the name space, which is Atwood Clinic language for a dwarf John Doe patient.

He said, "Someone is missing a boy. Let's get his fever down and his vitals stable. Let Larry know as soon as he gets out of the delivery room."

ᘉ ᘉ ᘉ

At 6:30 sharp, Mabel pulled into her parking place at the side of the Dine and Drive. As she stepped out of her car, she could see Katie McGuire and a man she had never seen before sitting in a booth. She wondered what

Katie was up to. Just looking at the woman gave her a strange taste in her mouth. She called it her that-girl-is-up-to-no-good-at-all bitter taste. She came in with a clatter, letting the heavy glass door slam behind her.

"Morning Mabel," Tully shouted from the kitchen as she placed a stack of heavy plates under the counter by the cook.

Jess reached down and scooped up two plates, mumbling, "New York bagel with cheese, eggs over easy and no salt or pepper."

Mabel put on her apron, watching the pair seated in the booth. She thought as she set napkin containers on the counter, *His silk shirt, wave of his hand, and tilt of his head; definitely gay. Her overdone makeup; maybe just normal for Katie, but the high heels and fancy clothes mean she's going somewhere.* She figured this to be her best observation for the whole week, though her opinion of Katie wasn't one she would share with anyone else.

Tully whispered, "They've been here twenty minutes," then she said louder, "No word on Dwain. The hospital had a medical emergency this morning. I saw the helicopter land and take off while I was getting ready for work."

Mabel nodded and moved to the tables, carrying filled napkin holders. Now she would be able to hear more of what they were saying and less of Tully. The man said, "Darling, you are the one. You are absolutely the one. It's Hollywood all the way, girl. Hanson wants your designs for the whole production—and we, girl, are going to the top with this."

Mabel leaned between them to reach for the napkin holder as Katie said, "My brother offered me thirty thousand for the horse."

He waved his hand, almost slapping Mabel in his overly dramatic exhibit of enthusiasm. "Darling, that is just perfect. We quick-like pay last month's rent, so no one suspects we even considered closing the doors. In two months the studio will begin making payments for using your beautiful designs. We will be in the money, honey."

Lingering between them, Mabel had to hold her breath to prevent her being overcome by the strong combination of perfumes. Katie said, "I don't know. I'll have to sign another lease for the office space. For me to commit to ten thousand dollars a month right now..."

"Honey." He touched her hand. "Appearances, appearances, appearances. We look like we have paying clients, and we'll attract paying clients. Trust me on this. We fly back this afternoon. It's already tea time in the Big Apple so everyone is buzzing like busy bees."

Mabel whispered under her breath as she walked back to pick up their order, "And it's her money you're busy buzzing with."

Returning to the table with their plates, Mabel had to ask, "Did you tell Brent you're leaving? Are you paying him for the fence he had to put up at the back of his field for your horses?"

Katie raised her coffee cup to her thickly glossed lips and extended her pinky finger. "What's between Brent Anderson and me isn't your affair, Mabel. It wasn't when we were in high school and it isn't now."

Before Mabel could respond, her boss yelled from the kitchen. "Give me a hand in here, Mabel."

She pushed through the swinging doors. "What are you doing here so early?"

"Haven't you heard? It's September 30."

"So?"

He pulled a stack of four large rectangular baking pans from a shelf. "We're going to make some birthday cakes."

Mabel crossed her arms and looked at him. She knew him too well to believe he'd just decided to contribute to the party at the school. Something was up. She moved to the mixer, opened a cookbook to the chocolate cake recipe and pulled three dozen eggs from the refrigerator. "Why are we making cakes?"

"My brother, Tony, he got an order at midnight from George McCain. It's a big order for Tony. He does a good job this time, he gets more catering calls."

She put her hands on her hips. "George is paying for catering a party that includes the patients of the Atwood Clinic? He would never do that."

The man motioned to the bin of flour. "Work while you talk. Why wouldn't George do it? He signed a lease for a dollar a year so handicapped kids can have a summer camp. So maybe George is not his old self. Maybe this George, we like better. It doesn't matter. What does matter is that we get the cakes into the oven before truckers start coming in for breakfast."

He called out to the front, "Tully, make a sign for the front door. We're closing from two thirty until four o'clock. Tell them to come to the high school if they want something to eat."

∽ ∽ ∽

At 6:33 Dwain opened his eyes and looked around what he recognized as a hospital's intensive care unit, and he wondered why the Lewiston hospital was so quiet. As he tried to sit up, he realized that his leg felt better. A lot better. And he was starving. He looked for a button to push to call a nurse. There was a button—on the wall, out of reach.

With no crutch to lift up and push the call button on the wall, he had only one option for getting someone's attention. "Hey, anybody? Can I have something to eat? Hey, anybody. Excuse me but I'm hungry. I'm hungry. Please can I eat?"

A nurse rushed to his side as he sat up. An all-too-familiar sensation alerted him to a catheter. He slipped his hand under the covers, pulled a plastic tube out of himself, and handed it to the nurse. "I don't need this. I can use the bathroom okay."

She tut-tutted him but took the tube. "You need to lie back."

He sat up straighter. "I'm hungry. May I please have something to eat? I feel great. Your doctor fixed me up just great." He moved the sheet to look at his leg. "It's better. It's not swollen. Can I get up now? Will you please bring me some crutches so I can get up?"

Hearing his friend Jeff's persuasive voice in the intensive care room, Dr. Larry Atwood stopped short and looked through the doorway. The teenager spotted him. "Hi, Doctor. Thanks for fixing my leg. It feels great. Would you please ask someone to bring me something to eat? I'm starving."

Fighting to hold back tears, Larry nodded to a nurse, sending her to the cafeteria for a breakfast tray. He then picked up the medical chart. "Well, what has one young man's faith brought to pass?"

The nurse said, "A medevac touched down just long enough to push him out. They picked him up along the side of a highway near Lewiston."

Dwain put his legs over the side of the bed. "Can I have a wheelchair please, so I can wheel down to your cafeteria? I'm really starving."

Larry turned around and closed his eyes. "Thank You, my Lord. Thank You. Thank You. Thank You, so very much."

The nurse said, "It's an absolute miracle. His leg isn't swollen or discolored in the least bit and"—she pressed her hand to his forehead—"his fever is completely gone."

Dr. Atwood placed a firm hand on Dwain's shoulder as he said to the nurse, "Wait until 7:30 and then get Judge Roy Bain on the phone. Call him at home and tell him I'll meet him at his office. Ask him what time he'll be there. Tell him it's urgent."

"You can go," Dwain said. "You don't have to worry about me. I feel great. I'm just hungry."

A woman placed a breakfast tray on a rolling table. "If you sit back, I'll put this in front of you."

"Great. I'm starving. Can I have another tray just like this one? I'm really starving."

The doctor crossed out Tiny Tot on the chart and wrote the name Dwain Campbell. The nurse leaning to see what he wrote slapped her hand over her mouth in astonishment.

After asking Dwain a few questions, he said to the nurse, "He can be placed in the children's ward." He pointed a firm finger at her. "No one is to say anything. Nothing leaves this room or this hospital. I'm going over to see Judge Bain. I don't want anything leaking out to Zelda the witch."

Dwain looked up quickly. "Does she run this hospital? I don't want to stay here if a witch is in charge around here."

Larry laughed. "No, no, you are perfectly safe here, Dwain."

Dwain's eyes opened wide as two little men no taller than he was stepped to the sides of his bed and lowered it to a height they could manage. One said, "Hang onto your tray, young man. You can finish that when we get you settled in."

He was pushed through a wide and brightly lit hallway and then into a long room lined with beds. After passing by sleeping children in two rows of beds, they slid him into an empty space between beds. One of the little men pressed a button that raised the bed, allowing him to sit up.

A teenage boy sitting up in the bed next to him said, "I'll have the same, Charlie."

He was a little person too. Dwain looked around him. Each bed held a little person. A weird feeling tumbled in his belly as he realized how weird, but how wonderfully normal it felt to be around people his own size.

The little man waved over his shoulder as he walked out. "Fifteen minutes, Chris. Hold your horses for fifteen minutes, and everyone will be served."

Dwain held out his plate. "Want some?"

"Na, I was just kidding. What are you in for?"

"Not much. Just my cast has to be put back on." He dug into his breakfast as they talked.

"So what are you going to do when you grow up?"

Dwain smiled. "I'm going to be a professional basketball player."

"That sounds like a great ambition, but I got news for you, you'll be striving all of your life to reach it."

Dwain laughed. "I've never even talked to another person like me."

"Really? You're in for a real surprise because you're in a hospital full of little people. This is the kid's wing of the Atwood Clinic. Babies are down the hall and adults are across the hall. If you get up and around later, you'll see that tall people are abnormal."

Dwain looked around as little children began sitting up and sliding out of their beds. He counted six girls and five boys, including him. "Are you foster kids?"

The boy stared at him. "No way. Why, are you?"

A younger boy, hurrying toward the bathroom, waved at Dwain and smiled. A little girl rubbing sleep from her eyes also smiled at him. Dwain, thinking aloud said, "This must be what heaven is like."

"I hope it's not," the boy next to him said.

Dwain watched a normal-sized couple come into the room. Or abnormally tall. He smirked to himself. They walked straight to the bed next to him. The man ruffled Chris's hair. "How are you feeling?"

"I'll be fine when this arm quits hurting, Dad. When can I go home?"

"We're going to wait for Dr. Atwood to come in to tell us, but what we do know is that at 2:45 this afternoon all of us are getting on the hospital bus to go to a birthday party."

"Great. So, which Dr. Atwood do I get today?"

A tall, elderly man stepped into the room. He said, "The old grumpy one, Christopher. How are you feeling today?"

"Good, but I want to go home. You only have twelve channels on your TV and I have a Game Slot 150 Turbo Gear waiting for me at home."

Again Dwain's eyes opened wide. Coming his way were three little people wearing the same type of white hospital shirt as the doctor. They stood before Dwain, who sat up on a bed appropriate for their height. "Good morning, new patient," one of the two women said, "I'm Dr. Atwood."

The woman next to her, who looked almost identical, said, "No, you must be mistaken, my good miss, don't you see by the name upon this"— she pointed a small finger at her name tag—"that I'm Dr. Atwood?"

The third one, a little man with the same wavy brown hair and twinkling eyes, raised a finger and said, "Be assured, young misses, you are both quite mistaken, for I'm Dr. Atwood."

Dwain laughed as they argued in this comical way. The two women shook a finger at the man as they retreated to different sides of the room to each greet another small patient. The man removed Dwain's empty serving tray and unplugged his bed. Leaving the head up, he gripped a side bar. An electric motor hummed as the bed moved along at the little man's side with no more effort than the touching of a button at his finger tips.

"So, who's really Dr. Atwood?"

The man laughed as he turned the bed, guiding it into a small room. "That is a very good question." He placed a towel under the cast on Dwain's right leg and lifted an electric saw. "A very good question, indeed." He smiled a warm and caring smile. "This will not hurt in the least bit."

"I've had casts taken off before. Are you really a doctor?"

He winked. "I am Dr. Atwood." And he touched the name tag. As the small curved blade sliced the cast, he explained.

"Forty-three years ago, my father, that man who referred to himself as a grumpy old man, came here to this hospital as the only doctor. It's a small community, so how many doctors are needed?" The saw whizzed through the fiberglass.

"Both of my parents are of normal size, as are their parents and their grandparents, so it completely baffled them both, as to the reason for all three of their firstborn children to have dwarfism.

"You know, there are over two hundred specific types of dwarfism in the world. My type is different from the type of almost every patient we see. Look at my hands and look at yours. Mine are large, and my fingers are long and slender in comparison to yours, but there are more dwarfs with your bone formation in the world than with mine. For my chosen profession, these hands suit me well, as I'm sure that the shape of your hands will not hinder you in the least bit in any profession you choose."

Dwain's eyes widened. "So you all became doctors here in the same hospital as your father?"

The man lifted the round blade, looked at him, and smiled. "Let me tell this story."

Dwain liked this man, very much. He bit his lip and forced himself to sit still and not interrupt again. The man continued to saw, saying, "While doing a great deal of genetic research, my parents became familiar with the patterns and problems that are present in dwarfism. After writing and publishing research papers, they found themselves in the role of consulting others, and began receiving so many dwarfism patients, the hospital had to add a special wing to accommodate them.

"Their first concern had been to minimize bone deformities in their own children, to allow us to have the physical ability to pursue a college education and the careers of our choice. The Atwood Clinic was established to provide bone surgery and physical therapy in an environment most suited for little people and their families. And often, we were sent little ones without families that my parents could not part with, thus, our family grew and"—he touched the name tag on his shirt again—"my father ordered these name tags by the dozen.

"Patients that came here twenty-five years ago come back to see us on a regular basis. Our patients come from all over the world. That young fellow you were visiting with, Christopher, has come to us all the way from Maine. One of the girls is from New York City, and last night a very well-known romance writer made medical history by giving birth to dwarf triplets. She came to us all the way from Seattle, Washington."

"Why do they come from so far away?"

"Because we specialize in what they need. Parents want the best care available for their child's specific body type."

After he removed the cast, he pulled up a stool and sat, waiting. Realizing this man cared, Dwain said softly, "There is something in the medical field I know I'm supposed to do, but it is so specialized, I would have to be in a big city. I've been in city hospitals, and I've never felt like I do here."

The man smiled. "I understand what you're saying. The medical skill that I have would be greatly hindered in another environment, such as a hospital that is not properly equipped to accommodate my size.

"Dwain, if you have a specialized practice, in time, those in need will come to you."

Dwain said, "But only the ones that someone cares about."

The sudden anger in his voice startled Dwain, and he could tell the doctor noticed it too. Dr. Atwood said calmly, "We have a veterinarian in this community who has a relatively new practice. Because of his stature"—he emphasized his size by motioning to his own body—"his business got off to a shaky start. But he made the best of it. He hung out a sign, shortened his office hours, and climbed into his vehicle and drove about the countryside making house calls. And in time, his office hours outnumbered driving time."

Dwain nodded, suddenly realizing what he could do. "If I had a specialized field, do you think I could work here in this hospital, and when something happened out there, I could fly to a city and take care of it and then come back here?"

The man smiled. "When you finish school, I'm sure my father will want to look at what you're proposing."

"Can I start now?" Dwain's face brightened. "I could help here in the hospital. I love babies. I really love babies. I can help with the babies and little kids. I could live here."

The man held up a hand. "One step at a time. First we're going to x-ray these legs and see what was done here." He put the parts of the cast into a trash container and the towel from under the leg into a hamper. Then by pressing the buttons on the side of the bed, he moved the bed back out into the hallway.

After waiting a few minutes for the x-rays and taking a quick look at them, the little doctor smiled and nodded his approval and then guided the narrow bed down the long hallway and through two electronically controlled doors that opened into the walls as they passed into another section of the hospital.

Here the doctor selected a wheelchair from an assortment of chairs hanging low on a wall. Placing it beside the narrow bed, he helped Dwain into the chair and covered him with the thin blanket from the bed.

Farther down the hallway, they turned into the nursery, where two tall nurses and a tall redheaded man stood looking down into an incubator. Dwain was pushed up to the thick plastic of the incubator. Inside were three tiny newborn babies. As he watched, the redheaded man reached in and carefully slid his fingers under the baby wearing a blue knitted cap on his tiny head. Holding him in the palm of one hand he wrapped a blanket around the baby, raised him up, and lowered him into Dwain's arms. Never in his life had he been in trusted with such a tiny, precious living being. He smiled in amazement at the baby as his fingers gently stroked the infant's similarly shaped tiny stubs.

The man knelt on one knee, lowering himself to be level with Dwain. He then lifted a dwarf little boy and girl up to see their new baby brother.

Dwain said to the baby, "You are beautiful."

The baby's father said, "He's perfect."

Dwain whispered, "What's his name?"

The man motioned to the radio speaker on the wall that was now filling the room with music. "It's September 30. He came to us today, so we decided that the only appropriate name for him is Dwain."

Dwain didn't get what his name could have to do with September 30, but when it hit him that today was his birthday, which he shared with these little babies, he almost cried. He swallowed twice before he could speak. "Hi, Dwain." The baby responded by moving his head, pressing toward him. "Are you hungry?"

Dr. Atwood said, "We'll wheel baby Dwain down to his mommy for a feeding."

Dwain could not believe his good fortune. He was being permitted to hold the tiny baby as he was wheeled in the hospital hallway. A tall woman leaned down and said, "Oh, how cute. Is this your baby?"

Dwain shook his head. "His name is Dwain. He was born today."

She touched his tiny fingers, lovingly. "The perfect name for a baby boy born on September 30. Happy birthday, Dwain."

He smiled. He had never heard those last three words spoken so lovingly. And he wondered again what was so important about naming a baby Dwain on the thirtieth of September. He decided it had to be the same reason he had been given that name. He would inquire about that later, but for now, they were moving again. One of the little women doctors said to another in passing, "Good morning, Dr. Atwood." The other said, "Good morning to you, Dr. Atwood." Dwain laughed and then he was turned into a hospital room with only one occupant. The normal-sized woman lying on the bed was looking at him, smiling.

Dr. Atwood said, "We brought you a hungry little one."

The head of her bed had been raised enough for her to easily accept the tiny bundle as Dr. Atwood raised him up above his own shoulders to place him into her arms. The little boy and girl from the nursery ran in saying, "Mommy, hungry babies are coming. Mommy, you have hungry babies."

As the doctor turned Dwain to leave the room, the tall man from the nursery stepped in holding two little bundles wrapped in pink. He said to his wife, "Two more hungry babies."

Dwain said, "This would be a great place to work."

From behind him, the doctor said, "So, I understand that you want to be a doctor."

A little doctor said softly in passing, "Dr. Atwood, I presume?"

The man pushing his chair said, "Good morning, Dr. Atwood."

Dwain said, "I guess I have to change my name to Atwood. Are there any tall Dr. Atwoods besides your dad?"

"My mother, and my brother, Larry. He's our surgeon. I don't think you will ever have need of his services. You must have had a very skilled doctor. I'm surprised that you had any trouble with your leg after surgery. You should be up and out of here today."

"But I want to stay here."

"First," the man said as he pushed the wheelchair into the casting room, "you need to go to the high school and enroll. I understand that the enrollment hour is three o'clock this afternoon. After you enroll, you go home and finish high school, and then go to college for a medical degree. I had to do it in that order myself. Eventually I was permitted to wear the white jacket with everyone else's name on it."

Dwain laughed. "Does this mean I'm not going back to the foster home I was at?"

The man looked seriously at him. "We would like to keep you close to us. The home that you're being released to is located close enough for you to come in and help here at the hospital after school and on weekends, if you would like to."

"I would love to. It would be incredible." The feeling of real hope filled Dwain for the first time in his life. There was, for the first time, something beyond today for him to look forward to.

Dr. Atwood began preparing the casting materials as a little black woman came in to help him. She spoke to the doctor in a high-pitched, squeaky voice. He said, "Dwain, this is my sister, Silvia. She's in nursing school and will assist me with your casting." To her he said, "He is just a few weeks away from taking off the casts, so we should put something light on him for the time being. Just enough to reinforce his legs in case he's bumped or he tries to put too much weight on them." He looked at his patient, "Of course he wouldn't do that."

Dwain smiled.

15

Dane heard his dad turn off the shower, and he stepped into the bathroom, more than ready to wash off the sticky feeling leftover from helping with Millie's triplet calves. "The girls are in the bathroom upstairs." He shed his clothes and stepped into the shower.

"Well, girls will do that," his dad said. "You know, you did really well today, Son. I'm proud of you."

Dane lathered up. "Dad, did you always want to be vet?"

"No. When I was little I wanted to be only one thing. I talked, walked, and lived the first six years of life as a munchkin in the Wizard of Oz. And then, when my dad made me a path out of yellow bricks, I decided that I had to be something else."

Dane heard his voice moving toward the door so he had to stop him before he left. He opened the shower. "What did you have to be Dad?"

He grinned. "After that, I was an Oompa-Loompa in search of a chocolate factory."

Dane laughed so hard he got soap in his mouth. He finished showering and toweled off, still laughing. His mother had set his clean clothes on the edge of the bathroom counter. He dressed quickly and stepped out into the bedroom, trying not to make noise in case his dad was already sleeping.

Tiredly his dad called, "You can go back to bed for a few hours if you want to, Son."

"I have a history test first hour, Dad and it's September 30. I don't want to miss a minute of today. I don't want anyone thinking I'm moping around at home, expecting nothing to happen."

He walked out into the kitchen and started up the stairs to his room. Tammy Rae was at the top of the steps, starting to slide down on her bottom. Teresa was gripping the low handrail, ready to take her first step down. The eyes of both girls lit up excitedly at the sight of their big brother. He took three steps up the stairs and scooped the littlest one up in one arm and then turned around and sat two steps from the top so Teresa could climb onto his back.

In the kitchen, he deposited each of the laughing girls on a high chair and then ran up to his room for his schoolbooks, then headed downstairs again. Back in the kitchen, he listened to a lengthy prayer by Teresa and ate as he reviewed a chapter in his history book.

His mom said, "The McCain boys were up early again this morning. I could see the top of their equipment moving over the hill at five o'clock."

Dane memorized a date and then said, "Teddy and Trenton finished baling the hay. They had to get up early and take it over to the Emery Dairy farm and then come back and start cutting straw. Teddy said it was dry enough this summer for his dad to turn the cut hay three times before they baled it. They should get a good price for it, because it's extra dry."

She smiled. "If you learn enough about farming from Teddy, you'll want to be a farmer."

He looked thoughtfully at her. "I don't know what I want to be, but I'm sure I don't want to be a farmer."

✂ ✂ ✂

Judge Bain had told everyone who was anyone that he was going out of town on a fishing trip, so he was surprised to get a phone message from Larry Atwood. The only reason he was here was because his fishing trip got rained out. He'd just come in the door a few minutes before the phone rang.

He assured the nurse on the phone, he would be in his office at the courthouse. All she would tell him was that a very important Tiny Tot had come in this morning, and the child's identity had to be kept secret. That sounded like the start of a political scandal, which wasn't something he was looking forward to dealing with. Especially, now while he was officially on vacation.

Later, as Larry Atwood walked into his office, Judge Bain rose and shook the doctor's hand. "So I understand you got a little John Doe. Who are we hiding and why?"

Larry slumped onto a leather sofa. A slow, broad smile covered his face. "What I have is a healthy young man named Dwain Jeffery Campbell."

Judge Bain was halfway into his chair when the impact of Larry's words hit him, and he sprang back up. "He came to your hospital? Do the Campbells know yet?"

Larry shook his head. "Not yet."

Looking at the wall clock, Judge Bain bit his lip. "I guess that birthday party is in just a few hours." He nodded. "And we don't want word getting out too soon—if the wrong person hears, it might be dangerous for Dwain. Let's wait and tell them then. So tell me what happened."

"He arrived early this morning on a medevac. All we know is that he was picked up on the side of a highway near Lewiston as a medical emergency. When I walked into the ER, he was sitting up wanting a double breakfast."

The judge smiled and brought his hands together in a single clap. "Just like that. Just like that, he is swooped up and deposited right here on the thirtieth of September. Doesn't that strike you as rather odd, Larry?"

"No." Larry winked. "It strikes me as absolutely wonderful."

Over coffee the judge had his secretary make some phone calls to backtrack Dwain's travels last night. After listening to Dr. Atwood in a brief conversation with the originating doctor, Judge Bain had his secretary place a call to the social worker in Idaho.

When his secretary stepped back into the office, he handed her the top page of his note pad, saying to Larry, "We might as well kill two birds with one stone and type up a restraining order on Zelda Cloud. You know she'll be a hot wire if we don't pull her plug. Why, she'll be on this like no-see-ums at a fishing hole, and be in contact with the social worker in Idaho before she has her coffee this morning. It won't take her long to figure out the only logical place for Dwain to have been taken in his condition is the Atwood Clinic for Dwarfism."

Larry sat forward. "There are a few other things I need you to take care of. Dwain told my brother."

The judge raised his hand. "Which brother is that?

Larry smiled tiredly. "Dr. Atwood."

He laughed. "I should have expected that. Go on."

"Dwain said he was awarded the Henderson Handicap Medical Professional Grant."

"Oh." Judge Bain lit up. "Wow, that doesn't just go to anyone. There could be another veterinarian in that family."

Larry's expression became serious. "I need you to make sure the grant money is deposited into a safe account. The person who did the footwork to locate and fill out the application for that grant didn't intend to use the money for Dwain's education."

Judge Bain nodded. "I'll freeze everything with Dwain's social security number on it, and notify the board of the foundation. We'll make certain the funds are where they need to be when Dwain graduates from high school."

He leaned back. "Medical. So he's following in his father's footsteps?"

Larry shook his head, sadly. "No he wants to work with children. He seriously believes it's his calling in life to do one thing in particular."

"What is that?"

"He wants to be a forensic pathologist specializing in the questionable deaths of infants and children."

Judge Bain winced. "He wants to slice and dice dead babies. Why, for the life of me, would anyone at his young age even think about something that morbid?"

Larry released a heavy sigh and bowed his head. "That's another thing we need to talk about. Dwain believes he was deliberately poisoned on his seventh birthday, by the caregiver in the children's home he was in. At the time, he told the doctors and nurses she threatened to kill him because he wouldn't stop accusing her of smothering one of the babies. Of course it was his word against hers."

Judge Bain squinted. "That is a long time ago and it could be easily attributed to an overly active imagination. Do you know if his social worker was involved?"

Rubbing his eyes, Larry said, "Let's put it this way. He has an abnormally high fear of witches. Most of my very young patients have heard the story of the Wizard of Oz too many times, but for Dwain, his witch is real. He told my brother that she was dressed in black and demanded that he shut up about being poisoned. She physically threw him onto the backseat of her car when he was still too sick to walk, and she yelled at him while she drove, saying she would kill him herself if he caused her any more trouble."

Judge Bain picked up a thick folder on his desk. "That's what I thought. Zelda said she was unaware of anything that happened in that home. The home is closed. The FBI started an investigation that opened up a whole can of worms."

The phone buzzed and he reached for it, saying, "That's an important line." He motioned to the doctor to excuse him for a minute. To the caller he said, "If you bring me a copy of those credit card charges. It's obviously unusual behavior for her and exceeds her means, as do the purchases of the house and automobile. I have to have documentation to substantiate this request." He hung up and smiled.

"Well, that was the FBI. Between you and me, it looks like Zelda has a shadow she's unaware of."

Larry leaned forward. "Doesn't the FBI investigate only federal crimes?"

As his secretary stepped into the room, Judge Bain held up a paper he had written on while on the phone. "Brenda, I need a search warrant for Zelda Cloud's home. The specifics for the search are written here, as is the address of her home. An FBI agent will be here shortly to pick it up. And no more calls directly to my phone. I'm going back on vacation as soon as Larry and I finish our coffee."

‽ ‽ ‽

In first hour at school, Dane forced himself to concentrate on the questions on the test. He looked over at Amanda. She was tapping her pencil on the paper as if she wasn't going to complete the test. She looked at him and then quickly down at the paper on her desk. He felt badly because he had only a few best friends, and she had always been one of them.

After class, he stopped at her locker and asked her what was wrong. She shoved a book into her locker and slammed the locker door. "Can't you just take a hint, Dane?"

"No. You never acted like this before. What's wrong?"

She leaned against her locker. "Maybe I'm just tired of this town and everybody in it."

"Millie had three calves. That would have made you awfully happy just a few months ago, but now you act like you don't even care."

She glared at him. "A few months ago you weren't spending all your time on 'Finding Dwain.'"

He asked, "Would you rather I spend the whole month moping around?"

Trenton McCain leaned on the locker behind Amanda and put his arms around her. "So are you going to the dance with anyone, sweet lady?"

Dane stepped back. Those words just did not describe Amanda. She was like a viper today. But when Trenton spoke to her, she seemed to melt in his arms. She rolled on the locker until she was facing him and smiled. "Are you asking me if I have a date or are you asking me for a date?"

He gripped her firmly with both arms around her. "I'm asking if you want to hit the dance scene with me."

She looked up at him. "I don't want to go to the dance with an eighth grader who doesn't know what to do with his hands. And I'd have done better on a test if you would've stayed home last night." She knocked his arms away and shoved him as she walked off.

Trenton shrugged and looked at Dane. "Sorry about Dwain and all. You got to admit it was a long shot, Campbell."

Dane smiled. "It's not three o'clock yet. I heard you were up early."

"I heard you were up all night."

⌀⌖ ⌀⌖ ⌀⌖

Brent Anderson stepped out of his truck onto freshly mowed grass at the edge of the cemetery. Noon was a safe time to walk down the rows of headstones with assurance of being alone in his thoughts. Under an old oak tree, he paused to read the inscription on Sid's headstone. He smiled, thinking that Sid would get a kick out of the Kawasaki with his sidecar attached to it.

There was no assurance in life. When Sid's number was up to be drafted, he enlisted in the Navy to keep from going to Vietnam. He wrote home from Hawaii, bragging about how he had gotten the best duty there was. That was the last letter he sent home. His stone read, "Fallen Soldier," but didn't mention that he fell off a bar stool and hit his head.

Brent walked on, thinking the inscriptions on most of the stones told only a part of the truth. He stopped and read his wife's headstone. "Emily Anderson, devoted wife, loving mother." He touched the stone. *Anything can be written on a headstone. God knows the truth.*

He looked back at a sound behind him. Katie was standing at a tenfoot-tall granite statue of an angel. Holding the rim of his hat in his hands, he walked slowly back to the McCain family plot and stood next to her. She said, "I was here after her funeral. I wanted to come back when everything wasn't covered with snow."

He asked, "You want to be alone?"

She nodded, so he walked to his truck and leaned on the door, waiting for her. She looked toward him and then looked down and said, "It's me, Katie. Hilda, I'm sorry. So much was my fault. We were going to be the finest designers in New York City, but I got caught up in everything. Well, you know all that, but I want you to know I have a chance now to be great. Two of my design packages were accepted by a Hollywood producer. Well, anyway, my agent says they're in the top choices." She looked back at Brent.

"Everything here is the way it always was. Daddy lost everything so I guess some things have changed, but then again, Daddy gambled everything away before and he always bounced back." She sighed. "But with

Momma being gone now and him being close to eighty, he may just settle down and quit his shenanigans." She smiled. "Now who am I fooling saying that, Hilda?"

She turned and slowly walked toward Brent. "It's getting windy. The leaves are blowing off the trees."

He knew, but asked anyway. "Are you leaving?"

She crossed her arms, closing her cashmere sweater at the neck. "I'm so close to making something happen. I can't just walk away."

"I thought you already walked away. You closed your business."

"Our lease ended on our office. The financing wasn't available to stay open while we waited for reviews on my designs."

He looked back at the cemetery. She knew him too well to not know he was disappointed, so all he said was, "I wish you well, Katie." And then he opened his pickup door and climbed in and rolled the window down.

She said, "I promise, I'll not stay away so long this time."

Without saying more, he nodded to her the way he always had when they were best friends in high school and she had something she had to do and he understood.

Watching him drive away, she sat in her car with her hands on the wheel. Something inside told her she needed to stop and think about what she was doing. But the need to succeed was overpowering the voice of caution. She looked up at the sky. "God, what should I do? I'm too old to start over. Whatever I do, I have to succeed. Will You talk to me? I'm listening. Brent always said that I'm not listening for You to speak to me. Well, I'm sitting here and listening and I can't hear You. I've never been able to hear You. Tell me, please, what to do. But please don't run over anyone else with a plow for me to hear You."

A few minutes later she found herself parking in front of the Dine and Drive. She wasn't hungry and didn't need a cup of coffee but she walked in and slid into a booth by the window.

Mabel glowered at her. "What can I get you, Katie?"

Katie looked at her and wondered what she did want. Looking around, she realized that she was the only customer. Mabel crossed her arms as if she was going to make one of her irritating comments, and Katie braced herself for it, and then she surprised herself by saying, "Mabel, would you sit down for a few minutes?"

Mabel slid into the booth across from her and tapped her pen on her order pad. Katie heard herself saying what she had never once considered saying to this woman. "You have always come right out and said what you think. Everyone else stands back and watches; just letting people do what they want to even if it's not the right thing to do."

Mabel raised her eyebrows. "What are you getting at?"

"What do you think I should do? I am open to what you have to say."

Mabel looked at the door as though hoping another customer would rescue her from having to sit with Katie, and then she scrunched her forehead. "When we were in high school, you designed all the costumes for the school and church plays. You are a gifted designer and everyone knows it. It's just too bad you let other people drag you off."

She laid her order book on the table, apparently deciding to stay where she was. "You weren't going to go to New York City or anywhere else when you graduated from high school. Hilda was harping at you to pack up and go with her, but that wasn't what you wanted. That was up until you saw something that scared you so badly, you had to get away from here.

"You refused to talk about seeing that plow go over Eddie, because you didn't want anything to do with whatever God might have expected from you.

"So you got out there to the city and you did pretty good for yourself. When your dad lost all his money on horse races, everyone knows you sent him ninety grand. We also know you had the guts to stand up to him, and get a lien against his mares before handing him the money.

"If you really want my opinion, I'll tell you. You should look at what you really want before you run off again. You can't live Hilda's life for her. It's time you started living your own life."

Mabel hadn't told her anything she didn't already know. Katie shrugged her shoulders. "I can't do what I want to here. The ranch is gone."

"Katie, those mares you have are worth three times what you lent your dad. Now, you're selling them to your brother for a third of what they cost you. You're gambling away everything, hoping to make it big in three months.

"You asked me what I think you should do. You should stay in that $300-a-month room over at Sadie's. Send your designs over the Internet to that producer the way you always have. Don't tell me you need someone to push the send button on the computer for you.

"The talent is yours. A fancy office isn't going to make what you offer any better. If you trust the good Lord, He'll clear a path ahead of you. But you better be prepared to take the path He clears and not be turning off every time the devil points at something you never even considered doing in the first place.

"When you make your first sixty grand, you can buy your folk's old place." She slapped the pen down on the order book.

"Mabel, you know George McCain bought that place."

"I don't know any such thing. George never bought the section with the house and barn. All he bought from the bank was the back one thousand acres that he can plow under and plant. The bank still has the section with the house and barn."

As three young men came in, Mabel stood and lifted her order pad and pen.

Katie looked up at her and said quietly, "I was there."

Mabel slid back into the booth. "Eddie Davis?" Katie nodded. Mabel asked, "Where were you exactly? And don't leave out a thing. Tell me everything you saw."

Bobby Miller motioned to Ted Briggs to get the coffeepot. He turned on the counter to listen as Katie spoke. She hesitated, but now that she'd started, she had to finish—no matter who was listening. It struck her that choosing Mabel as her confidante had been a way of deciding to lay her soul bare before God and everyone she knew. "It's been more than thirty years, but I can see it like it just happened. I was on the Coby road just past that tree Bobby Langley fell out of and broke his arm."

Mabel asked, "What side of the Langley tree were you on, the stream side or the highway side?"

"I was past the tree going toward the wooden bridge."

Bobby motioned to Artie to forget the booth and sit next to him on a counter stool. He asked Katie, "You talking about when Pastor Davis was run over by the plow?"

Mabel hushed him with a wave. "She was there. Now let her tell what she saw."

Artie sat on the stool staring at Katie. "What did you see?"

As the three young men leaned toward her on their counter stools, and Mabel hung on every word, she said, "I was looking at him. He was plowing the outside row, and I was thinking that he was just about finished with the field. Like slow motion, he leaned back and let go of the steering wheel. It seemed like he was being lifted slowly up and then lowered down between the tractor and the plow. The plow rose up like it was floating just over him. After it was past him, it lowered down so it was plowing again. Then the tractor turned all by itself and went out of the field. Eddie was lying there with his eyes wide open like he was seeing something up in the sky."

"Was he bleeding?' Artie asked.

She shook her head. "He was looking up and then his dad's old gray pickup went by me and stopped. Mr. Davis was yelling, 'Eddie, oh no,' and his brother Mike yelled, 'Dad he's been killed for sure.' Then Eddie sat up and looked right at me. His dad grabbed his shoulder and yelled, 'You hurt, boy?' Eddie said, 'I must a fell off the tractor,' and he stood up.

"The tractor was spinning a tire, pushing against a tree. Mike ran over and turned it off."

The door opened behind her as two long-haul truck drivers came in. Artie announced, "She saw Pastor Davis run over by the field plow. Keep telling us, ma'am, what happened next?"

Katie swallowed, then she took a deep breath and continued. "He said something to his dad and his dad yelled at him. 'If that's what God told you to do, you should've just said, "Yes, Sir," and come and told me,' and Eddie said, 'I figured you'd never believe me, and besides, I'm going to be a farmer, not a preacher.'"

Mabel jumped up out of the booth. "I knew it. He went off backward and the plow went over him and never touched him."

A truck driver slid into the booth where Mabel had been sitting. "Three years ago up in Washington, I was behind a ten-car pileup when a tanker went off the road and tipped over. Fuel poured out of it, heading right at my rig. All of a sudden I was standing off to the side. I can't tell you how I got out of that cab. To this day, I just don't know. I was standing there watching my rig burst into flames."

Another driver slid in next to him and told a similar story as Mabel took the coffeepot from Ted and snatched up more cups. Katie smiled as she realized a heavy weight had been lifted from her shoulders.

❧ ❧ ❧

As Dr. Larry Atwood drained the last drops of coffee from his cup, Judge Bain said, "Last night Jeff and Dane helped my granddaughter's milk cow deliver three calves. I stopped by there on my way here this morning. They are the smallest calves I've ever seen."

Larry had to chuckle. "And last night, I delivered three of the tiniest triplets I've ever seen. Flora Ann Kindle and her husband, Bill, flew down from Seattle to have their at-risk triplets. We had no trouble at all. They now have five under the age of five years old, and they're all little people."

Judge Bain rubbed the side of his head. "That name is familiar. Flora Ann Kindle is the author that writes those romance novels?" He squinted and said, "That little couple that ran the travel agency were Kindles. They had a tall redheaded boy."

Larry nodded. "They moved to Seattle about ten years ago. Their son Bill was farming for Mac Edwards and dating Flora Ann. She's Jess and Tonya Murray's daughter. Got pregnant pretty young."

Judge Bain nodded. "I remember now. George and Thelma adopted her baby boy. They named him Thomas. I remember that because they always name their boys the same first name as the real father, but George didn't like the name William so he named him Thomas. That was his brother, Sid's, real name. Thomas Sidney McCain. I remember that from his obituary."

Larry chuckled as he got up to leave. "George McCain would have a heart attack if he knew that his eleven-year-old has five dwarf siblings."

Judge Bain smiled. "Let's not tell him."

Larry smiled as he parked in front of the Campbell house a little while later. He was thinking about George McCain being so outspoken about planning the perfect farming family.

Not seeing anyone outside, Larry knocked on the kitchen door. When no one answered, he reached over and moved a frog figurine and took the key out from underneath. He put the key back after unlocking the door.

What he had come for was something Dwain could wear when he left the hospital. He wanted to see if Dane had anything that would fit his shorter twin. When he entered Dane's bedroom, he was impressed with the change in the room.

Jeff had said Dane was ready for Dwain to come home. On a low rod in the closet were shirts and pants that had to be for Dwain. He recognized one shirt, and chuckled as he lifted the hanger, remembering how proud of that Donald Duck shirt Jeff had been. He called it his "lucky shirt" and even wore it when he took his college entrance exam.

Brent stepped into the room and studied Larry without saying anything, a knowing glimmer in his eyes. Larry put back the lucky shirt and removed what he thought would be a more appropriate shirt from another hanger. Selecting a pair of wide-leg, recently shortened blue jeans, he laid the clothes on the foot of Dane's bed and opened a dresser drawer looking for underwear.

He said to Brent, "When Jeff and I took the college entrance exam, we got the same score. Our tests were exactly identical. The only reason we weren't required to retake the test was because we were sitting across the room from each other." He pointed at the shirt hanging in the closet. "I told him that if he wore that stupid Donald Duck shirt, I wouldn't sit by him. If he hadn't worn it, we'd have had to take that test over again." He smiled and shook his head. "I never thought about that before. It really was a lucky shirt."

Brent looked at the clothes on the bed. He cleared his throat, and when he spoke, his voice shook. "You got him?"

Larry looked at him and smiled.

Brent asked, "He's on his way home?"

Larry took a pair of tennis shoes off of the bottom shelf. Recognizing his own etching on the side of one of the shoes, he remembered teasing Jeff while writing on his cast. "Judge Roy Bain prepared a court order to have Dwain legally returned to Jeff and Sara at three o'clock this afternoon."

Brent crossed his arms, nodding his head again, and again as tears ran down his face. "He was never adopted." He shook his head. "I knew she was lying. I knew he was never adopted."

Larry's phone beeped. "This is Larry."

He let out a long slow breath and looked at Brent as he said, "No, I have court approval to treat this as a Tiny Tot case. I don't care what Zelda says she knows. When she calls again or if she comes to the clinic, just follow Tiny Tot procedure. His name is not in our records."

He listened and then said, "She can watch the bus all she wants. I'll be there in fifteen minutes with his clothes. Have one of the nurses ready to drive him to the school. If we do this right, Zelda will be watching for him to get on the bus at the back door while he gets into a car out front. Just tell him he's enrolling in school."

Brent blinked and wiped his eyes as Larry closed his phone. "I'll go get him."

Larry pulled a folded paper from his shirt pocket. "Zelda has been on the phone all day trying to locate Dwain. If she shows up at the school, someone has to be there to present her with this restraining order."

Brent slid his fingers into his jeans pockets as Larry tried to hand him the restraining order.

Knowing this wasn't what Brent wanted to do, he explained, "We have a very tired, hurt little person who has had his hopes shattered all of his life. If we rush into this, he may get more than just emotionally hurt. He may get trampled."

He picked up the clothes.

Brent snatched the folded paper as Larry stepped past into the hallway.

He looked back at Brent from the top of the steps. Touching the folded electric stair-chair, he said, "He's going to need this for a few weeks. Jeff said he put the leg supports somewhere."

After the doctor left, Brent reached into his pocket for his cell phone. He opened it and then closed it, realizing that Larry was right. Too many people knowing that Dwain was coming could be dangerous for the little guy. He reached into the hallway closet for the leg attachments to the electric stair-chair.

As he finished tightening the last bolt he said, "Dear God, thank You. Thank You so much." He heard a cough below him, wiped his face on his arm, and looked down at Gramps standing at the bottom of the steps, with Tammy Rae seated on his arm. The old man said, "What's gone wrong now? You forgot to come and get this munchkin, so I brought her over so you can take her to that birthday party before she drives us all crazy."

⌇⌇ ⌇⌇ ⌇⌇

Larry listened to the news from his car radio. "Social Worker Dennis Allen Drake didn't think he was making enough money, so he grasped an opportunity to extort a hundred thousand dollars from an unfortunate family that has been searching for their child for seventeen years."

"Judge Roy Bain called this a hideous crime. "In his words, 'The efforts of a whole community to find Dwain have turned what was filled with hope into a parent's worst nightmare.'"

"The whereabouts of Dwain Campbell is still not known."

Larry looked at his watch. It was almost time. He pulled into his parking spot in front of the clinic and smiled as he stepped out onto the yellow brick entryway. He rushed through the front doors and handed the clothing to a nurse hurrying along behind him saying, "Your father is allowing us to take twenty-two children and seven adult patients on the bus to the birthday party."

Larry ran out the back door of the hospital, spotted the bus driver standing near the long white bus, and waved to him. "Is everything ready?"

"I'm ready, Dr. Atwood."

He turned and almost walked into nurse Helen Tims as she said, "My car is parked at the front entrance. Zelda Cloud has driven around the building three times. Our plan is to start loading the bus and hopefully she'll be too busy watching the bus to notice when we put him in my car at the front door."

He nodded, "What did you tell him?"

"What you said to tell him. Just that we're going to the school to enroll him—and we didn't tell anyone at the school. We're so afraid for him. My husband called me and said that there are more than a thousand people in the gymnasium. They had to send boys over to the church for more tables and chairs."

He closed his eyes. "This really scares me."

She said softly, "Dwain doesn't want to leave the hospital. He really doesn't want to go."

"Maybe…" He looked at his watch. He felt a familiar feeling and smiled. "When God helps me during a surgery so all the pieces come together, I could stand there and wonder how it all went so well, or close the incision and return the child to his parents."

He watched children and adults gather at the side of the bus as Nurse Tims rushed back into the hospital. A line formed at the open bus door and another at the wheelchair lift. Standing between the two bus entrances, with her legs apart and feet firmly planted, stood Zelda Cloud. Larry stepped out of her view, not wanting to give away the plan by accidently smiling.

Zelda scanned every face in the lineups. She knew Dwain Campbell had to be here. Which one was he?

"That one." She blocked a little boy's first step into the bus. A baseball cap hid his face. "What's his name?"

The woman behind him said, "He is our son, Chris."

"Let me see him," Zelda snapped. If she had to personally examine each child here, she'd do it. She wouldn't let them get away with making a fool of her.

The boy tipped his head up. "I'm Chris Patterson, you old witch."

She gasped. "What horrible manners. You little beast."

"We know what you're here for, and we already told you that Dwain isn't here." The boy stuck his tongue out at her.

She rolled her fingers into fists, and then made herself relax her hands.

She forced a smile and softened her voice. "Did a new boy come here very early this morning?"

His mother's hand moved to his shoulder, and her fingers compressed the puffy fabric. Zelda's senses went on high alert. These people definitely knew something about the Campbell boy, and she was going to get it out of them.

Chris rubbed his chin, clearly faking deep thought. "Aaaa, lady?" He squinted as if trying to remember. "Is he from a foster home?"

Her eyes widened, and her pulse raced. "Yes. Where is he?"

"Never saw him." The kid smirked.

"Do you know *who I am*?" She stomped her foot.

Chris stepped up two more steps and looked straight into her eyes. "I know who you are." Of course he knew. She was in a position of authority. "You are the wicked witch, Zelda Cloud."

Of all the nerve. Zelda felt sick to her stomach. "What is *wrong* with you people?" she hissed through her clenched teeth. Then she threw both hands up, searching for one sane face in the bunch. "You aren't raising children, you're raising monsters."

A little girl looking up at her screamed. "A wicked witch. *Mommy*, a wicked witch."

Her tall, redheaded father scooped up the brat. "Mommy is with our three new babies, remember? We are going to Dane and Dwain's birthday party." He looked squarely at Zelda and said, "I will see you in court, Zelda. If you lied to Jeff and Sara Campbell, you probably lied to us. You'd better have proof our son was adopted into a good family."

She stared at the man and then at the child in his arms and then at all the hideous little bodies below her and moved away, raising her arms to escape by squeezing between the chairs at the wheelchair lift.

In her car, she sat thinking. She couldn't remember ever seeing that red-headed man. "Finding Dwain" was causing her so much trouble. Too many people were questioning her ethics. Old cases were being opened by the state headquarters for review. But she did not believe she had anything to do with that man's child. She was certain that Dwain was her only dwarfism case.

ᴕᴥᴧ ᴕᴥᴧ ᴕᴥᴧ

At the small-town airport, Nash Manish secured two seats on a commuter flight by assuring the owner of the little airline operation that his business partner would bring her credit card. Then he drove to Mike's Rent-a-Car and turned in his car and keys and waited for his credit card to be approved.

"I'm sorry, sir. It has been declined again."

"Oh, now what has that bank done this time?" He reached into his pocket and withdrew four twenty-dollar bills and his cell phone. As the man counted back his change, he said into the phone, "Katie, darling, I'm at Mike's. He's being fabulous and giving me a ride back to the airport. I'll meet you there, dear, in say, half an hour."

He turned quickly away from the counter and lowered his voice, saying, "You have to be kidding me. Honey, you are the greatest thing that ever hit New York City. I don't understand. You can't mean it." Losing the connection abruptly, he snapped the phone shut and stood looking out the window.

Mike asked him, "Do you still want a lift to the airport?"

He fingered the few bills left in his pocket, and feeling queasy, he asked, "Bus station?"

The man pointed across the street. As he crossed the street carrying his sleek leather travel bag, he tapped a number on his cell phone. "Momma, it is so wonderful to hear your voice. This is your favorite son, Theodore. How is my wonderful momma doing this beautiful day?"

"What do you mean, what am I up to this time? What kind of a question is that? I just want to tell you that I will be in your area on business and I would like to visit you for a few days, Momma.

"That's okay if the spare room is full. What about that space over the garage?

"Momma, but I could sleep on the sofa?"

He closed the phone and dialed another number as he waited in the ticket line at the bus station. "Hello, Elton, how are you, darling? I've been thinking about you. Wasn't the opera absolutely divine?"

Hung up on again, he laid fifty dollars on the counter. "To the closest city, leaving as soon as possible in any direction."

16

As Brent slowed to let Gramps and Tammy Rae out near the front entrance of the school, he saw his grandson look at him from a passing car. The car parked where the sidewalk sloped for handicapped students. His heart pounded as his eyes filled with tears—then he saw Zelda. She was getting out of her car. The long white hospital bus parked at the gymnasium doors. Five boys, four carrying two folded tables and the fifth with his arms full of folding chairs, stepped out of the way of the bus. One motioned to Brent's pickup. "Hey, look, Gramps is here."

"Gramps," Brent said, "We got trouble. Dwain is in that car with Helen Tims, and Zelda is over here, closing in fast. You take the baby in." He snatched the restraining order off the dash.

Dwain looked around, watching the movement in the parking lot. That woman! He knew that woman dressed in black. His mind brought back his nightmare. *You think she poisoned you. Just wait and see what I do, if you cause me any more trouble.* Now she was yelling, "Stop right now. I demand that you stop. You're not taking him in there. I'm ordering you to stop this instant."

Someone whistled the sharpest whistle he had ever heard, and the sound made Dwain jump. He turned to see a very tall white-haired man stepping out of a pickup truck. The man held up his hands, with five fingers up on one hand and one finger on the other, and then moved his hand like he was slicing the air.

With a crash, the big boys dropped the tables and chairs. They were running straight toward Dwain, so he raised his arms to protect his head.

One boy said, "Block the old witch. Five on one, and Gramps said don't foul."

Dwain was shaking. "I, I don't feel good. Let's go back to the hospital. I can register for school on Monday." He looked over his shoulder. "Please, nurse, I don't think I'm supposed to be here."

He felt her weight press heavily on the back of his wheelchair. A red-headed boy pushed open the glass door of the school. Over his shoulder the nurse shouted, "Hold the door, Tommy. We're coming through."

Tommy yelled, motioning for her to hurry. "The witch is coming, hurry, Mrs. Tims."

Inside the school, ten feet down the hallway, his wheelchair stopped, and Nurse Tims panted for breath. A man rushed around in front of Dwain—the tall man with the white hair—and plopped a little girl on Dwain's lap. The man said, "You sit right here for a ride, little Munchkin."

She grinned up at Dwain as though this was the most fun she'd ever had, then wrapped her short arms around him and pressed her cheek to his chest. "I knew you'd come, Dwain."

Nurse Tims rushed back to the glass doors, calling to Tommy, "You take him from here. I'm going back to have a talk with Zelda Cloud."

Dwain held on to the little girl. Tommy gripped the handles on the chair, and he and Dwain looked behind them. Dwain hoped Tommy wouldn't have to escape at a run. He didn't want the little girl to get hurt if they crashed. Five athletic-looking boys were standing between Zelda and the front door. A cowboy, wearing blue jeans and a leather jacket, was taking off his hat and handing her a sheet of paper. If she got past him and pushed through the big boys, she'd have to get past the tall old man with the white hair. The old guy stood loose and ready, with his arms out to his sides.

"I'm Tommy McCain," said the redheaded boy pushing his wheelchair. "I'm in the sixth grade and"—he looked around, cocking his head as a grin spread over his face—"I'm your tour guide this afternoon. Tammy Rae, hang on tight, we have liftoff."

They passed the office, and Dwain said, "I have to go in there and register."

Pushing hard and picking up speed, Tommy called out louder and louder as they moved down the empty hallway, "On our left is the cafeteria where we eat lunch. Coming up on the right is the science lab, the girls' restroom on the left, the boy's restroom on our right, and taking this turn we are now heading for our final destination. Tighten your seat belts, we are heading for turbulence."

Ahead the hallway was blocked by students. Dwain clung to the chair with one hand and held tightly to the little girl. He shouted, "Tommy *please slow* down!"

As Tommy yelled, "Out of the way, coming through," a girl touched Dwain's shoulder and waved, smiling at him. He looked back at her, thinking *cute girl*, and almost tipped out of the chair as Tommy swerved it into the gymnasium.

A man who looked like a principal stood in the middle of the gymnasium speaking to what had to be the entire community. "We're all looking forward to our Fall Festival tomorrow. I think we're all going to have a good time. I know I will be out on Main Street with my horses and wagon full of hay, so if any of you would like to ride through town, jump on. If anyone wants to shovel up behind the horses, just feel free to do so."

Everybody chuckled.

"Hey, Principal Campbell." Tommy charged forward with the wheelchair as though racing for a finish line in the center of the gym, precisely where Principal Campbell stood. Realizing they were moving too fast to stop as they approached the circle, Dwain wrapped both arms around the little girl to shield her. Tommy's sneakers squealed on the floor behind him. Only the quick response of his principal kept both riders seated in the chair. Once they stopped, Tommy started babbling, and the principal had to ask him to slow down.

Looking around at all the silent faces, Tommy pointed behind him and shouted, "Witch Zelda was after Dwain. Mrs. Tims yelled, hold the door, we're coming through. Then she said, take him and run with him as fast you can and don't stop for anything."

Mr. Campbell narrowed one eye at Tommy as though he didn't believe him. He placed his fingers on Tammy Rae's shoulder. "And where did you get this little rider?"

Tommy's eyes widened. He pointed back at the door and looked up at Mr. Campbell. "Gramps."

A little man burst through the crowd and was almost to the wheelchair. Both men looked worried. Then the cowboy and the tall man with the white hair—Gramps, Dwain figured—came in. The cowboy raised his hand and put his thumb in the air. Dwain figured that meant everything was under control.

Principal Campbell broke the silence. "Well, Dwain, so you decided to come to your birthday party after all."

Dwain looked around. Was that a question or a statement? He looked up at the man, still shaken. He didn't know what to think. Then the man said, "Dwain, I'm your grandfather."

Dwain considered this quickly. He'd a few grandfathers in foster care. Some were nice and others were hardened in how they felt about dwarfism and foster children in general. The little man still stood next to his chair, and he kept squeezing his eyes shut and taking deep breaths. The grandfather gestured to the little man. "And this is my son, Jeff. He's your father, Dwain."

Dwain looked at the little man standing next to him, but the words wouldn't sink in.

The little man hugged his neck. "Happy birthday, Son." And he kissed the side of Dwain's face. The kiss didn't bother him as much as the dampness from the tears on the man's face. Then, the little man said, "Welcome home, Dwain. Welcome home, Son."

Someone motioned for the band to play. As they struck a loud note and burst into a victory song, a group of girls pulled up a long banner. Dwain read, "Welcome Home Dwain Campbell."

"You knew I was coming?"

A pretty blond woman leaned down and put her arms around his neck. "I'm your momma, Dwain. And this is your dad and this"—she pulled a tall teenager forward—"is Dane, your twin brother."

The little girl on his lap had turned in his arms. She had her thumb in her mouth and had closed her eyes, perfectly comfortable for her afternoon nap. Her mother—*his* mother too—said, "This is your sister Tammy

Rae." She pointed up at a little girl standing on the stage at the end of the gymnasium. "And there is your other sister, Teresa."

Little Teresa held a microphone with both of her hands. She pressed it to her lips. "I need the band to stop now. Everybody has to stop now."

The pretty woman who said she was his mother hugged Dwain's shoulders. "Dwain, Teresa has been practicing to sing for you."

He wondered what the meaning of this strange dream was and then he heard the woman whispering close to his ear. "I'm your real Momma, Dwain. You're home."

Once again, the room was silent. A lady slipped behind the piano and smiled to let the little girl know that she was ready. She began with four notes on the piano, and the little girl, holding a large black microphone in both of her little hands, smiled down at Dwain.

She said, "This song is for my big brother Dwain." She waved to someone behind Dwain, so he looked back at the doorway. The cowboy raised his thumb and smiled as if telling her he was ready for something. Dwain looked back at her as she sang in a sweet, pure voice, "Jesus loves me this I know." She pointed at the cowboy, who then sang, "For the Bible tells me so."

She sang, "Little ones to Him belong. We"—she put her hand on her chest and pointed at Dwain as she sang—"are weak but He is strong."

Struggling to hold the microphone with one hand, she pointed at all the people, starting at her left and going around to her right. "Everybody sing."

Everyone stood and sang. "Jesus loves me this I know, for the Bible tells me so. Little ones to Him belong, we are weak but He is strong."

As Dwain tried to wrap his thoughts around the news that he had a real family, one who maybe even loved him, Tommy moved along the gym floor at the front of the stage, keeping his head down until he was in line with Teresa. He put his mouth close to her ear.

She smiled. "Today is a very special day. My brothers' birthday is today, and my brother Dwain finally came home."

Tommy fidgeted. He opened and closed his mouth silently, and waved his hands in a hurry-up gesture. She fluttered her eyelashes at him and said, "Tommy McCain, you are just too cute."

His face became redder than his red hair. He turned around and sank to the floor, clutching his chest as though he had been hit in combat.

As everyone sang happy birthday, Dane leaned down and pressed his face to Dwain's shoulder, saying, "You got here."

Dwain looked around, still not completely comprehending. He looked up at the tall teenager. "Are you and I really twins?"

"Yes. I asked God to bring you home by today. I knew God would bring you home."

Seeing familiar faces from the hospital, he asked Dane, "Did my doctor tell you I was coming?"

Another boy leaned in close. "Hey, Dwain. I'm Kevin." He grabbed Dwain's hand and pumped it. "We asked Dr. Atwood to help us to find you. He told us it would be impossible. Like finding a needle in a haystack."

Dwain's eyes widened. "You were looking for me?"

The cute girl from the doorway of the gymnasium squeezed up to the side of his wheelchair. "Hi, Dwain. I'm Cathy." She smiled that pretty smile again.

His face heated to a million degrees. "Hi...uh...hi," he said.

Kevin said, "We were all looking for you. First, just the senior class, and then the whole school, and the town, and the television news and the radio. We made a Web site called "Finding Dwain" just for people to contact us if they knew anything about you."

The cowboy put his hand on Momma's shoulder. "Judge Bain officially gave him back to you and Jeff at three o'clock."

She looked up at the clock. "It's five minutes after." She looked at his dad, blinking away tears. "Jeff, he's ours. He's ours. He's really ours."

Dwain figured he could get used to having so many family members and friends. His chest felt like it might pop with the happiness of it all.

The man still had his hand on her shoulder but he was looking at his dad when he said, "I gave Zelda a court order in the parking lot. If she causes any trouble, she'll be in contempt of court."

Dwain's momma hugged him around the neck and looked at his dad and his twin brother. "Dwain is ours. Jeff, Dane"—she let go of Dwain and hugged Dane—"he's home. Dwain is home. Dwain is really home."

A woman shoved a microphone in front of Dwain. "I am Jackie Angels with Light-Night News. Dwain, did you know you were coming here to be reunited with your family?

"No, I thought I was registering for…" This was really happening to him. Suddenly, he was crying. "My…my real family. I didn't know."

The news lady turned to Dane. "Dane did you know he was coming here today?"

"No one told me, but I asked God to bring him home by September 30 for our birthday. I asked every September, but this time I asked with faith. Jesus said that whatever you ask for in His name with the tiniest bit of faith, you will receive. I asked and then I believed. We got everything ready, just believing."

Dwain's dad—what a great word—leaned on the wheelchair. "I want to take my son home now."

Dane gripped their dad's shoulder. "Look, someone brought balloons." Dane turned around, raising both hands, and yelled to everyone, "It's time for the party. Dwain is home."

The band played the victory song again as Dane leaned down, pressing close to Dwain for the television camera. Gripping the microphone, he said, "This is my twin brother, Dwain. I want to thank everyone for helping us find him. My class is going to put pictures of our birthday party on our Web site so if you want to see the new pictures, go to www.findingdwain.com and click on the word, "found."

The news camera high up on the bleachers panned the room below. Jackie Angels of Light-Night News, standing in the doorway, looked back at the students and parents gathered around a long row of tables, where plates were filled with cake and ice cream. A catering service cart with whistles, balloons, party hats, and lots of other things sat in the center of dozens of excited children.

She said to her television audience, "This is an incredible celebration. Truly this community believed that Dwain Campbell was going to be here for his and Dane's seventeenth birthday party. We are invited to celebrate with this town tomorrow. Their annual Fall Festival will begin with a parade on Main Street at nine in the morning. This year, heading the parade will be Dane Campbell riding his motorcycle with his twin brother, Dwain, riding in the sidecar.

"After the parade, there will be booths, games, and fun for everyone, followed by the Fall Festival dance. So come out and join us. I know, I for one, would not miss this for anything."

Greg crossed the room to where his grandfather was sitting on the bleachers. He handed the big man a plate filled with cake and ice cream and sat next to him. He said, "So if you think that old fish will bite a good fishing worm, we should dig some up as soon as my chores are done in the morning."

His grandfather said, "I was thinking that I could come over and help you with your chores and then go and watch the parade with you. I want to see Dwain riding in that sidecar. I can't believe he's actually here. You know, I have two brothers that are just like him. They're both back home in Minnesota, but they come to the Atwood Clinic for checkups about once a year. Butchie is about your age. He'll be here next week. I hoped to have a little one myself, being that I live so close to the clinic and all, but it skips a generation now and then."

Shelly shyly sat on the bleacher next to Greg. Alex set her plate on her lap and turned to a boy behind him. "This is my sister. Billy, you can sit by me and my sister."

Katie, standing next to Mabel by the bleachers, spotted Brent heading her way. He smiled, and she knew he was seeing the old Katie he had known standing there in her blue jeans, western boots, and long-sleeved red flannel shirt. He walked slowly toward her, stepping carefully around running children.

"You look nice." Brent sat on the bleacher as she sat down. "Does this mean you're staying?"

"Mabel talked some sense into me. Paying ten thousand dollars a month for an office plus fees for an agent, and being where I don't want to be, just doesn't make sense." Her cell phone rang, and she checked to see who was calling as Brent reached up to take sleeping Tammy Rae from Dane.

The ring was her e-mail line. She scrolled down, looking at the message, and then frowned and backed to a deleted message from three days ago. She had never read that message or the one before it. Something wasn't right. She watched Brent holding the little one while trying to take his jacket off. Wanting to help, she carefully slid Tammy Rae onto her own lap. She smiled as a new warm feeling she had never felt before flowed through her.

He spread his jacket to wrap Tammy Rae in. Katie helped him place her in the center and watched as he pulled the sides over her and cuddled her in his arms. She smiled as he kissed the sleeping little girl on the top of her head. She opened her cell phone again. Something had to be wrong with her e-mail account. Messages had been deleted before she'd read them. She scrolled through all the deleted messages.

She was shocked when she realized that Hanson Production had e-mailed her three times, offering her a substantial amount of money for her designs. A reply had been sent, from her account and in her name, accepting the offer. Now they were requesting a mailing address to send her a check.

She had a growing suspicion that her former agent, Nash Manish, was able to check her e-mails. Now, she realized that the production company had contacted her directly rather than through Nash. He had read her e-mail, responded, and deleted the messages. After she'd severed her business dealings with him, she hadn't expected to hear from him again. She quickly changed the password on her e-mail account and then replied to Hanson Production, giving the company her address at the small-town post office.

Katie closed her cell phone and said to Brent, "She's pretty."

He gently touched Tammy Rae's face as he watched Teresa trudging toward him, her little lips pursed in a frown. "She looks like her mommy." He slipped the bundled little one over onto Katie's lap and reached down and lifted Teresa. Hugging her, he whispered, "What's the matter, honey?"

"I can't even get close to Dwain. Everybody is all around him and they're all bigger than me."

"There will be lots of time to talk to him when we get home."

Dwain looked toward Teresa and tugged lightly on Dane's sleeve. "Who's the cowboy?"

Dane lifted a piece of chocolate cake and placed it on a little boy's plate. As he licked frosting off his fingers he looked in the direction Dwain was pointing. "That's Grandpa Anderson, Mom's dad."

Dwain backed up his wheelchair, saying, "Excuse me. Please excuse me." He wheeled around the end of the table and rolled across the floor toward the bleachers. As he rolled to a stop before Teresa he said, "Thank you for singing."

Their grandpa lifted her as she reached out to wrap her arms around Dwain's neck and crawl onto his lap. Dwain couldn't get enough of her. "Will you sing for me again?"

She nodded, smiled, and sang, "Jesus loves me this I know"—she pointed at their grandpa, who sang, "for the Bible tells me so." She sang, "Little ones to Him belong"—she pointed at Dwain and then at herself. Grandpa sang—"they are weak but He is strong."

"Grandpa, that wasn't your part."

He laughed, "I'm sorry, I forgot."

Dwain looked at the man. "You're my grandfather." Having such a big family, who seemed so happy to see him, still felt surreal.

Brent leaned forward, placing his hand on Dwain's shoulder, "I am, and I want you to know, I messed up when I gave you up. I tried right from the start to get you back, and none of us ever stopped loving you. I'm very sorry."

Dwain swallowed, his eyes burning at the unfairness of it…and the happiness that he finally had a real family. Every foster kid's dream. "I appreciate your telling me that. Thank you."

He looked at the woman next to his grandfather. She shook her head. "I'm just a friend. My name's Katie. I'm very pleased to meet you, Dwain."

Teresa shouted, pointing at two women walking slowly toward them. "That's our grandma and that's our Grams."

The younger of the two leaned down and lightly kissed the side of Dwain's face. "Hello, Dwain. I'm your grandma, Tamara Campbell, and I'm very happy you're here."

The older woman beside her snapped at Dwain, "Jeffery, go and get me a plate of that cake and ice cream."

Dwain smiled and wheeled away. Teresa rode along as Grandma Tamara walked next to them, explaining red faced, "Your great-grandmother has memory lapses. You look very much like your father when he was your age, and he was also in a wheelchair."

"It's all right. She's cool. Chocolate or vanilla cake?"

Returning to the bleacher he handed the old woman her cake and ice cream on a small plastic plate. She looked at him through pale blue eyes, as if trying to see something she couldn't quite make out. Her eye brows rose and her eyes opened wider, and she said, "Yes, you're Dwain. I remember now. Dane said you were coming home today."

Standing by the bleachers, Jeff looked up at his friend as Larry touched his shoulder. "So, you figured out where he was?"

Larry sat on the bleacher to be at Jeff's height. "No, I didn't. In fact, I was doing what you were doing when he arrived." He smiled. "Delivering my first set of triplets."

Together they watched the happy faces in the gym—kids from this school, the elementary school, the Atwood Clinic, and all their families. Larry quickly recounted the early morning events, ending with, "So Brent took the restraining order, and Helen Tims brought Dwain over here."

Jeff asked, "So, Dwain is all right?"

Larry leaned forward, looking past Jeff toward the twins. "He's just missing one thing."

Jeff felt his eyes snap wide open. "What?"

"A Donald Duck shirt." Larry chuckled and then ducked as though expecting Jeff to whack his head with a textbook. "Where did all this stuff come from? I was expecting just cake and ice cream. This is quite a party."

Jeff raised his hands. "We ask God for rain and He sent a waterfall." He motioned to the clock. "And right on time."

✧ ✧ ✧

Fuming by her car at the back of the full high school parking lot, Zelda Cloud could hear the excitement emanating from the open gymnasium doorway behind the parked white bus. She crumpled the restraining order in her hands and threw it angrily onto the seat of the passenger side. Standing beside the car, she closed the door. She was not through.

As disjointed thoughts tumbled through her mind, she shrieked to the space around her, "This cannot happen. Sara sat there and told me that she wasn't worried because what is in her is greater than what is in the world. Greater!" She threw up her hands. "No one has that kind of power in them to make this happen."

A profoundly calm presence drew her eyes toward a man she had not seen approaching. She knew he must have been standing there long enough to hear what she'd said. He lifted his worn, brown Bible and said softly, "What's in here is a hidden treasure. Without help from the Author, it is impossible to find that treasure. Many people who pick up this book, don't know that the Author has a special key to unlock the meaning of it. They toss it aside and believe that those who found the treasure are just pretending."

Something stilled her urge to snap at him. What he said made sense, in a way that she could almost grasp. And suddenly, she felt an overpowering desire to understand what he was talking about. As though he could read her thoughts, he winked at her. When he resumed speaking, his voice was low and mellifluous and filled her with a sense of longing.

"The Author patiently stands at the door, knocking. But He will not come in unless you open the door. If you open the door and invite Him to come in, then"—he held up the worn brown book—"He will open your eyes and your understanding."

Tears slipped down her face. "How do I ask someone to come in when I can't even see Him?"

He smiled. "By having faith. Knowing He is here when you can't see Him, and trusting that when you ask Him, He will come in."

The man bowed his head to her, turned, and walked away. She dashed the tears from her eyes and looked for him. He was gone, but the Bible lay on the hood of her car. She lifted it and stared at the cover; unable to decide whether to toss it on the ground or hold it closer to herself, unable to part with it. She set it carefully on the passenger seat.

Zelda drove home with the top up on her sports car. Still caught up in the dreamlike encounter, she never looked in her rearview mirror or used her turn signal when she left the freeway and turned toward home. Just inside the entrance to the state park, three police cars were parked with their lights flashing. She slowed and then saw Marcus, standing with his head down, being placed into the back of a police car.

She drove on, her hands shaking on the steering wheel. She had suspected something wasn't right, but she had wanted everything to be as she dreamed it could be. He had never returned the calls she had made to the hospital. She was always told that he wasn't available or it wasn't his shift. She feared he had a wife or another lover. She feared. She always feared, because nothing ever turned out right for her.

Approaching her dream home, she slowed as a man she recognized as the FBI agent she had yelled at in her office held up his badge and walked toward her. The garage doors on the neighbor's side of the house were open. She could see her love's silver sports car parked inside. The agent allowed her to step out of her vehicle. He frowned at her.

"Zelda Cloud, you are under arrest."

She smacked his face. "That is entirely ridiculous. I am a state employee and I have never, in my entire life, been in any kind of trouble. What is going on here?"

With a handprint blooming on his cheek, he clapped handcuffs on her wrists. "You just assaulted a federal officer. In addition, a major felony has taken place in a home that you own. Because you are living in that home, you are an accomplice in the crime. I'm sorry, but you have the right to remain silent. Anything you say can and will be used against you in a court of law...."

17

In a rundown hotel on the shady side of the city, Arnold reached into his pocket for a large bill to pay a prostitute. She finished buttoning her blouse as she waited for her money. The news station was interrupted for a special bulletin. He moved away from her as he turned the volume up.

"Pay me an extra twenty dollars for the room," she demanded. "I paid twenty for an hour."

He stared at the TV. He couldn't look away from it, even though the bulletin made his insides churn like the industrial mixer. "After an intensive FBI search spanning more than seven years and covering almost every state in the nation, agents have in custody Archibald Dunkin Walters; but somehow his younger brother, Arnold Darien Walters, has once again eluded apprehension." They put up a picture of Arnold that made him look extra stupid, and that made him madder. "This is Arnold. If you have seen him, call the number at the bottom of the screen. There's a hundred-thousand-dollar reward for information leading to this man's arrest. Be very careful and do not approach him. He is a suspected serial killer and extremely dangerous."

The annoying hooker had finished putting her clothes on. She turned toward the door, and as she did, she pushed his shoulder. "What the hell, keep your twenty bucks. I'm out of here."

His hands moved. Silent. Fast. Deadly. Gripping her neck, he twisted sharply, heard the familiar *crunch*, and then let her limp body fall to the floor. He then sat on the bed, thinking that next time he told her to shut up, she would shut up. It was her fault. If she would shut up, she already would have her money and would be gone. But no, she didn't shut up. It was her fault because she didn't shut up.

Archie had always sent him far enough way to allow him to escape. Something must have gone wrong when he met with the buyers. Archie always planned ahead, and now Arnold had to do the same thing. He tried to think. He couldn't call his dad. Archie told him not to, if he was caught.

The plan, the plan, what was the plan? If he followed the plan just as Archie had told him to do, everything would be all right. He concentrated hard. It was important to remember. And he did. He took the key to the rented storage garage out of his pocket and sat looking at it. He had to go across town, get the boxes of money they had stored there, and then head for the coast. Archie's high-paid lawyer would get him out on bond, and he would come to the boat by Dad's workplace. Then Arnold and Archie would leave the country, and no one would find them again.

Maybe they'd go somewhere the hookers weren't so annoying.

He opened his cell phone and looked in the directory. When Amanda called him about the FBI agent being at the high school, her phone number was on the screen. He had saved it in his directory, and now he called her.

Hearing her soft voice, he said, "Amanda, what you said about God means a lot to me. You are the only one who ever talked to me like that, and I want to know more about God loving me even before I was born and what I can do to be forgiven and live the way God wants me to live. So I'm calling to ask you to come here. I'm just sitting here, all alone." With his foot he pushed the woman's legs under the bed, thinking that he would have to hide the body better before Amanda came.

In her bedroom, Amanda listened to Arnold's plea for a friend to talk to. She was thinking that she also needed a friend to talk to. She closed her cell phone and went downstairs. In the kitchen, she passed her mother scooping her special recipe of spicy tomatoes into canning jars.

"Amanda, I think this batch is even better than last year. This is a blue-ribbon batch for sure."

Tell someone who cares. Amanda reached up for the key to the car. "I need to check the class bulletin board and see what I missed this afternoon."

Her mother looked at the clock. "That McCain boy won't be there, will he?"

She pressed the key in her fingers. *Just stay calm.* "It's just people setting up for the food tasting." She motioned to her mother's row of filled canning jars.

Her mother looked sadly at her, "I wish you would just go over and see Dane, and meet his brother. I don't understand what is wrong with you lately. We are doing everything we can to make sure you go to Oregon State with the other kids. Ever since we got into this financial mess, you've been unhappy. Is that what's bothering you? Are you worried about college?"

She squeezed the key in her hand. *I don't know what is wrong with me. Stop asking me!* "I just want to get my homework assignments, Mom."

"Be careful. You're all we have, dear."

"Whatever." Glancing back at the house on her way out of the yard, she saw her mother standing by the window, head bowed, lips moving.

Amanda wiped tears from her eyes, almost forgetting her unhappiness when she saw Millie and her three long-legged little calves standing at the fence, watching as she passed by.

It's all Trenton's fault. Why can't he just stay away? She sighed, and thought, *I had a choice. When he said he wanted me to climb out my window. I didn't have to. It's my fault I failed the history test and had to come home early to sleep. It's my fault Dad is disappointed with me.*

She tried to not look toward Dane's home as she passed, but couldn't help but see Brent's pickup truck and both Principal and Dr. Campbell's cars parked between the two homes in front of the barn. She forced her eyes ahead and realized she was coming up on a motorcycle with a sidecar parked in the middle of the road. Dane stepped off and waved, stopping her.

"Amanda, I want you to meet Dwain. Come on. *Please.*" He opened the car door and pulled her to her feet. "He is really happy to be here, and the bike runs great."

In the sidecar, Dwain lifted his helmet as Dane said, "Amanda is my best friend. She helped me on the motorcycle. We worked on it for years, right Amanda?" Dane put his arm around her in a friendly hug. "Isn't this great? Amanda, take it for a ride." He handed her his helmet. "Just stay on this road. Grandpa won't let us go out on the highway."

She looked at the car. *Arnold's waiting.* "I can't. Maybe tomorrow."

Dane was now speaking into his cell phone, "Mom, will you tell Kevin that we're going to take Amanda's car to the Dine and Drive for"—reaching into his pocket, withdrawing a few bills—"fries?"

He said to Amanda, "Help me get Dwain in your car."

She grinned, as Dane's enthusiasm won her over. *Arnold can wait for a half hour.* With one on each side and Dwain's arms over their shoulders, they carried him to the car and set him on the backseat. Dwain's eyes looked into hers. She blushed and then smiled.

Dane pushed the bike off the road and waved to let Kevin know he saw him running across the field from the house. Seeing Amanda in the backseat, Dane slipped behind the wheel and looked back as he pushed the seat back, keeping it clear of Dwain's legs.

Kevin slid into the front. "Amanda, great idea. I have twenty bucks. We could get more than just fries."

Amanda looked shyly at Dwain. He smiled at her. She thought, *He looks older than I thought he would. He's handsome. I wonder if he has a girlfriend. My heart is pounding.* She said softly, "You look like your dad."

He beamed. "I consider that to be a very nice compliment."

A few minutes later, with Dane on one side, Kevin on the other, and Amanda holding the door, they had no trouble getting Dwain into the Dine and Drive. Mabel followed them to the corner booth at the back, saying, "You are a sight for sore eyes, Dwain Campbell. We have been watching for you for a long time."

As Dwain pulled himself to the back of the U-shaped booth, Amanda pushed past Kevin and slid back to sit next to him. Mabel lifted her order book and shot Amanda a secret smile. "What will it be?"

Her boss yelled from the kitchen, "Anything they want. It's on the house."

Dwain said, "Wow, I'll have a chocolate shake."

Amanda laughed. "That's what your dad always has."

He smiled, tilting his head the way his father often did. "And what else does he always have?"

She blushed. "Fish and chips."

"I've never had that. Actually I've never eaten out before."

Everybody looked at him funny when he said that, but Dane said, "Then it's about time," and the moment passed.

Mabel wrote their orders down and moved back as others gathered around. Joe, the owner of Joe Bob's Service Station, was the first to offer Dwain his hand. "Hey there, Dwain, it's good to have you finally home."

At least a dozen others spoke to them before Amanda happened to look out the window and saw Dane's motorbike. She poked him in the shoulder. "Hey, it's your Grandpa, and look. Your dad rode here in the side-car."

As they came in a man seated at the counter said, "Brent how you doing? Dr. Campbell, good to see you."

Dane and Kevin slid farther in, forcing Amanda and Dwain to move closer together. Amanda put her hand under the table. Her hand touched Dwain's. She smiled. Sitting down, he was almost as tall as she was. She looked at Dr. Campbell and smiled. He smiled, letting her know she was still welcome with his family. She liked the feel of Dwain's fingers holding her fingers.

Looking up at the television as Mabel turned the volume up, Amanda saw Arnold's face. The announcer was saying, "The street value of the cocaine was more than a quarter of a million dollars, but this mixture was so lethal, if it had been sold on the street, it would have killed thousands of people. "This is Arnold. If you see him, don't approach him. Just call the number at the bottom of the screen. This man is *extremely* dangerous."

Amanda pushed Kevin. "May I get out, please?" *Arnold lied to me. He could have killed thousands of people with those drugs.* She looked at the phone number on the television screen.

Jeff slid out and then Kevin. Amanda rushed toward the restroom, say-ing the phone number from the television screen over and over again in her head.

When she returned she felt much better until Jeff slid out to let her slide into the booth but Kevin slid toward Dwain. She glared her most threatening glare at Kevin. "I'm sitting there."

"What?" He shrugged his shoulders and slid out. He looked questioningly at Dane. Dane shrugged too.

As Amanda slid closer to Dwain, Jeff asked him, "Is there anything besides a medical career that you would like to do?"

"Lots of things." He took her hand in his under the table. "I want a driver's license and pilot's training, so I can fly a small plane. I want to drive heavy equipment, and maybe even a semi truck."

Brent smiled. "How about if we start you out on a tractor?"

Dwain beamed. "Say when. I'll be there."

Dane stared at Amanda, then caught Kevin's eye. His dad intercepted with a warning look. Then Jeff said, "Dane, you and Dwain were awake almost all night, and we have to be on Main Street early in the morning for the parade. As soon as you finish eating, we need to go."

The boys shoveled their food down, then they all headed out to the car. Amanda sat close to Dwain again, letting him rest his head against her shoulder. Kevin turned on the radio. Dane drove carefully, keeping a safe distance between the car and the motorcycle and sidecar ahead of them.

Amanda rubbed Dwain's fingers between hers and whispered close to his ear, "Will you go to the Fall Festival dance with me tomorrow night?"

He whispered, "You couldn't stop me with a convoy of semi trucks."

✧ ✧ ✧

At the hotel, Arnold wasn't expecting Amanda yet, but he was expecting her. She had to come. He needed her to drive him to the warehouse to get the money. He pushed the woman's body farther under the bed and turned as someone knocked heavily on the door.

"Listen lady," a man yelled, "You paid for an hour. It's been three, so if you're staying the whole night, pay me fifty. Otherwise, get out so I can clean the room."

He pulled the fifty-dollar-bill out of his pocket, thinking, *I would've gave this to her but she had to make me mad. She made me kill her. It was her fault for making me mad.* He opened the door just enough to hand the man the bill. As the money was taken from his fingers, he felt the slap of metal on his wrist.

Jones felt seven years' satisfaction as he pulled the serial killer from the room and pushed him toward the waiting hands of the captain of the SWAT team. He stepped into the grungy motel room, gun ready. Seeing a woman's shoe protruding from the foot of the bed, he knelt and looked underneath, then pressed two fingers to her neck. She was too cold to be alive, but he checked for a pulse anyway, hoping. There was none.

"Why did you hide her?" he yelled at Arnold. "You've never done that before." Jones got to his feet and glared at Arnold, who gave him a stupid look that might hide more intelligence than he let on. "Who were you expecting, Arnold? Who did you call so you could get a ride out of here? Who were you going to kill next?"

Amanda said he called her and he said he was alone. If he had a hooker, why did he call Amanda? I'm going to make him admit he called Amanda. The perverted piece of crap. "Isn't one dead tonight enough? Did you call a girl to lure her into your trap? Why? You knew you would kill her, so why did you call her?"

Marshall stepped between them, speaking in a low voice meant to calm him. "Arnold, Archie needs help from your dad. Where is your dad so we can tell him, Archie needs him?"

Still, Arnold kept his mouth shut.

"What did he have in his pockets?" Jones demanded. "Look for a list, a phone, a PDA." *I don't want this creep getting off on any loopholes. Amanda called us. I want proof he was setting her up.*

A police officer started pressing buttons on a cell phone taken from Arnold, and another handed Jones a notebook he had taken out of the killer's back pocket. Opening it and following the dates, he came to Evelyn Ann Kramer, dated today. The name matched the dead woman's driver's license. He ran his finger down the list of names and dates. "There're at least a hundred names here, going back"—he looked at Arnold—"*way* back to the first one."

Jones flipped through the book, pausing briefly as he noticed a recipe.

He recognized the ingredients for cocaine. Maybe Arnold was smart enough to keep his mouth shut, but apparently he wasn't smart enough to mix a batch of drugs from a recipe. He shook his head.

Behind the recipe was an address for a warehouse on the waterfront in Seattle, Washington. Marked with the words: Dads Werk.

Marshall called in the address, requesting a raid as soon as possible, saying, "Keep the media out of this until we hit that warehouse. If he finds out Arnold has been arrested, he'll close up his operation and disappear. Archie, he can trust. He knows Arnold is an idiot."

The officer with the phone held it up. "Bingo." He handed the device to Jones, who didn't need to recognize the number to know the girl whose picture accompanied it.

Jones yelled at Arnold, "You knew you would kill Amanda. Why her? Why did you call her? Why did you tell that girl to come here? Arnold, you knew you would end up adding her to this list of yours, why did you call her?"

Arnold whined, "I like Amanda. I wouldn't hurt Amanda. She's my friend."

Jones had to look away. "Get him out of here."

Amanda, Arnold's next intended victim, would be the one to receive the reward money, and to Jones that seemed like a ray of light in the darkness.

18

Standing before federal court Judge Andrew Gorman, Zelda Cloud looked across the courtroom at her mother and her sister. In her mother's hand was Zelda's most treasured possession, the one item the court had allowed her in prison, the Holy Bible that belonged to Pastor Edward Davis, until he gave it to her in the school parking lot on the thirtieth of September. The day she'd thought her life would end, and the day it truly began.

The judge was speaking to her. She looked back at him with an attitude of respect and humility that was growing less difficult for her each day. He said, "You are one of the fortunate victims of these two men. This court does not believe you were producing cocaine or selling the drug; however, you are considered an accomplice, for which this court must sentence you to ten years in prison. Due to the circumstances, I am releasing you with the time you have already served and placing you on probation for the remainder of the ten years."

As she left the courtroom, her mother handed her the worn brown Bible. Zelda smiled, holding it close to her heart. "You know, Mom. I have no job, no home, no car, no money, and an incurable disease, but what I have now is greater than anything I've ever had."

Becky cuddled close to Zelda. "You can share my room with me. I have two beds now, one for you and one for me."

Zelda stopped right there and wrapped both arms around short, sturdy Becky, who had taught her more about love than she'd ever dreamed possible. This was the kind of love that had kept Brent Anderson going all these years, the kind of love that made an entire community follow one teenage boy on his quest to find his brother, the kind of love that for-gave…as she had been forgiven. She held Becky tight. "Thank you. That will be very nice, Becky."

"I love you, Zelda. Now let go of me, please." Becky ducked out of the hug and rushed toward the front doors, calling over her shoulder, "Hurry up, Zelda, I need to show you my room."

"I love you, too, Becky." Zelda wiped her eyes. "And I'll never let you go."